THE IMPOSSIBLE PREFECT

THE IMPOSSIBLE PREFECT

NANCY BREARY

BLACKIE

London and Glasgow

To the Skipper of *Whitewings*,
with Love and Apologies

Blackie & Son Ltd., 16/18 William IV Street, Charing Cross, London, W.C.2
17 Stanhope Street, Glasgow
Blackie & Son (India) Ltd., Bombay; Blackie & Son (Canada) Ltd., Toronto

Printed in Great Britain by Blackie & Son, Ltd., Glasgow

CONTENTS

CHAPTER		PAGE
I	Prefects' Meeting	7
II	A Dreadful Beginning for Jennifer	18
III	Meeting the Others	27
IV	Sailing Interlude	41
V	Two and Two Together	51
VI	Trouble With a Squirrel	65
VII	The Agony Inter	76
VIII	Thanks to Jennifer	88
IX	Christmas Shopping—and After	106
X	The Stocking Party	127
XI	The Loofah	138
XII	Neither Frail Nor Pathetic	148
XIII	Influence	159
XIV	Really, Jennifer!	175
XV	Getting Round Lindsay	190
XVI	" A Pretty Rancid Plight "	202
XVII	Worse and Worse	213
XVIII	The Kidnapper	226
XIX	It Pays to be Practical	236
XX	Picnics in the Moonlight	244
XXI	Running Away	254
XXII	Ragging Olive	265
XXIII	A Meeting in Hall	277
XXIV	The Regatta	287

CHAPTER I
Prefects' Meeting

" But fancy the Head choosing *Lindsay* of all people!" said Olive Sanders.

" Surely she *knows* what an incompetent prefect she'll make," said Mary Cooper.

" It will be a very dashing incompetence," said Rachel Anderson with a sigh.

The three prefects, lounging at their study window, stared blankly out at the wide view of trees and river and sloping lawns, while beyond the cosy security of the little room the school assembled for the winter term with all its customary fuss and bustle.

" It isn't as if we could manage without her help," Mary went on, breaking an apprehensive silence. " The juniors were pretty badly out of hand last term, and I don't imagine two months at home will have improved them. Generally, in my experience, home has exactly the opposite effect."

Rachel nodded and then sighed. She did not approve of Miss Hazell's choice of the new prefect. Lately Lindsay Dysart had been too vague and casual about almost everything to take any new responsibility seriously, but she secretly wished she possessed just a touch of Lindsay's dash to garnish, as it were, her own more substantial qualities. She had captained River Place for two terms now, and, although she knew herself to be both persevering and conscientious (her reports for years past had rather laboured this information), she was not very satisfied with the general tone of the school. Sometimes she wondered if the rule of herself and her prefects was perhaps a little uninspired—ponderous, even, had occurred to her in this connexion during a moment of unusual illumination.

"I expect Lindsay will pull herself together when she knows she has been made a prefect," she said, in the resigned voice which she generally used. "After all, she is one of us. She's soaked in the traditions of the school. She's been here since she was ten——"

Olive gave an unpleasant little laugh.

"As if that makes any difference to a person as completely self-centred as Lindsay! I'm not suggesting that once she might not have been useful, but lately she's simply too slack for anything."

"And even if she does rouse herself as Rachel says, I'm not sure she'll have a *repressive* influence on the kids. In some odd way she almost seems to excite them," put in Mary, an expert on the niceties of working up a general depression. "Oh, I agree absolutely with Olive," she went on emphatically. "At a time like this the Head might at least have given us somebody efficient——"

She was interrupted by an impatient movement

from the depths of the big armchair, where Prudence Grenfell lay, her legs stretched out to their longest extent, her arms clasped behind her head.

"You are all being most awfully unfair," she quietly protested, "and as for calling Lindsay inefficient, that's simply absurd. She's in the first eleven and the tennis six. She's the best swimmer we've had here for years, and she's forgotten more about sailing that the rest of us will ever know."

This support of the new prefect was seconded immediately by Anita Bostock, the games captain, who was half sitting on the table swinging one leg.

"Of course she's not inefficient, and how you people do love making a fuss about nothing," she scoffed. "Lindsay can do anything with the juniors when she takes the trouble."

"Yes, *when* she takes the trouble; that is exactly our point," murmured Mary, her eyes still fixed on the river, where a yacht, tacking downstream, lazily ignored the self-important bustle of a motor cruiser with a noisy radio on board.

"Oh well, as I said before, she'll have to take trouble now that she's a prefect, and I think perhaps we are being unfair," fluttered Rachel, looking apologetically across at Prudence, who was Lindsay's special friend. "Lindsay certainly couldn't be called inefficient, but even you must admit, Prue, that lately she hasn't seemed interested. Her heart isn't in school things."

Prudence said nothing. Rachel was right. It was only too obvious that lately Lindsay's heart was in none of these things she did so well. She was scarcely more than politely interested in the real concerns of the school, and even Prudence could not discover the reason. She was always scribbling, of course, but surely that alone could not account for so complete a change in her.

Olive, however, had no such doubts.

" Of course the trouble started when she first began to see herself as a modern Thackeray or Dickens," she asserted with malicious amusement. " Our Lindsay is nothing if not ambitious."

Anita made a bored and inelegant sound through tightly compressed lips.

" Oh well, I vote we don't *fuss*," she begged. " The longer I live the more convinced I am becoming that it *pays* to co-operate with the inevitable. The Head has made her a prefect and we've got to make the best of it. Anyhow, the kids will be pleased, and in my opinion when the kids are pleased they are less likely to make plagues of themselves than when they are peeved."

" I couldn't more passionately agree with you," drawled Prudence.

Mary and Olive exchanged despairing groans. As usual, Anita's point of view combined a quite idiotic optimism with such a hearty disregard of facts, that the effect was simply infuriating.

" I shouldn't be surprised," went on Prudence, neatly forestalling their protests, " I shouldn't be a bit surprised if Lindsay hasn't grown up more quickly than the rest of us."

" *Grown up?*" shrilled Olive and Mary in an outraged duet. And Olive added caustically:

" You must be mad, Prue. Why only last term Miss Hazell caught her sailing paper boats in Willow Dyke; don't you remember? Lindsay had the nerve to say she was working out a theory which would revolutionize navigation."

Prudence grinned over her shoulder at the depressed trio on the window-seat.

" Well, that showed remarkable presence of mind, if nothing else."

" What do you mean exactly, that she has grown up more quickly? Surely we are all more or less grown-up?" Rachel was beginning, when a commotion outside the door resembling nothing more closely than an elephant descending the stairs in a galvanized bath caught their attention.

" I thought," remarked Anita, as discreet squeals and muffled giggles mingled with the disturbance, " that juniors were supposed to walk in silence through the corridors. Hadn't you better go out and *be firm*, Rachel?"

Rachel looked irresolute.

" Oh well, it's the first day and they have their unpacking to do. I think we must allow a certain amount of running about. We don't want to appear tyrannical."

Anita glanced at her almost pityingly.

" My very dear old friend, they are ragging, *not* running, and they are doing it right outside our study door. Deliberate insubordination, as matron would say."

" Perhaps they don't know we are in here," suggested Rachel hopefully. The bumping had ceased now, but the giggling and the hissing commands continued. A scuffling in the neighbourhood of the keyhole suggested that turns were being taken to peep through.

" Surely you are being rather feeble, Rachel?" remarked Prudence gently from her big armchair.

Anita had bounced off the table.

" I should think so indeed. Look here, Rachel, if you don't want to cope, let me go out there and knock their heads together."

" Well, if you really think it necessary——"

" Of course it is necessary," Anita persisted, and threw open the door. Outside, six small girls, bobbing about behind garlands of laurel leaves, seemed surprised but by no means disconcerted at the sudden appearance of the prefect.

" Oh, good afternoon. We have come as a deputation from Rotten Row to offer our congratulations to Lindsay Dysart on the occasion of her preferment," began a particularly skittishly wreathed little girl all in one breath, " and to invite her to become our dorm prefect——"

" We want Lindsay," shrilled the five in the background, as mechanically as if they had been turned on and off by some hidden switch.

" We've brought a nice big tray with us, and a lovely laurel wreath, and we mean to carry her up there now in all glory, laud and honour——"

" We—want—Lindsay."

"—So if you will kindly tell her we are here, Anita——"

" We—want—Lindsay!" screamed the chorus.

A faint protesting sound came from inside the study which acute third-form ears had no difficulty in associating with the head girl—Fluff and Feathers as she had been nicknamed by a discerning lower school.

Anita intensified, if such a thing were possible, the severity of her manner.

" What do you mean by coming here, dressed up like sights, and making all this row?"

" We—want—Lindsay!"

" Pat Thompson, answer my question at once, please; a fine captain of the upper third you make, I must say."

" We—want——"

Anita took a threatening step towards them, and the chorus, abandoning their laurel leaves, scuttled for refuge behind the enormous tray, which had been borrowed from the pantry. Once there, they peeped at the indignant games captain over the top with expressions of exaggerated terror.

" If you say that once again, you'll write it out five hundred times; first day or no first day," she stormed. " Lindsay Dysart has not come yet, and even if she had, that could not excuse this disgraceful exhibition. As to your dorm prefect, you have no choice whatever in the matter, besides which you already have Olive Sanders."

" We don't like Olive and we do like Lindsay," interrupted Pat woodenly.

Anita felt slightly at a loss. She could have told Pat how heartily she agreed with her. Most people did prefer Lindsay to Olive, but it was shockingly impertinent of juniors to express their views so frankly, and she did not relax the severity of her expression.

" You know quite well your tastes are not considered, and anyhow you probably don't know what they really are. Now go back to your dormitory at once, please, and do not leave it without permission until tea-time—Pat, do you hear?"

" Oh yes; we hear," agreed Pat politely, but neither she nor her chorus moved.

Inside the study Rachel, listening helplessly, was in a flutter of apprehension. Olive had certainly heard that wretched child's remark; she was, as Rachel knew, already jealous of Lindsay's much greater popularity, and now she would feel it her duty to oppose the new prefect at every opportunity. Rachel sighed. Peace at any price was the guiding principle of her life, but peace was such an elusive luxury at River Place.

She glanced across at Olive who, with a heightened colour, was pretending to read a letter. No doubt whatever that she had heard. Rachel sighed, wishing that Prue, instead of Anita, had offered to cope with the children. Prue's quiet manner was often more impressive than Anita's exuberance. She even began to wish she had gone herself. Pat was arguing with Anita now, not exactly rudely, but there was a cheerful insolence about her tone which was impossible to notice officially because so difficult to define. If Anita did not successfully get rid of the juniors soon she would really have to go out there and assert herself. Not very dignified at this late hour, and Anita would be annoyed at any interference, but still—Oh, goodness, what was happening now?

More feet were scampering down the corridor. There were more squeals—of wrath this time. There were shrill cries of " Oh, you horrid pigs! We'll pay you out for stealing our idea of serenading Lindsay!" Then there were thumps, giggles, much pushing and scuffling, and the lower fourth had arrived to fall upon their rivals and drive them away in a running fight.

Rachel hurried to the door. Outside, the floor was strewn with laurel leaves. On the landing, at the end of the corridor, where a desperate battle was in progress, the tray had been captured by the lower fourth and was coming in nicely as a weapon for banging the heads of the enemy.

" Go back to your unpacking at once," Rachel ordered. "And you will each take an order mark. Do you hear? Pamela—Pat—Gretchen."

Nobody answered, but after a dreadful moment of giggling defiance they moved quietly away.

Prudence laughed to herself as Rachel and the games captain, both looking pink and disconcerted, came back into the room, but there was very little amusement in the sound.

" Not a particularly promising start for the new term," she commented dryly.

" No; wasn't it simply frightful? And things are sure to get worse instead of better; they always do," moaned Mary.

Anita glanced angrily at the head girl.

" Rachel, I do think when you hand a job over to another prefect you might allow her to finish it without interfering."

" I thought you needed help." Rachel had returned to the window-seat and was staring miserably down at some first-form children, playing on the little wooden bridge over Willow Dyke, which divided the playing-fields from the garden.

" I can't imagine how you could think I needed help; and anyhow, surely it's very undignified to hurl order marks at people fifty yards away?"

Rachel flushed painfully.

" They had gone by the time I arrived."

" You could have called them back."

" I was afraid they wouldn't come."

Anita appeared to be getting so dangerously angry that Olive quickly interposed.

" I don't think arguing among ourselves will help much. It's Miss Hazell's fault. If she will do such idiotic things, what can you expect? Lindsay is starting to make trouble even before she arrives, just as I knew she would. The juniors are all right as juniors go. They only need a firm hand."

The others did not look very certain about this. Firm hands were all very well as long as the juniors respected the owner, but respect for the prefects was sometimes most noticeably lacking among the juniors of River Place.

It was Anita who, in spite of her annoyance, had a brilliant idea.

" How about putting Lindsay in charge of

Rotten Row? She will have to rouse herself to keep order there. You wouldn't mind moving, would you, Olive?"

Olive had decided to forget Pat's foolish remark about liking Lindsay better than herself. If she forgot it, perhaps the others would soon forget too. She shrugged, smiling pleasantly at Anita.

" Not in the least, as I haven't unpacked yet. Lindsay is welcome to try; and if she makes a muddle of the job, as she is almost sure to do, perhaps Miss Hazell will realize her mistake and give us somebody more efficient as a prefect."

" What do you others think?" asked Rachel, never happy unless her decisions were endorsed.

" It seems rather as if we are encouraging them to behave badly, but perhaps it is the best arrangement," Mary agreed unhopefully.

Prudence said nothing. Rotten Row was so very far away from the west wing, where she supervised the seconds, that intimate chats with Lindsay before senior " lights out " might be difficult to arrange.

" Prue?" persisted Rachel.

Prue stretched lazily, and getting up, joined the others at the window.

" If you mean, do I think Lindsay can cope with Rotten Row, naturally I do. If you want to know my personal wishes, then I would rather you put her in the west wing with me."

Rachel nodded, satisfied. As long as they all agreed, nobody could blame her if things went wrong.

" Then that is settled. Lindsay takes over

Rotten Row. Thanks, Anita, for suggesting it.
Now how about running through the club lists;
there is still time before tea?"

CHAPTER II

A Dreadful Beginning for Jennifer

" There's not the slightest need to sprint about
the platform like a scalded kangaroo."

" But, John, we shall miss the Norwich train."

" We've missed it already."

" *Missed it?*"

Jennifer Windgate, her freckled face pink and
dismayed, her school hat clinging more precariously even than usual to the back of her riot of
red curly hair, refused to believe such a disaster
could have happened to her.

" But, John, I'm new. There will be an awful
fuss. They may even think I'm not coming and
phone Mummy; or perhaps they'll send out an
S.O.S. on the radio. Oh, are you sure we've missed
it? It's simply awful. I don't suppose a new girl
has ever been late at school before."

" Well, at any rate you won't be overlooked
when you arrive, and you'll like that," John, her
brother and twin, assured her cheerfully. " As to
the radio, I wouldn't worry about that; you're
not half as important as you think you are."

Jennifer was too anxious to argue even on a
point so bristling with good opportunities.

" How long have we got to wait?"

" Two hours."

" *Two hours?*"

" Oh crumbs! Don't repeat everything I say in that fat-headed way."

" But, John, the buses will have left Norwich."

" Naturally they will."

" Then, whatever shall we do?"

" We'll ring up River Place presently and ask for somebody to meet you at Horning. You can get a train from Norwich to Wroxham and a bus from there and—look here, I vote we stroll out into the town now and get some food. After that we might go to the cinema, if there is one in this scraggy little place."

" But will the ticket collector let us come back on to the platform?"

As this question was obviously too idiotic to answer, John picked up their cases and strode out of the station into a leafy road which led uphill to a little town.

" Let's both say what we'll have to eat. You can have first go," he suggested over his shoulder to Jennifer, still pink with anxiety and trotting along behind.

Jennifer cheered up immediately.

" Vanilla ice, sausages, cauliflower, chipped potatoes, treacle pudding, some kind of fruit tart, and cream, and a double strawberry ice."

A very short time later they sat eating their lunch at a cosy table overlooking the crooked little High Street of Appledene.

" I simply don't know what Mummy would say about this, or what will happen when I don't turn up at River Place, but I am enjoying myself," remarked Jennifer between delicious mouthfuls.

" Well, what about me? I shall be late back too," John reminded her.

" Yes, but you've been at Peerbury for years, so it doesn't matter much. You'll feel different about being late next year when you are going to Shrewsbury for the first time."

John declined to discuss this matter. Partly because for once Jennifer was right, and partly because it would take some of the taste away from a jolly good meal.

" I can't think how Father made that mistake about the trains," he said presently, when they were waiting for the treacle pudding to be served.

" Oh well, he probably looked up a bus time-table by mistake. You can't expect an archæologist to understand modern things," Jennifer replied.

" Sometimes he's quite up to the mark, though," John reminded her. " Do you remember when I dared you to put two dummy eggs on his plate at breakfast and he just leaned over, even before he attempted to crack them, and exchanged them for yours? Jolly silly you looked, I must say."

" Yes, and jolly silly you looked when I dared you to go down the well in the pail and the chain broke," Jennifer cried in a huff.

" But not as silly as you looked when I——"

" I bet you did, I bet you looked a lot sillier."

" I bet you twopence you looked sillier when I

dared you to hide six spiders in the bishop's chair and he politely made you sit in it yourself."

"Well, I bet you twopence ha'penny that you looked sillier when I dared you to recite ' Friends, Romans, Countrymen ' in front of that theatre queue."

"Not at all; I made rather a hit. Somebody gave me threepence. Anyhow, I bet you wouldn't have done it."

"I certainly would if it was a dare."

"All right, then. I dare you to sing a song outside a cinema queue."

"All right, then, I will—but—but—I shan't be able to until next holidays," Jennifer reminded him faintly, as she suddenly realized what a dreadful thing she had let herself in for now. Perhaps by Christmas John would have forgotten.

John, feeling remarkably victorious, leaned towards her across the table. Better to change the subject before Jennifer started to argue.

"Look here, shall we have double chocolate and double vanilla ices or——" he began earnestly.

"Oh, double definitely," Jennifer replied.

"And now for a film," said John, when, packed with food and in a glow of well-being, they went out into the High Street.

Jennifer started. The film! She'd forgotten the film. Supposing there was a queue outside the cinema. Supposing—— Suddenly the brightness was gone from the afternoon and her troubles, the old nagging one about arriving late at school, and the fearful new one concerning the dare, came back to her with a rush. She must keep John away from cinemas at all cost. She must. Oh, she *must*!

" How about going and looking at the church?" she murmured, trying to sound excited at the prospect.

John did not even pretend to share her enthusiasm.

" I say," he called to a passing errand boy. " Can you tell me the way to the cinema?"

Unfortunately the errand boy could.

" First turning to the right, second to the left, and it's just across the square, but it doesn't open until two," he yelled over his shoulder.

" Then we needn't—er—I mean, it's not worth going!" cried Jennifer, her spirits starting to skip.

" May as well go and see what's on, though. It's something to do," John replied laconically.

It did not take long to walk to the cinema, although Jennifer loitered as much as she dared, taking an excited interest in everything displayed in the shops. John was beginning to look impatient when at last they turned into a little square roughly framed in trees and saw on the opposite side a modern white building, outside which straggled—oh help! oh horrors!—a long bored queue! No one else was about in the sleepy dinner hour, but a splendid car with a smart chauffeur was drawn up in front of some old-fashioned shops near by.

" M'm, not much doing here," John grumbled, but just as Jennifer was all ready with a wild suggestion about walking on to the next station, he grinned suddenly.

" Now's your chance."

" My chance?" echoed Jennifer innocently.

" To carry out the dare, of course. There's plenty of time, and it's not nearly such a big queue as mine was."

Jennifer was in despair. Until to-day she had been as keen as her twin on the intricate system of dares with which, since nursery days, she and John had satisfied a certain recklessness in their make-up, but this was carrying a good thing rather too far. To be expected to sing anything, any-where, on her way to a new school—and in her school uniform too—simply proved, as sometimes happened, that John's love of ragging was too much for his sense of fairness.

" Don't be an ass," she summed up, rather over-doing the scornful unconcern.

" You're afraid."

" I certainly am not."

" Then, why don't you sing?"

" But, John——" So many important reasons were in her mind that she couldn't sort them out.

" Those people look so bored they would even be interested in a cat fight; and you don't sing badly for a girl," John encouraged her.

" But, John, my *uniform*." Jennifer could have howled in the face of a truly terrible situation. " I'm wearing my *uniform*," she repeated feebly.

John was not even slightly impressed. What the dickens did a uniform matter when there was no one about to recognize it?

" You can take your hat and coat off and hang

them on the fence. I'll see no one bags them."

" But, John, suppose somebody from school sees me? I'd be expelled even before I arrive."

John looked bored, an expression Jennifer had cause to dread.

" Gosh! It's pretty bad luck having such a queasy miss for a sister. I've always wished you'd been a boy. ' Suppose someone from school sees me '," he mimicked, wagging his shoulders in outrageous imitation of poor Jennifer's gestures. " You don't really think anyone from your precious River Place is going to walk through this square, now, do you? We are fifty miles from Norwich, and farther still from Horning; besides, this place doesn't lead to anywhere; it's right off the map."

Jennifer cast an anxious glance across the square. There was some truth in what John said. Nobody from River Place was likely to be anywhere near, but it was the gibe about not being a boy which really settled the matter.

" I'll take your things," John offered again, more amiably now, and quick to push his advantage. " Heaps of girls wear green frocks, and that red sort of colour—or at least, I suppose they do," he added bracingly.

Jennifer was peeling off her hat and coat. Her only desire now was to get through her ordeal as quickly as possible. Besides, the queue was getting longer all the time.

" What shall I sing?" she gulped.

" Oh, ' Cherry Ripe ' will do."

" Only one verse."

" No, it must be to the end. I recited to the end."

Feeling she was walking through the distorted terror of one of her own nightmares, Jennifer approached the long line of people, who smiled expectantly at the embarrassed, but rather striking-looking little girl in her green cloth frock, smartly braided in rust. Then desperately she started to sing. In spite of her agitation, she sang very well.

Leaning against the fence on which was prominently displayed a selection of the uniform of River Place, John listened almost appreciatively. It was true, Jennifer did not sing badly for a girl. The queue looked enthusiastic, and would probably ask for more, he was deciding, when his interest was caught by movement close at hand. The chauffeur had got out of the car to open the door for a tall girl, in a green tweed suit and rust silk blouse, who had just emerged from one of the shops.

Already impressed by the splendour of the car, John stared at her with interest. She was not very young; to John she seemed quite grown-up, and there was an air of rather nonchalant distinction about her which, while summing it up in his mind as " cocky but not too bad ", John had to admit, went well with the car. Instead of getting straight in, the girl stood on the pavement staring at Jennifer, but it was not until her very purposeful glance had moved from the singer to her hat and coat hanging on the fence that a flicker of anxiety lit in John's mind. Surely a person with such a super car was not in the habit of listening so critically to street singers, and where had he seen clothes like that before? The answer sprang up and knocked him back against the fence! Jennifer had a green suit and reddish silk blouse like that. He remembered now. She had prinked about the drawing-room in them, wanting to be admired, only last Sunday, and Mums had said the colour of the blouse shrieked at Jennifer's hair. On this person the same suit and blouse looked so different that he had not recognized them at first.

" Crumbs!" summed up John, feeling hot and then cold. She was someone from River Place. Probably a prefect. Gosh! Somehow he must stop Jennifer making that infernal row.

Fortunately Jennifer left off, and, refusing to sing another song, in spite of the applause, ran towards him across the square. The tall girl had got into the car now but she still watched Jennifer through the window. As the car moved away Jennifer saw her there, recognized her uniform, and for one terrible moment met an inquiring, faintly quizzical glance from a pair of wide-set eyes, which were neither green nor grey, before she turned and fled from the square.

When the car had gone too, John, feeling horribly guilty, snatched the hat and coat from the fence, and raced after his twin. He overtook her in a little lane leading out into the country.

" My whole life is ruined!" Jennifer gulped, struggling to keep back her tears.

For once John looked ashamed of himself.

" Look here, I'm sorry, Jen."

" S-s-she'll tell Miss Hazell."

" Oh, I don't know about that," he encouraged her, trying to look more certain than he felt. " She didn't look half as knocked back as she might have done. I say, hadn't you better put on your things? We don't want to miss another train."

Gulping hard, Jennifer put her arms into the coat he was holding out for her.

" It doesn't matter how late I am now," she whispered in a sad shaky voice, " because I'm sure to be expelled directly I get there."

" Rot!" John scoffed. At girls' schools they didn't expel people for a silly bit of a rag—or did they? John wasn't sure, but he felt uncomfortable.

CHAPTER III

Meeting the Others

Jennifer would never forget that first journey to school. It wasn't quite so bad while John was with her, but when he had seen her on to the bus at Wroxham and, bracing to the last, had cheerfully yelled out good-bye, black despair settled over Jennifer like a sooty blanket.

That beautiful car would have covered the sixty-odd miles to River Place in no time, and probably at this very moment the girl with the lovely odd-coloured eyes was telling Miss Hazell how dreadfully a new girl with red hair and a squeaky voice had disgraced the school. Almost certainly, too, the girl in the car was a prefect, and even if Miss Hazell did allow Jennifer to stay at River Place, the other prefects would be told about this shocking thing she had done, and would, of course, be particularly severe for terms to come. Choking back tears of self-pity, Jennifer stared out of the window, but everything looked blurred, and she was too miserable to notice where she was going. She knew her school was beautifully situated among little rivers and quiet broads, and that the neighbourhood was a famous haunt of yachtsmen. Occasionally she saw a sail moving slowly through the flat green fields, but she couldn't feel excited about it as she would have done if only her father had not made that muddle over the trains. It was all his fault really; and John's, for suggesting such a stupid dare. Families—sniff—might be more careful—gulp—how they ruined people's lives.

At Horning village Jennifer could hardly force herself to get into the car John had arranged by telephone should meet her there. In ten minutes' time from now she might be on her way back to the bus in this very same car, her luggage piled depressingly about her. In ten minutes from now . . .

Actually, in ten minutes' time Miss Hazell, her new headmistress, small, extremely alert, and as brown as the nut her name resembled, was being unexpectedly reassuring.

" And so you missed the connexion to Norwich?" she smiled, welcoming Jennifer in her very un-schoolish sitting-room.

" M-my father made a mistake about the

trains," Jennifer explained with flaming cheeks.

Miss Hazell noticed, in some surprise, her new girl's extreme embarrassment, which must, she thought, be caused by something deeper than ordinary shyness. Curiosity, too faint to be called suspicion, flickered in her mind.

"Well, never mind, you are here now," she said.

"Yes, Miss Hazell," Jennifer smiled, her spirits leaping. The headmistress hadn't been told. She didn't *know*. What luck! What marvellous luck! Then the obvious explanation occurred to her, and she felt leaden again with anxiety. The girl in the car had not yet arrived. Probably she had stopped to visit friends on the way. She would be sure to tell Miss Hazell directly she came and——

"You had no trouble or special excitement on your journey here, Jennifer?"

"Oh *no*, Miss Hazell." The words were out before she could stop them and Jennifer faced a new trouble. Now she had not only disgraced her new school, she had told an untruth, and before this day was over Miss Hazell would know about both. The suspense would be awful. In fact, it was beginning to be awful already. Miss Hazell was looking at her kindly. Impulsively Jennifer decided to confess what had happened and get it over, but she was not brave enough, or quick enough, to seize the opportunity, and it passed.

"I'm sure you must be very hungry," the headmistress said, "but as it will so soon be time for school tea I expect you would prefer to have it with your companions than here with me. I will send for Pamela Cameron, your form captain, to be introduced to you," she went on, giving a message to the maid who had answered her bell.

For the next few minutes, which dragged incredibly, Jennifer tried to answer questions about her home and the day school she had attended, knowing instinctively that her awkwardness was making a bad impression; and then Pamela Cameron was standing in the doorway, and mercifully, Miss Hazell's bright, probing eyes were fixed on her.

" Ah, Pamela." The Head's voice became sharper and her manner more crisp. "This is Jennifer Windgate. I am now going to put her in your charge. She will be in the lower fourth with you and also in your dormitory. Mind you look after her carefully and tell her everything she should know. Now go with Pamela, dear, and next time we meet I shall expect to see you looking more cheerful."

" Next time we meet," Jennifer thought, almost resigned, " you will be sending me home for good." She managed, however, a shy, submissive smile before following Pamela out into the corridor.

Pamela was a cheerful, bouncing person with a round face, two thick brown plaits, and an air of such complete ability to cope with her surroundings that Jennifer, quivering inside like a half-set jelly, could only envy.

" You are jolly lucky to be in our form," Pamela remarked, as they walked together up the wide staircase and through many polished corridors. " We have lovely times, and we are a frightfully decent crowd. Quite the nicest set in the whole school, I should say, if you asked me to be absolutely candid. You would have had an awful time in the upper third, they are so crude, and as for the upper fourth, well, when I tell you they are simply prigs —dull, deceitful, conceited prigs—you'll see what I mean. Now this is our dorm." She flung open a door, but before Jennifer could catch more than a jumbled impression of sunshine, blue curtains fluttering to reveal small white beds, and, from the nearest window, a lovely glimpse of the river, there was a stampede of feet towards them, while half a dozen voices volunteered shrill scraps of news.

" I say, Pam, whatever do you think? It's up on the board——"

" Lindsay Dysart of *all* people——"

" She's *actually* going to be our dorm prefect——"

" She'll sleep in the study at the end of the corridor——"

" Of course the upper third will share her too——"

" The upper third don't *count*——"

" Rather not; we won't let them."

" Pamela, isn't it *super*?"

When they were satisfied that Pamela was absolutely staggered by their remarkable luck, the capering ceased and everyone turned to stare at the new girl. She seemed very scared, they thought, but that would wear off, and although her hair was rather on the bright side it was certainly lovely and curly. Apart from her hair, and a lot of freckles and that odd, frightened expression, her appearance was much the same as any other in the room and would therefore pass. Whether her behaviour would pass a similar test Jennifer had still to prove.

" Now first I'll introduce you to everybody," fussed Pamela, " and then we must start to get Lindsay's study all beautifully ready for her. I'm Pamela Cameron, and I expect you'll soon notice that, compared with other captains, I'm pretty efficient. This is Anthea Ward," indicating a quiet nondescript person with a reassuring smile, " and this is Rosalie Wayne, only we call her the Duckling because of all that yellow hair and her downy sort of face. If only that was yellow too and she was walking through a violet wreath she'd look *exactly* like something on an Easter card, don't you think? Where was I? Oh yes. This tall one is Caroline Rand, who is quite useful because she often knows an answer that has slipped even my memory, and this is Gretchen Withers, who can eat twice as much as anyone else twice as quickly; she is rather too fat, I expect you are thinking, but —oh, all *right*, Gretchen, there is no need to be so cross, the Nutkin said I was to tell Jennifer everything she ought to know—and this is Geraldine Crator, a poet of much promise. That's all. Now what do you think of us?" Pamela waited hopefully. The others looked alert. General discomfort made Jennifer reckless.

" Well, as we are all strangers, p'raps it would be more polite not to say."

A giggle from Duckling broke the flabbergasted silence, and Jennifer, now shocked by her own tactlessness, glanced at her gratefully. Not that it mattered what her new form thought of her. They wouldn't be her new form for long. After to-morrow morning, at the very latest, they probably would not be her form at all. But all the same she did wish now that she had not said the very first words that came into her head.

Pamela was the first to recover her presence of mind. As form captain she was excessively aware of her responsibilities, and she prided herself that she never failed to give a lead—even when, as often happened, it was in the wrong direction. Now she decided that a pose of splendid indifference —the sort of thing at which Lindsay was so expert when annoyed—was the only way to cope with the new girl's shocking manners. Yes, that was the only way to treat ill-mannered people. A poised and splendid indifference as à la Lindsay Dysart as possible. She set her shoulders, stretching out her neck to its fullest extent—that gave you a poised appearance. A frigid eye on the ceiling and a bar or two of the National Anthem, hummed through the nose, would do the splendid indifference.

She held the pose until a meaning cackle of laughter from Caroline made her drop it rather hurriedly and begin to hustle her audience.

"Now come along all of you, we must get Lindsay's room ready. No time to stand about discussing the—the weather. Anthea, could you go and get some flowers? There are some lovely zinnias in the staff-room, if nobody is about, and it is nearer than the garden. We've got to hurry.

She may come at any minute now. It's a pity we arranged our ovation too early, but, anyhow, the upper third ruined that by stealing our idea. While Anthea is borrowing the flowers the rest of us must go and see how we can improve the study. Come on, let's all bustle about."

They bustled obediently out of the room. Only Pamela herself remained in the doorway. After thinking for a moment she called to Jennifer, standing lonely and irresolute in her cubicle.

" I suppose you had better come too, Jennifer, even if you do find our appearance so depressing," she remarked, aware that she had descended with a nasty thump from her previous elevated level, but unable to resist the thrust. " We must all do our best to improve before we leave off being strangers, because we should hate to make you say anything that wasn't polite, you know," she went on, hammering the point well home. There was, however, no malice in her tone, only the admirable intention of showing a badly brought-up new girl her place and seeing that she stayed there.

Jennifer, too shattered to say a word, followed her down the corridor to the prefect's study. She was not particularly interested in the immensely popular Lindsay Dysart. The girl in the car, almost certainly a prefect too, would very soon tell the dorm prefect what a simply frightful sort of new girl she had in her charge, and Lindsay therefore would be turned against her from the beginning.

Jennifer sighed forlornly as she leaned against the desk in the window watching her new form crashing about the room. What a dreadful beginning to a new life! She had been seen entertaining a cinema queue. She had told Miss Hazell a sort of lie, and she had offended the lower fourth when they were only being friendly. Then she remembered this particular new life would be abruptly ended at any moment now. To-morrow she would be back again in her old life and, in spite of a twinge of apprehension about her parents' reaction to quite so brief a boarding-school career, she felt a little cheered. Anything was better than staying here among strangers who thought her a show-off and a liar and a disagreeable bore.

Presently Anthea came in with a flaming bunch of zinnias, and now there started a noisy argument about how they should be arranged.

Pamela wanted the bunch divided so that both the vase on the desk and the one on the mantel-shelf could be filled, and when Pamela wanted a thing she believed in saying so. The others all thought that a great jugful in the empty fireplace would look simply marvellous, and Caroline, showing much determination, was actually filling a jug at the hand basin behind the screen when the door split open and the upper third tumbled in.

" What are you doing here?" they cried.

" Minding our own business," retorted Pamela, with more spirit than truth.

The upper third were not impressed. They knew their rivals too well for that.

" You horrid things! You are spoiling our beautiful apple-pie bed——"

" Your *what*?" The lower fourth looked really concerned.

" We've made an apple-pie bed to pay Olive out for being our dorm prefect again and——"

" But, Pat, you dreadful little idiot, she isn't any more. Lindsay is dorm prefect this term."

" *Lindsay?*" Pat stared blankly at Caroline, and the rest of her form tottered back through the door, round-mouthed with dismay and astonishment. " But those are Olive's trunks over there," faltered Pat, pointing a quivering finger.

" Well, it has all been changed at the last minute. Lindsay is prefect here this term; it's up on the board."

Pat leapt at the bed. " Quick! We must unmake it before she comes!" she cried over her shoulder to the rest of her form, who all dashed back to help.

In a moment the blue silk cover and all the blankets were pulled off the little divan, which did duty as a sofa by day, and anxious hands started dragging out the holly leaves and hair brushes from between the sheets. Then a neat design of pins was hastily removed from outside the pillow-case, while three large books, a tablet of soap, and a pair of hockey boots were collected from inside. Over by the window the argument about the flowers continued with unabated fury.

" But who ever *heard* of flowers in a fireplace? Huh!" That was Pamela.

" Anybody has with *any taste*." That was Caroline, always more restive than the others under her captain's too domineering rule.

" Allow me to tell you, Caroline, my taste is a lot better than yours." Pamela again.

" And allow me to tell you that it isn't." Caroline, still holding the jug, moved undaunted towards the fireplace. The flowers *were* going to stand there. She would put them there herself. Why should Pam always expect to decide everything?

Pam, equally determined, sought wildly about for a proof that Caroline's taste was inferior to her own. Not being particular, she found one immediately.

" Well, what about that hat your aunt wore last speech day?"

" I didn't choose my aunt's hat, and anyhow she didn't eat a whole plateful of cream buns at tea, and then throw the plate through the window as your little brother did."

Caroline became convulsed at the memory. Other people joined in the yells of laughter. Pamela scowled about her aggressively, and then without warning snatched the jug from Caroline's hands. The jug came at once, but not the handle, and it came so easily that Pamela, unprepared, let it crash to the floor. A stream of water shot towards the fireplace; another trickled purposefully beneath the pile of blankets on the rug. The handle hung uselessly in Caroline's hand. Alarm and despondency enveloped the study.

" *Pamela!*"

" Oh help, what have you done?"

" Hadn't we better clear up the mess?"

Then:

"Quick!" cried everybody in one voice. The lower fourth and upper third united for once in the face of this common disaster. Suppose Lindsay came in now? Whatever would she think of them? Horrors! She might even refuse to be their dorm prefect and walk straight out again.

Clean towels were grabbed to mop up the water. The blankets, already damp, were hurriedly shaken. The books, the holly, and the hockey boots were piled in the middle of the floor, where they sadly hampered movement, but nobody could think of a better place to put them. Lindsay mustn't come and find her room in this frightful state. She simply must not. Quite apart from the fact that she would probably be very angry, it was such a different welcome from the ovation they had planned for her. The shaking and the mopping and the argument continued with feverish haste. In the confusion nobody heard footsteps outside or realized their antics were being observed, until a small case was suddenly thrust into the nearest chair, and a voice asked dryly from the doorway: "What exactly is going on in here?"

They stopped their mopping and poking and pulling as simultaneously as if an electric current had been switched off. They looked in guilty silence at the tall prefect in the doorway, trying to judge from her cool scrutiny of the scene whether she was going to pass it over with an indulgent shake of the head. They rather thought not.

"Slightly amateurish, all this, isn't it?" she commented presently.

" Amateurish?" Both forms were solidly of the opinion that they were experts in the technique of getting up any rag.

" If those are your idea of suitable ingredients for an apple-pie bed," indicating with a contemptuous gesture the holly and the hockey boots, " I should call them decidedly amateurish."

" Oh!"

" Holly," continued Lindsay patiently, " should have gone out with your first-form days. Hockey boots in the pillow-case with your second. If you must play practical jokes you might at least try to be efficient. Be your age, people, and remember your proud position in the school."

There was a flourish in her voice which the juniors would have found very fascinating if only they had not suspected irony as well. They could not be sure. Lindsay's manner was so gentle, but she didn't often talk like that. They exchanged uneasy glances, not knowing what to do or say next. Nobody noticed the new girl, who had silently turned to stone.

Pamela started to pick up the holly.

" Lindsay, could you tell us, please, how to make a really efficient apple-pie bed?" she asked experimentally.

" I could," Lindsay said with truth, " but I'm not going to. Now please clear up this mess, all of you, and then run away, and if you come into my study again without permission—*my* permission—there will be a row."

They hurried to obey, trying at the same time to wriggle themselves back into favour.

" We didn't make this bed for you, you know, Lindsay," faltered Pat, carefully spreading the sheets with some help from Anthea.

" I didn't suppose you had," Lindsay replied, noting Olive's trunks still piled in the corner.

" A-and we brought you these flowers," stammered Rosalie, trying to look her most appealing.

" Thanks; that was nice of you, but I'd rather you didn't give me flowers, or anything else."

" We're very sorry some water got upset by mistake," attempted somebody else.

" So am I, if those bedclothes on the floor are mine."

Certainly Lindsay was not forthcoming, and it occurred to Pamela that a change of subject would be nice for them all.

" Lindsay, we've got a new girl; may we introduce her to you?"

" A new girl? Where is she?"

They looked about the room.

" She was here just now."

" Where can she have gone?"

" Jennifer—where are you?"

They found her lurking nervously behind the screen, and with fussy exclamations led her up to the new form prefect.

" Fancy hiding from Lindsay!"

" Nobody ever does."

" Lindsay, this is Jennifer Windgate—she's

awfully funny and shy, and she seems worse than ever now you've come in."

Lindsay smiled at her charmingly.

" How do you do, Jennifer?"

Jennifer swallowed hard. Suspense and embarrassment made her throat so dry that it hurt her to speak.

" How do you do?" she whispered, staring up with a sort of dreary fascination into the odd-coloured eyes that had watched her so intently through the car window in Appledene Square. The same expression was in them now, an inquiring, half-bantering look which betrayed nothing of their owner's intention.

" She knows it's me, and she knows that I know she knows," Jennifer decided resignedly. " I wonder how soon she will tell?"

CHAPTER IV

Sailing Interlude

On the first Wednesday half of term Prudence sought out Lindsay, whom she presently found curled up in her study window. A large notebook was propped against her knees, in which she was leisurely writing.

" Letters?" suggested Prudence, beaming.

" Not exactly." Lindsay smothered a sigh. She hated being disturbed just then—even by Prudence. " Have some peppermint creams?" she invited, for fear Prue had noticed her impatience. "There's a box in the cupboard; and throw me some over."

"I came to suggest we go sailing," Prudence went on, rummaging about the untidy shelf. "It's a heavenly afternoon, and next week hockey will have started and the Windrush will be out of bounds."

Lindsay crossed out a word and wrote another over the top.

"I'm rather busy just now, old thing; if you could get somebody else."

"Somebody else?" Disappointment clouded Prue's face. "As if I wanted anybody else!"

Lindsay smiled at her over the top of her note-book, wrinkling her nose derisively.

"You'd have a better chance of winning."

"Oh, I didn't mean to do any racing," Prue objected quickly. "I didn't even mean to sail myself. I thought it would be nice to come with you in *Whitewings* so that we could have a jolly good chat."

"H'm! You've planned a nice lazy afternoon for yourself, haven't you?" Lindsay commented, but she put the notebook aside and, after stretching lazily, stood up.

Prudence was full of smiles.

"You are a saint to let me disturb you, but it isn't as if you were doing anything important."

"I was writing a story."

"Well, that's what I mean; it isn't important."

Lindsay pulled a green polo-necked sweater over

her head, thrusting her hair, which was crisp and curly, back into place before her mirror.

"You can write any time," persisted Prue, loyally trying to force an interest it was only too obvious she did not feel.

"Or no time," Lindsay murmured ruefully, as they ran downstairs and out into the leafy drive. A relaxed, holiday air hung over the place. People were strolling about with books under their arms, sounds of cheerful activity came from the tennis courts, and a gramophone was blaring near an open window. "Fluff absolutely insists on me taking over the Agony Inter, and you know what that means," she went on, turning out into the old country road, lined with willow trees, which ran on for miles between the flat fields, intersected with reedy dykes and little waterways. From the river close at hand came the chugging of a motor cruiser, and beyond the playing-fields a couple of sails could be seen running before the wind.

"Nice wind," Prue remarked, sniffing hard. "About the old Agony Inter. I'm not surprised that it's a difficult thing to run, and I think Miss Hazell should have abolished it long ago. It's a terrible ordeal for some of the juniors, especially the new ones, to have to stand up and sing and recite or whatever it is to nearly a hundred people with hardly a moment's notice."

"The names are put up on the board at break and the Inter doesn't start until after supper," Lindsay reminded her.

"Well, in some ways I'm not sure that doesn't

make it worse. I remember I could hardly eat a thing, and I always got a good crop of returns on the days when my name was up on the board."

Lindsay nodded rather sympathetically.

" I know, and I agree with you; the whole thing is beastly, but they get used to it in time. We did, Prue."

" I've never got used to it," contradicted Prue, " and that was one of the good things about being made a prefect. As for you, even as an infant, you were so indecently brazen that I don't believe you minded at all." There was exasperation as well as admiration in her voice, and Lindsay laughed.

" That just shows how little you really know me, but as a matter of fact I think Fluff should have given the job to you. You would have been so much more sympathetic with all the protests and pleadings. I shall absolutely dread Wednesdays now. Thank goodness we don't start until next week."

Prue glanced anxiously at her friend striding along beside her. Lindsay's tone was so much more bored than her words, and this boredom with school interests and responsibilities was, as Rachel and Co. had predicted, growing more noticeable than ever. Prue tried hard to understand but it was difficult. Surely, *surely* a person so expert in all the things which really mattered, and one who could lead anywhere in her nonchalant way when others had to push, would not lightly throw away these advantages for a stupid craze? Wasting time writing stories, which no one wanted to read, was all right for some people—for Olive perhaps, or even herself—but not for Lindsay. Besides, Lindsay was not only bored by her new responsibilities, she was beginning to neglect them. There was that affair in Rotten Row before lights out last night. Prue determined to give Lindsay a tactful hint when she could make an opportunity.

They had left the road now and were walking down a sloping field. At the bottom lay Windrush Broad, the sprawling reed-fringed stretch of water which Miss Hazell rented for the use of her school. Here in the summer term the girls learned to swim and dive, row and sail. Here also each July the regatta was held, when various aquatic sports took place and the sixth raced their little sailing boats against competitors from local clubs.

In the middle of the broad there was an island. Near by lay anchored a derelict houseboat known as " The Junk ", on which diving-boards were fixed. A big boat-house sheltered the sixth form's boats, and the three old tubs known as *Winkin'*, *Blinkin'* and *Nod*, in which juniors learned the thrilling art of sailing, under the expert eye of the games mistress or occasionally one of the prefects. Tall trees grew near the boat-house, making a shady place for lounging on hot afternoons, and on all sides fields and little woods rolled away pleasantly from the water.

" What a spot, and we've got it to ourselves!" Prue sighed in deep content.

" Almost." Lindsay pointed at two small sails, a white one and a brown one, beating against a freshening wind beyond the island. " Rachel and Olive," she went on. " Odd none of the fifth are out, but sailing the tubs isn't much fun for them. I expect they have all gone to Horning shopping."

" A good thing too; this place isn't half so nice in the summer when it's simply bulging with bodies like Brighton Beach on Bank holiday," Prue said, following Lindsay into the dark boat-house.

Whitewings, gleaming and spotless, nozzled the bank invitingly as they got in. To Lindsay, bringing her out into the sunshine with an oar over the stern, the little boat seemed as full of life as a friendly horse or puppy. Soon the sails were up and they were flying over the water. They passed Rachel and Olive sailing companionably side by side but, although both waved, there was a reserve about them which was not lost upon *Whitewing's* skipper.

" They haven't forgiven me yet for last night," she remarked, as they rounded the island and the wind sent the little boat heeling over.

Here was the opportunity for which Prudence had been waiting. She seized it greedily, reminding herself at the same time to be tactful. Lindsay, when she tried, was very wily at changing a tiresome subject.

" What happened exactly?" she asked, watching some coots among the reeds.

Lindsay, never happy unless she was sailing as hard as possible, appeared to be intent on getting all she could out of the wind.

" Oh, nothing much. A row, I think, between

Pamela's gang and Pat's. As a matter of fact I wasn't there. Olive discovered it—I can't think why she happened to be in Rotten Row just then —and reported it to Rachel."

"You weren't there?" echoed Prudence, a shade too indifferently. It was an unwritten but rigid law among the prefects that they should remain in their studies during the half-hour before junior lights out, while the dormitories in their charge were preparing for bed.

Lindsay guessed a lecture was coming. Prue was being too cautious for words.

"Afraid not—boom coming over!—I was in the library, looking something up."

"Prep left-overs?" Prudence persevered.

Lindsay laughed, wrinkling her nose in a way which never failed to fascinate the juniors.

"No, you old nannie, it was not prep left-overs as you are perfectly well aware. I was looking up some material for my new story. Carry on. I know you are dying to pitch into me."

"Oh well, it was only—" Prue blurted out, looking confused, "that Olive and one or two of the others did rather hint that you might be too casual for a prefect, and of course we *are* supposed to stay in our studies until lights out, and—and— oh, Lindsay, I'd just hate them to be able to say to each other ' I told you so '."

Lindsay flushed.

"When did they say I was too casual for a prefect?"

"Oh, on the first day before you came—just a few

words, nothing much—and, of course, it isn't true."

" But it is true," Lindsay murmured, busy with the ropes.

Prudence looked perplexed.

" Then, Lindsay, if you know it's true, why not do something about it?"

" I'm doing as much as I can," Lindsay said, after a thoughtful pause, " only lately school just doesn't seem very important. There are so many other lovely things to do."

" Other things? You mean writing?"

" Yes."

" But, Lindsay, *is* that important yet awhile? You could be such a marvellous influence if only you bothered."

" I wonder. Anyhow, that was a slip last night. I went down to the library, only meaning to stay a minute, and then I simply forgot the kids existed. Sorry, Prue, I'll try not to let it happen again."

Prue smiled her gratitude.

" I think you are a saint to let me preach at you," she said, " but I can't help it sometimes. I can't bear you to—to *waste* yourself. You are so good at all the important things, and even now you've got more influence with the kids than the rest of us put together, and—and—oh help, but I must say it. Honestly, Lindsay, if you ever do write a book you'll probably only find it among the ' reduced in price ' on one of Smith's bookstalls."

It was out at last. It had been in her mind for weeks and now she wondered in a panic what Lindsay would say.

" Boom coming over!" Lindsay said.

They sailed on in silence down the little dyke which lead from the broad to the river, turning upstream towards the school. As they passed the playing-fields, where Anita Bostock was spending an energetic afternoon looking out for hidden hockey talent among the thirds, it occurred to Prudence that while this silence lasted she would never know how deeply Lindsay was offended.

She started to talk wildly about the first subject that came into her head.

" Why, there is that new red-haired child in the lower fourth. What is she doing on the towpath? I suppose she doesn't realize it is out of bounds?"

" They ought to be looking after her," Lindsay said, " but she doesn't seem to be settling down awfully well."

Prudence assumed a look of exaggerated interest.

" Perhaps we'd better go across and tell her?"

" I suppose we had."

Lindsay brought *Whitewings* round into the wind and then sailed across to where Jennifer was standing watching them, her eyes two round pools of awe and admiration.

" You shouldn't be out here, Jennifer. Didn't you know the tow-path is out of bounds for juniors?" Lindsay asked, leaning out from under the gently flapping sail.

Jennifer coloured furiously.

" Yes—I—I did know."

" Then what are you doing here?"

" I was watching the boats."

" In that case, if you knew you were breaking rules you must take an order mark. Run away now."

Before Jennifer could obey Pam's pink and anxious face was pushed through a hole in the hedge.

" Oh, Lindsay, it's my fault. I told her to stand there."

" Then as she is so new you must take the order mark instead," Lindsay said, not bothering, as Prudence would have done, to go into the reason for Pam's admission.

Pam nodded cheerfully.

" All right, Lindsay, I knew I'd have to. May we give you a push off from the bank?"

" What an odd child Jennifer is," Prudence remarked when they were out in the river again.

" She looked as scared of you as if she expected to be murdered; I suppose she's awfully shy?"

A flicker of amusement crossed Lindsay's face. She would scarcely have called Jennifer awfully shy—not when she was away from school at any rate. Awfully shy people seldom sang to cinema queues.

" She certainly does her best to keep out of my way," she agreed. " I say, Prue, let's run down to Horning and eat ices at The Coot's Nest. Remember, this is the only really free afternoon we shall have until the end of term."

Prudence, quietly enthusiastic, agreed. It was lovely to think that her dreadful remark about

Smith's bookstall hadn't offended Lindsay. Perhaps even Lindsay, who was always so generous, might realize the justice of Prue's few words and give up this silly craze of hers.

That would be lovely too.

CHAPTER V

Two and Two Together

" Well, you are a muggins, you really are," remarked Pam to Jennifer as they clambered back through the hedge.

" I'm sorry," Jennifer apologized in a small voice, " but what could I do? "

" Bobbed back into the field until they had passed, of course. You must have seen them before they saw you. And now I've got an order mark; that's three already, and if I get another——"

" I'd love to sail a boat like that," sighed Jennifer, watching until *Whitewings* had skimmed out of sight round a bend in the river.

" Well, really! " Pam addressed a hovering gull in mild exasperation. " *She* get's herself caught on the tow-path by a couple of prefects. *I* get the order mark, and all she can talk about is sailing a boat like Lindsay who——"

" I'm sorry," said Jennifer again. " It was decent of you to say it was your fault."

" Oh that! " Pam, who had been waiting for a little appreciation of some sort, brushed it aside with a noble gesture. " You looked so jolly scared. Besides, in a way it was my fault. You are scared of Lindsay, aren't you? Don't you like her?"

" Oh *yes*!"

" Then why do you always hide from her when you can?"

" I—I—didn't know I did," muttered Jennifer untruthfully, but she meant: " I didn't know you knew I did."

" Well, you do. Everybody has noticed it and I should think Lindsay must have too; but there is no need to look so red. You can hide from Lindsay if you want to; there is all the more of her for the rest of us to share. Did the *Jolly Roger* pass, by the way?"

Jennifer joyfully seized this change of subject.

" No, it didn't. Only one motor boat passed all the time I was watching, and that was called *My Girl Sue*. The others were sailing boats except one big black wherry. Why are you all so interested in the *Jolly Roger*, Pam?"

Pam assumed a darkly conspiratorial air.

" Well, we *had* decided not to tell you——"

" Oh!"

" —because you are such a frightened little rabbit——"

" Oh, I'm *not*. Not really—I—I——"

"—and we thought you might go and give the whole thing away, but as you didn't behave too badly on the tow-path—I mean it was quite clever of you to tell Lindsay you were watching the boats; it was true, you see, without being *expansive.* Just the sort of thing I should have thought of myself. I'm very quick and tactful that way as I expect you've noticed. I always have been even in the first form—where was I?"

Jennifer wasn't quite sure.

" On the tow-path?" she attempted.

" Oh yes. Well, as you didn't rouse Lindsay's suspicions by telling her you were watching for the *Jolly Roger* and that we had told you to do it, it may be that you are not as queer in the head as you appear, and that the greatest crime mystery of modern times will be safe in your hands."

Jennifer's eyes glistened. She loved mysteries almost as much as she had loved dares until her whole life had been ruined by one.

" Oh, it will be safe. I promise you it will be safe. What is it, *please*?" she cried in shrill curiosity.

" Come up to the bridge where there is no one to hear and I'll tell you."

Tense with dark mysteries they walked across the field, skirting the hockey players, and on to the bridge which spanned Willow Dyke. Having sat down carefully on the curved wooden boards with her legs dangling out over the water, Pam invited the new girl to join her. When they were both settled she began her story.

" The skipper of the *Jolly Roger* is a notorious kidnapper, masquerading as a shipbuilder," she muttered, with a minimum of movement from her mouth.

" A kidnapper? *Crumbs!*" Jennifer shuddered, staring down the dyke towards the river, as if she half expected to see the *Jolly Roger* forcing its way in under the willow trees.

" Oh yes." Pam was satisfied with the impression she had made. " He kidnapped a girl called Rose Gubbins last July *and he is still holding her*. Obviously can't get a big enough ransom."

Jennifer was bursting with sympathy for the unfortunate Rose.

" But what a *terrible* thing. However did you find out?"

" We put two and two together," Pam explained.

" Oh!"

" You see "—Pam was trying to hit a floating leaf with little pieces of wood—" Rose Gubbins disappeared from her home in Cow Street, Yarmouth, last July. It was all in the papers, but actually we heard about it from Doris—you know Doris, the corridor maid—oh no, I forgot, she didn't come back this term. Well, anyhow, Doris told us about it and we were awfully interested because, although it was generally believed that she was being held captive in the neighbourhood, the police simply couldn't trace her."

" And you did trace her?"

" We did."

Jennifer was frowning thoughtfully as she too tried to hit the twirling leaf. Thrilled and interested as she was by the story, she couldn't help feeling it sounded more like a book than real life.

" You see, we had a clue," Pat informed her importantly.

" But if you had a clue, surely the police could

find one too," worried Jennifer—and indeed it did
seem possible.

Pam would not tolerate even the slightest hint
of scepticism from a new girl.

" Of course, if you don't want to hear any more,"
she began huffily.

" Oh, but I do. I do. I'm sorry, Pam, I was only
trying to understand. What is your clue?"

" The Frail Pathetic Hand."

" Gosh—how thrilling!"

" It certainly is. We saw it the very next day,
hanging out of the port-hole of the *Jolly Roger*,
and we saw it again each Monday, Wednesday and
Friday at exactly 10.25 until the end of last term.
Rose was obviously trying to signal to us. She still
is, but we never have been able to make out what
she is trying to say."

" Oh, Pam, how *awful*. Poor Rose!"

Pam, her good humour completely restored,
nodded complacently.

" It certainly is, and the lovely—I mean sad
thing is that he is *still* holding her. We saw the
Frail Pathetic at break on Monday and again this
morning. We were certain she would have
been discovered during the summer holidays and
that is why we didn't do anything definite to
help."

Jennifer, her doubts forgotten, was struck all
of a heap with excitement. The kidnapper had
passed that very morning. His helpless victim
had fluttered her signal from the port-hole and
Jennifer, contentedly nibbling ginger biscuits, had

not known that tragedy and drama were passing by on the other side of the hedge.

" And you've never seen her face?" she asked breathlessly.

" Never. No. She is probably fastened up in some way and only one hand can reach the port-hole."

" But aren't you going to tell the police?"

Pam had obviously expected this question and the vigour with which she parried it cleverly fore-stalled criticism.

" Oh, dear me, no. They would be sure to mess things up. We are going to rescue her ourselves."

Jennifer, however, was in no mood to criticize. All her private troubles were forgotten in this new interest.

" Oh, Pam, please may I help?"

" Certainly." Pam's manner became slightly sublime. " You were helping in a very small way this afternoon. A new girl couldn't expect to play a very spectacular part such as—such as bearding the bully in his boat."

" Are you *really* going to do that?"

" It is the climax of our operation," Pam in-formed her loftily. " We haven't quite decided yet on all the minor moves. We shall have to be careful or he may get wind of our activities and take her away somewhere else."

" And all this wickedness just to get a ransom," marvelled Jennifer, deeply moved.

" It takes all sorts to make a world," Pam ob-served profoundly.

At tea that afternoon Jennifer felt more at ease with her new form than she had ever done before. She shared a secret with them—and what a secret! It was as if in some odd way the secret had made her belong. They had forgotten—or forgiven—her dreadful remark about appearances and were giving her a fresh start. If only she didn't have to feel so uncomfortable whenever she met Lindsay's thrilling but inscrutable glance, how happy she would be!

" What I can't understand," Caroline remarked when the whole form had discussed whether or not the new girl should have been let into the secret just as coolly as if she had not been there, " what I can't understand *is* why so little has been said officially, you know, about Rose's disappearance. I mean, you'd have expected there to be an S.O.S. on the wireless, or the police to put up notices and offer a reward."

" Probably the police are keeping quiet because they don't want to admit they've failed," said Pam, always ready with an opinion whether she knew anything about the subject or not.

" Pretty rancid of them," remarked the Duckling, leaning over for a scone.

Gretchen was tucking into the bread and butter. When she had demolished half a plateful she turned a glazed eye upon Jennifer.

" You're certain the *Jolly Roger* didn't pass while you were on guard?"

" Oh yes, definitely. Does it often pass, except at break, I mean?" Jennifer asked meekly.

" It does sometimes, and quite often at night. We can always recognize it. It's got a most peculiar-sounding *chug*. Instead of going chug-chug-chug like an ordinary motor boat, it goes chug-chug*ger*-chug-chug*ger*-chugger-chugger-*chug-chug*-gererer."

" *Really?*" Jennifer said, looking bewildered.

" An absolutely *rancid* row," put in the Duckling.

" I suppose you never see it at night?" again ventured Jennifer, breaking a thoughtful, bread-and-butter-munching pause in the conversation.

" We've seen its lights," Anthea answered emphatically.

" But what we don't know," added Pam, " and what we mean to find out soon, is whether or not the Frail Pathetic is on board at night."

" Pretty rancid for her if she is," observed the Duckling.

Pam winked at Jennifer.

" The Duckling has got a new word. Isn't it nice for her?"

" No, I think it's pretty rancid," giggled Jennifer, rapidly growing bolder, and everybody laughed approvingly. The new girl seemed to have improved a lot since dinner-time.

That evening, while the lower fourth were preparing for bed in a most exemplary manner—the row last night had had unpleasant consequences—the door was pushed open and Alison Marks of the upper third peeped nervously in.

" Oh, Pamela, Pat and the others told me to

tell you that we've bagged to fag for Lindsay, and that you had—had better not interfere."

The nightly scramble against lights out stopped abruptly and everybody stared at Alison, trying to look bold and defiant in the doorway.

Although shaken, Pamela showed self-control.

" Oh really? How interesting!" Swaggering purposefully from her cubicle she gave herself time to think what to say next. The idea of those crude little scraps in the upper third thinking they could fag for Lindsay; and fancy their getting hold of such a lovely idea first!

Alison backed a step.

" Then what shall I tell them?"

" Tell them? Dear me, what does it matter? *We* don't mind. Lindsay is such a friend of ours that, of course, it never entered our heads to suggest fagging for her. It's different for you, and I hope you enjoy yourselves. Mind you wash the cups cleanly. When we are having tea with her next time we don't want to find the china stained."

Alison may have been simple but she was not as simple as all that.

" You've never been invited to tea with Lindsay in your lives."

Pamela appeared conveniently deaf to the interruption.

"—And mind you wash your hands before you get out the cakes. That will do, Alison. Run along now. And close the door, please," she added in her form-mistress's voice.

Slightly at a loss, Alison departed. The moment

she was gone Pam flung on her dressing-gown.

" Quick!" she cried. " We must go and ask Lindsay if we may fag for her too. It's a lovely idea, and one of you ought to have thought of it first. It's a shame to expect me to think of every tiny thing."

They found Lindsay sunk deep in her armchair, dreaming of wonderful situations which only needed words—the exactly right words unfortunately—and skilfully drawn characters to bring them to life.

She sighed and then smiled as she looked at the group of solemn, well-polished faces in the doorway.

" Well?" she invited, moving lazily. " You all look very brushed and scrubbed to-night. What do you want?"

Everyone started to talk at once.

" Lindsay, we want to fag for you."

" Lindsay, it isn't *fair* that the upper third should have all the fun."

" Lindsay, won't you *please* let us fag for you too?"

Lindsay looked surprised.

" But I don't want any fags. Prefects at girls' schools don't generally indulge in such luxuries."

" But we *want* to fag for you."

" Well, that's very nice—why?"

" Partly," Pam explained carefully, " because we don't think it's fair for Pat and Co. to do it and not us, and partly because we want to—to— help to give you a lovely time."

" I see." Lindsay eyed them benevolently.

" What makes you think fagging for me would be such fun?"

This was slightly disconcerting.

" Oh—er—em—because we *do* like you Lindsay and you've got such nice things and—and—we'd just make it fun."

" Yes. Well, I'm sorry. I don't require any fags just now. You might mention that to the upper third in case they should be thinking of applying for the post too. As for giving me a lovely time, you can do that best by behaving yourselves. I know that's a frightful bore for you, but after all you are the senior form in Rotten Row and you might be expected to set a good example, don't you think?"

Sniffs, bashful wriggles, and a guileless glance or two were the only response.

Lindsay smothered a laugh. The interview so obviously had not gone according to plan.

" There are some peppermint creams on the table," she said. " You had better finish them up. Peppermint is a good stimulant after shock."

Pam, all smiles again, picked up the box.

" These, Lindsay? Do you mean we can have them all?"

" Yes, and please don't forget to clean your teeth afterwards, whether you've already done so or not. Good night."

" Good night, Lindsay. Thanks awfully."

No sooner were they outside the door than Pam stopped to open the box. " Six each," she murmured, calculating rapidly.

Each took her share and, munching contentedly, they sauntered down the corridor. Half-way along they met Olive. There was an absent-minded air about her, rather too emphasized, and she appeared to be going to pass them without comment, but when she noticed their bulging faces she stopped.

" Lower fourth again," she began, speaking in a stern undertone. " Is it quite impossible for you to refrain from breaking rules when you are not being supervised?"

" We're not doing anything," muttered Caroline.

" Not doing anything? You call eating sweets in the corridor, when you should be in bed, not doing anything?"

A door had opened behind and Lindsay's voice spoke lazily.

" Olive, I gave them those sweets myself. And they are in the corridor because they have no other means of getting from my study to their dormitory. If you want to make any comments will you make them to me, please, in here?"

Olive, looking, for her, almost embarrassed, coloured a little.

" Oh, well, I just happened to be passing and I thought you might be busy again——" She made an apologetic gesture.

The prefects went into the study, closing the door, and six juniors trotted happily to bed.

" Trying to catch Lindsay out again," giggled the Duckling. " Didn't Olive look small?"

" She certainly didn't expect Lindsay to appear

just then," Gretchen said. " It served her right for snooping."

Caroline threw off her dressing-gown.

" You got an order mark the other day for saying ' Snoop '," she reminded her virtuously.

" Well, it so exactly describes Olive. She's so very nosy, I can't think of anything else," Gretchen cheerfully defended herself.

" Wasn't Lindsay *nice*?" Geraldine gushed. "I'm going to write a poem about her. I'll start it at prep to-morrow."

They lounged on their beds finishing the sweets and allowing themselves to be just a shade sentimental about Lindsay. Only Pam was silent, and it was soon evident that she had something important on her mind.

" Look here, all of you," she began, when the last delicious mouthful was finished. " I vote we don't give Olive a chance to catch Lindsay out again. She was obviously on the prowl to-night. I expect she's jealous because she has been taken off Rotten Row and Lindsay put in her place, and she certainly scored a point last night when we were making all that noise and Lindsay wasn't even *here*."

The others nodded. Pam's reasoning was sound. It was obvious that any prefect taken away from Rotten Row and parked in East Wing with the talkative, spindle-legged first form had everything to make her jealous. It was equally obvious that Lindsay must be loyally supported against the horrid interfering Olive.

" It'll mean we shall have to be *good*," Pam reminded them sternly. " No ragging about, but we shan't be bored; we shall have our hands full with the upper third."

" How do you mean full? Lindsay said we were to set them a good example," Caroline reminded her.

" Well, that's only her way of asking us to keep them in order," freely translated Pamela. " And that will *certainly* take us all our time."

" So it will," the others agreed rather doubtfully.

It was not until they were getting into bed that they noticed Jennifer was already there.

" Why *ever* didn't you come with us to Lindsay's study?" Pam asked, lost in wonder at the peculiarities of the new girl.

" I—I—felt tired."

" Well, you are a muggins, you really are. She was an absolute *pet* and now we've eaten all the peppermint creams; we quite forgot you even existed."

Jennifer, snuggling down under the blankets, said nothing, but she felt rather sad. It was awful feeling so awkward with Lindsay, and worse still not knowing whether Lindsay had told about her or not. Sometimes she thought the other prefects looked at her very oddly. Then she remembered how nice Pam and the others had been over their secret and felt better. It would be lovely to catch the kidnapper single-handed.

The lights-out bell had sounded and they were all getting comfortably drowsy when an ominous sound came from the dark river.

Chug - chug*ger*-chug - chug*ger* - chugger - chugger - *chug-chug*-gererer.

"The *Jolly Roger*!" Pam's thrilling whisper crept across the room. In a moment they were out of bed, piling themselves up on the window-sills. Jennifer arrived last. By the time Caroline had moved her head out of the way the *Jolly Roger* had passed.

CHAPTER VI

Trouble with a Squirrel

Lindsay, curled up as usual in her big armchair, was starting a new short story.

Rachel and Olive were arguing helplessly about how best to cope with an outbreak of lurid novel reading in the lower fifth.

Miss Hazell was entertaining a few important friends in her drawing-room.

Miss Matthews had gone to lie down with a headache.

Cook was cutting sandwiches.

The lower fourth were waiting for someone to come and supervise their preparation. When, after ten minutes, nobody came, they began to feel hopeful.

"What can have happened? Miss Matthews is always so prompt," remarked the Duckling to nobody in particular. "If the school blew up she would arrive on the stroke of six to take prep among the ruins."

3

They lounged at their desks chatting contentedly. It did not occur to anyone, not even the moderately industrious Caroline, to start her work. The topic in front of their minds that day was the *Jolly Roger*. After their decision to make life easy for Lindsay they had abandoned — with much reluctance —their first idea of all going out together to discover if the kidnapper's victim was on board at night and, instead, they had drawn lots for the privilege of adventure. Two people would be less noticeable than seven.

The lots had fallen to Geraldine and the Duckling, who had crept away importantly down the fire escape, well coached as to what to do in every conceivable emergency. They had waited, shivering on the tow-path, for half an hour, but the boat had not appeared. The incident was not quite without interest, however, for on the way back to the house the Duckling had found a squirrel. It had been so drowsy with cold, or with fear of their torchlight, that it had made no attempt to escape, so she wrapped it in her scarf and carried it up to the dormitory, where it received a most tropical welcome. All the next day it had lived on a diet of apple and horse chestnuts in an empty desk in the back row. Now it occurred to someone that it might be as well to see how it looked.

" I will!" Anthea cried, always ready to be helpful, and, cautiously opening the lid, she put her hand inside. In a second it was out again, bleeding freely from one finger. He had *bitten* her—the beast! The others clustered round, shocked as well as sympathetic. Fancy, after all those nuts! And now he was actually trying to escape. Their very cautious attempts to reimprison him in the desk failed. He also evaded their efforts to catch him in the waste-paper basket. During the scuffle which followed, somebody sent a small blackboard crashing to the floor, a vase of flowers was knocked over, and nobody had the presence of mind to shut the door. Soon he was careering madly down the corridor, the lower fourth following with stealthy gestures of dismay.

The house was so quiet! From behind closed doors came that indefinable hum of people at work. The maids were shut away in their own quarters. The staff, not on duty, were out or resting. Down the warm corridors the squirrel scampered, and after him scampered the lower fourth. Across the hall, out into the entrance hall which the juniors were not supposed on ordinary occasions to use— and then—oh horrors!—straight through a half-opened doorway on the left. Miss Hazell's drawing-room. Horror-struck, they stood still listening to sounds of surprise and confusion from inside. There was a cry of fear, a crash of falling china, some polite murmurs of astonishment from the guests, and then the door was pushed violently open and Janet the parlour maid rushed out, an empty tray in her hand, and a trickle of blood on her crisp organdie apron.

" Something jumped on the tray and bit me!" she cried as she brushed past them.

The juniors stared at her stupidly. Inside the

room, now the door was open wide, could be seen a dreadful dark brown trickle from the overturned coffee-pot spreading across the carpet amongst a lot of broken china. Some of them noticed, too, the startled faces of the guests, the angry squirrel shrilly chattering from the mantelpiece, and, worst of all, Miss Hazell herself, grim and resolute among the ruins.

"Quick, we must *go*!" muttered Gretchen, swinging round. The others, turning to follow, ran into the hostile arms of Rachel and Olive, who had just hurried into the hall. At the same moment Miss Hazell came out of the drawing-room. On these dreadful occasions she always seemed to know without being told what had happened, even down to the murkiest detail.

"In the morning I shall wish to hear, lower fourth, why you are playing with a squirrel instead of doing your preparation. Olive, perhaps you will take them back to their form-room now and see they have some work to do. Rachel, just one moment, please."

The supper-bell was almost due when Lindsay, having spent a cosy creative evening in her study, strolled into the prefects' room. She looked dashingly attractive in her green velveteen frock, which emphasized the odd colour of her eyes, and the gay ease of her manner contrasted noticeably with the nervous tension of everyone else in the room. They stared at her resentfully. Even the loyal Prudence was looking shocked. It was Prue's expression which reminded Lindsay of something important she had forgotten.

"Great Scott! I should have taken prep in the lower fourth this evening."

"You should have done," Rachel agreed, going ponderously into action, "and thanks to the fact that you did not, Miss Hazell has still another proof of what she is pleased to consider our aimless inefficiency." With some smug assistance from Olive she sketched the details of the latest trouble.

Lindsay was shocked not only by her own carelessness but also by the Head's criticism of their efficiency.

"But surely she didn't say that in front of the kids?" she marvelled when she had attempted to apologize.

"No," Rachel sighed. "She sent them away with Olive and kept that titbit for me. If she hadn't been giving a party, she would probably have said much more."

Impulsively Lindsay slipped her arm across the head girl's shoulder.

"Rachel, don't look so worried, *please*. I'll tell her in the morning that it was absolutely my fault and nothing to do with any of you."

But Rachel refused to be comforted.

"I'm afraid that isn't good enough. Surely, Lindsay, you can see that we are all involved in this? Your slackness must reflect on the rest of us, but especially it reflects on me."

"I do see that—and I'm sorry." Lindsay spoke very quietly.

The others, feeling the unusual tension, reacted

to it characteristically.   Anita, hating scenes
bustled about opening windows. Olive was glowing
with hateful triumph. Mary's sigh was reminiscent
of a winter wind moaning among reeds. Prudence
as usual, ransacked her mind for something she
could say in Lindsay's defence.

Presently she found it.

" I think it hardly fair to blame Lindsay for
Miss Hazell's criticism," she objected. " After all,
the children were getting rather out of hand last
term when Lindsay wasn't a prefect."

" Hasn't Lindsay rather brought things to a
head, though?" Olive was suggesting smoothly
when Anita bounced into the conversation.

" Well, look here all of you, I vote we don't
fuss. Lindsay has apologized; she really can't do
more than that, except to see that nothing of the
sort happens again. This scribbling ramp is at the
root of the trouble. Why not give it up, Lindsay,
and be yourself for a change?"

" But somehow nowadays I must write or I
wouldn't be myself," Lindsay replied quietly.

Anita, of course, had no patience with so fat-
headed an attitude.

" Oh, rot! Look at us; we don't have to scribble
all the time. Be a sensible soul and give it up,
my dear. Save your brain, as we all save ours, for
the things that really matter. Plenty of time for
that sort of thing at the 'Varsity."

A long silence followed, during which they all
stared encouragingly at their new and quite impossible prefect, who presently broke it herself by

quoting rather movingly something beautiful she
had found in the holidays:

"'If a man does not keep pace with his companions, perhaps it is because he hears a different
drummer. Let him step to the music which he
hears, however measured or far away.'"

They were obviously impressed, and she smiled
at them in whimsical amusement.

"That isn't just gluey sentiment, it's extremely
sound advice," she said, adding, in the hope of
changing a difficult subject: "And now, weren't
we going to discuss that affair in the lower fifth? I
suppose the first move will be to discover who
supplies them with their lurid love stories?"

The atmosphere, which had certainly been mel-
lowing, now became exceedingly frigid again.

"I hardly think," Rachel began, spurred on by
some significant eye-play from Olive, "that you
can expect us to have much faith in your advice
or judgment in a really serious matter until you
have proved to be rather more efficient at the easy
humdrum jobs; and so—and so, Lindsay, we
should prefer to manage this affair without your
help."

"Just as you like," Lindsay shrugged, smiling
compassionately at the head girl, who was looking
so much more uncomfortable than the culprit
herself. Poor old Rachel. She had hated saying
that, and only her fear of Olive's tongue and Mary's
dismal forebodings had made her do it.

"In that case," Lindsay went on, after thinking
for a moment, "I'll leave you to carry on. I hope

you are all seething with good ideas; you'll certainly need plenty if you are going to make any impression on Marjorie Blake and Co."

They watched her almost reluctantly as she sauntered from the room. She seemed so unconcerned; even slightly amused by their solemn decree. Apparently she wasn't pretending not to care. She didn't care and her nonchalance was enviable.

Prudence, making a move to follow her, was hauled back into her chair by Anita.

" But we can't let her go like that," she whispered miserably.

" Oh yes, we can. Lindsay won't be nasty about it. She'll see our point of view."

The others nodded. That was one of the good things about Lindsay. She generally did see other points of view as clearly as her own. It was only in this small matter of the story-writing she was being so obstinate, but she would soon give it up if only they were firm. Not that anyone, with the possible exception of Olive, really wanted to be very firm. It was always so much easier to like and admire Lindsay than to criticize her, but in this matter of her slackness they felt they had a very definite grievance. She was letting them down badly, and secretly they knew they were not strong enough to carry her carelessness as well as their own less obvious shortcomings.

" If only Lindsay had not been made a prefect how nice it would be; we could go on just liking her for herself," Mary resumed presently.

" Well, naturally we shall go on *liking* her. Don't look so depressed, all of you. I'm sure she'll improve in time," proclaimed Anita, the unfailing optimist.

" Odd that Lindsay has never been really intimate with any of us, and I'm sure we should have liked her to be," Rachel said, staring dreamily into the fire.

Prudence shot round in her chair.

" Well, really, Rachel," she flared, roused out of her usual quiet good-humour. " Surely she's intimate with me?"

" Is she?" Olive sneered. " Officially you're her friend, of course."

Prudence coloured ominously and as usual Rachel hastened to prevent the quarrel.

" By the way, that was a good point of Lindsay's about stopping those novels from the source," she suggested eagerly. " I wonder it didn't occur to any of us. We must find out where they get them."

Olive's mouth twisted into an irritating smile.

" My dear old Feathers, the idea is so very obvious I should have said it was hardly worth mentioning."

" Was it? And would you?" retorted Prudence, imitating Olive's manner. She was furious with her for using the word officially in connexion with Lindsay's friendship. Perhaps because there was a suspicion of truth in it; just enough to make it sting.

The supper-bell was ringing through the house

and thankfully Rachel led the prefects downstairs. There was a dignity about the procession which fortunately concealed from prying junior eyes the unenviable state of its feelings.

"Lindsay and I have been great friends since we were ten," Prudence, unable to leave the subject, was saying to Anita.

"Don't you think this is going to be an utterly awful term?" Mary was saying to Olive.

"We must all do our best; we can't do more," sighed Rachel over her shoulder to no one in particular.

Next morning Lindsay confessed her share of the previous night's trouble and found Miss Hazell, at least as far as she was concerned, unexpectedly indulgent.

"We are all thoughtless at times, and as you know, I am always ready to encourage you people to take up useful and creative hobbies," she said, smiling as she motioned Lindsay to a chair. "Of course, it was unfortunate that you should forget to take preparation in the lower fourth, but that does not excuse their disgraceful behaviour. They are old enough now to know better and I am exceedingly angry with them."

Lindsay was instantly on the defensive.

"They are very sorry about it indeed, Miss Hazell. It really was an accident and—and—one thing led to another."

"You do not expect me to believe, Lindsay, that a squirrel found its way into the house by accident?"

Miss Hazell's voice sounded grimmer than before. " No—not exactly, but they didn't mean it to do any harm. Some of them were going to use it as a model in the studio, I believe."

" I see. Perhaps we had better not discuss the matter any further," Miss Hazell said, smiling dryly at the new prefect, whose guileless expression reminded her of Lindsay's own riotous days in the fourth. " I do not wish to put your imagination to too great a strain in defence of your charges. But there is something else I want to say to you. You were surprised possibly when I made you a prefect at the beginning of the term?"

" Yes, I was, Miss Hazell," Lindsay agreed, wondering where the question could be leading. " I think," she added seriously, " that the other prefects expected you to choose either Vivien or Greta or Audrey instead of me."

" And they would have preferred one of the others?"

Lindsay flushed.

" Yes."

Miss Hazell said nothing for a moment and then apparently started to talk about something else.

" I am not very happy about the tone of the school just now," she said. " Nothing serious, of course. The children are a little out of hand. There is a certain amount of silliness abroad in the lower fifth, and I am wondering if the school as a whole requires a more inspiring—even possibly a more unconventional—type of leadership. That sort of thing, I believe, you can give. The staff and the other prefects can attend to mere discipline. Think over what I have said, Lindsay. It may mean some sacrifice, of course, but I have never found you selfish when wider issues than your personal interests were at stake. There is the bell, dear. I won't keep you any longer now. Don't hesitate to come and discuss any difficulty with me, and I know I can trust you to be tactful and discreet."

CHAPTER VII

The Agony Inter

" I say, Jennifer, did you know? Your name is third on the list for the Agony Inter to-night." Pam, full of news, burst into her dormitory, where bed-making was in progress.

" *Oh!*" Jennifer's heart somersaulted violently, and the room started to move round her in the oddest way. " Oh, but—but—I can't," she stammered, clinging to her dressing-table to prevent herself from revolving with the furniture. " Where is it? Show me, Pam. I must go and tell Lindsay."

Pam eyed her with benevolent curiosity.

" It's up on the board," she said. " And it's no good you going to Lindsay, she won't let you off. You went, didn't you, Anthea?"

Anthea, punching up her pillows, nodded resignedly.

" What did she say?" demanded Jennifer, looking so pink and overwrought that they all stopped their bed-making to stare at her. Nobody *liked* standing up in Miss Hazell's drawing-room to sing or recite to a hundred people who were not only bored, but exceedingly critical; still, there was nothing in it to make one look as half-witted as Jennifer was looking now.

" Oh, let me see. She was quite nice," Anthea answered in her comfortable way, " but sort of *firm*, you know. She said if she let me off crowds of other people must be let off too, and there would be no point in having the Agony Inter."

" There is no point in it now," Caroline proclaimed decisively. " Everyone loathes it except a few people like Pat and Pam, who adore showing off, and they would show off anyway. It's life itself to them."

" Well, *really*!" Pam's indignation at this quite unprovoked attack was so great that words actually failed her. Not, however, for long.

" If," she observed, rallying nicely, " you don't know the difference between social gifts and showing off, Caroline Rand, you are even more ignorant than one might have supposed, judging by your remarks about the Danube in geography yesterday. Just because you sing like a waste pipe and dance like a feather bolster, and when you recite there is a general stampede for the exits——"

Gretchen threw a pillow at Pam, not in support of Caroline but as a hint that she had said enough to make her meaning clear. Pam immediately threw it back, followed in rapid succession by her own and Jennifer's. Jennifer's pillow sent the

Duckling's precious lavender water crashing to the floor, at which unfortunate moment Lindsay appeared in the doorway.

" An order mark for anyone who threw a pillow," Lindsay announced crisply, before strolling on down the corridor.

" That means you've got three," muttered Caroline to Pam with malicious delight.

" Now what are you going to do at the Agony Inter, Jennifer?" bustled Pam, not so much changing a painful subject as crashing into a safer one.

Jennifer swallowed hard.

" Why not sing?" suggested Anthea helpfully. " I always think that's easiest, because even if you do forget the words or go all flat, Lindsay will play the accompaniment beautifully and the audience will clap that."

" But—I—I—can't sing," protested Jennifer feebly. Nor could she now. Singing—any sort of singing—always brought back to her mind that dreadful moment at the cinema queue, contracting her throat in some odd way and making singing lessons an agony. Besides, it would remind Lindsay of something much better forgotten, she fumed, her common sense so warped by suspense that it did not occur to her that if Lindsay, who must have had a number of opportunities to expose her, had not already taken one, she would hardly choose the middle of the Agony Inter to make the announcement.

" I simply *can't*," she repeated with wild finality,

a decision which met with hearty support from Pamela.

" Of course she can't. Have you ever heard her sing? She sort of buzzes like a bee——"

" I shall recite," announced Jennifer, suddenly calm in a resigned, despairing way. " I shall recite the lines ' On the Extinction of the Venetian Republic '!"

" Oh, but you can't do *that*! Wordsworth is so crudely Victorian," protested Caroline, looking superior.

" Besides, everybody knows the ' Extinction '," objected the Duckling from the edge of the pool of lavender water which she was sadly mopping up.

Once more Pam came to the new girl's support.

" Well, that's all the better; we can prompt her. Do you know the deaf and dumb alphabet, Jennifer?"

" No."

" That's a great pity; it would have been such a help."

" Why, do you know it?"

" No."

" Do any of you know it?"

" No."

" Then we must think of something else," Jennifer said, too unhappy to have any intention of irony.

Pam thought of something else immediately.

" You learn the words so well that they are *tatooed* on your brain, Jennifer, then you'll have nothing to worry about," she assured her cheerfully. " There is the bell, we must hurry. You've got five long periods to revise it in, and I'll hear it for you after dinner."

In the letter rack that morning Jennifer found a letter from John. He did not often write to her, and when she had torn it open she was not surprised to find it was chiefly concerned with dares.

" That was a pretty good one about the cinema queue, wasn't it?" John wrote. " And I suppose as you weren't sent straight home things have cooled down by now. It's your turn this time, but don't forget that whatever you dare me to do you must do it yourself either before or afterwards. Let's each get a good one in this term, and then we can think out something a bit extra special for the hols——"

Jennifer crushed the letter into a ball, stuffing it away at the back of her desk. John would choose to-day to write to her about those idiotic dares. The day that was to celebrate the climax of her ruined school life. Listlessly she got out her *Golden Treasury* and started to turn over the pages. Here were the verses she intended to recite. Page 241. Her face was glowing already in anticipation of the mess she was going to make of it. She never had been able to recite, but she knew that she could sing. If only, *only* her father wasn't so vague, or John so keen on dares, or Appledene hadn't possessed a cinema, or the cinema hadn't possessed a queue, or Lindsay hadn't——

Pam came into the room looking full of business.

" I say, Jennifer, have you heard about the

upper third? They had an obstacle race in their dorm last night and some water got upset. It trickled through into the staff-room and made quite a pond, I believe. Of course it was after lights out, so no one could blame Lindsay, but still it just shows we must start setting them that good example Lindsay spoke about. We've been neglecting our duty, that's what we've been doing, but we won't any longer. To-night we are going to creep upstairs after prep and hide all their bed-clothes—blankets and everything—down the laundry chute. We may do something to their mattresses too if we can think of anything clever. Anyhow, we mean to teach them how to behave properly in their dorm in future and not to make life difficult for the best prefect on earth."

Jennifer smiled wanly.

" I think it's a super idea, but you won't mind if I don't help, will you? It's the last chance I'll have of going over my recitation."

Pam nodded understandingly.

" But I just thought I'd tell you," she said.

There was dancing for an hour in the hall that evening followed by supper, before the whole school and staff assembled in Miss Hazell's drawing-room for what was generally known as the " Agony Interlude ".

Lindsay, the organizer, looking most enviably self-possessed, stood near the grand piano, and from a list in her hand read out the programme, while the audience, festive in light frocks and evening shoes, arranged themselves about the room.

There was a chair or a perch on the arm of a chair for all seniors. Most of the juniors sat on the floor. Sometimes Miss Hazell made an encouraging little speech about the need of acquiring poise and social grace in one's youth. Sometimes Mademoiselle, who had a lovely soprano voice, sang a song, but to-night there were no such merciful delays.

Jennifer, her heart pounding, grasped a ball of paper in her hot hand and wondered if she dare risk a last peep at her words behind Gretchen's back, while Linda Severn of the upper fifth was singing " Who is Sylvia?" in a politely dispassionate way. The song was followed by a piano solo from a perky, pig-tailed first-form child who was loudly applauded, and then it was Jennifer's turn.

Afterwards Jennifer never remembered getting up from her obscure place on the floor—both Gretchen and Geraldine complained that she trod on them hard as she passed—but she found herself presently standing beside the piano, the paper ball still clutched in her hand and a stifling sensation in her chest. She was conscious of faces. Faces besieging her. A great semicircle of faces, reaching from the floor almost, it seemed, to the ceiling and all closing in on her. Pretty faces, plain faces, vivid faces, pudding faces. Faces— faces—faces.

She could hear Lindsay at her side announcing the title of her poem, and then, after waiting encouragingly for a moment, she nodded to her pleasantly to begin. But, having by now forgotten the first line, Jennifer couldn't begin. If only she

had supported a poet who used the first lines for
his titles! If only——

" Once did She hold the gorgeous East in fee,"
Lindsay prompted very low.

Jennifer repeated it in a silly voice. Then she
forgot the second line and stood waiting open-
mouthed.

" And was the safeguard of the West," prompted
Lindsay again.

She repeated the second line in a despairing sort
of roar. Then amid discreet titters she forgot the
third.

"—the worth of Venice did not—" Lindsay was
continuing patiently when something dreadful
happened. Something that Jennifer could never
remember all the rest of her schooldays without icy
shudders of dismay. She burst—exploded almost
—into tears and rushed from the room. The faces,
startled now or shocked or amused, bobbed about
in front of her until, with all her strength, she
banged the door on them and only an empty hall
lay ahead.

For a long time she hid in the dark form-room
trying to realize that this dreadful thing had
happened to her—not to Anthea or Pat, or some
obscure person in the lower second, but to her.
To Jennifer Windgate, who would never, never live
the horror down. Crouching against a radiator,
which was warm and a little comforting, she heard
the wind hurling the rain against the windows.
She would have liked to run away, but she felt
too shivery inside to be able to face the driving

November rain. Presently, as no one came to look for her, she crept upstairs to bed. Funny, when her whole school life had been ruined, how almost calm she felt, and in some odd way snugly withdrawn into herself.

Some time during the long hour which followed Matron brought her, without comment, a glass of hot milk. She gulped it down meekly and afterwards, feeling wonderfully drowsy, went to sleep. She did not hear her form come up to bed nor Lindsay's whispered instructions while they were undressing.

" But wasn't it awful? Fancy crying! Why do you think she did it, Lindsay?" Pam asked in a shocked voice.

" I don't know. But, remember, you're not to say a word about it—*ever*. Do you all understand?"

" Oh, of *course* not, Lindsay," agreed a virtuous chorus, and Lindsay, satisfied, went quietly away.

The promise was not so difficult to keep as might have been expected, because next morning the lower fourth happened to have something else of great importance on their minds. Matron's assistant, on the prowl, had prevented them from setting the good example they intended to the upper third the night before, and now as they dressed they were too busy elaborating their plans for doing it to-night to bother much about Jennifer. Their indifference suited Jennifer very well. Her only desire was to run away and hide herself, and it was in a spirit of gloomy resignation that she obeyed, after breakfast, a summons to Lindsay's study.

Lindsay, who was staring thoughtfully out of the window, did not look round as Jennifer entered.

" Jennifer, I shall have to put you down again next week for the Agony Inter; otherwise you'll get some dreadful kind of complex and never be able to speak in public again."

" I shall if you do," gulped Jennifer.

" Oh, nonsense! You'll manage much better next time."

" But, Lindsay, I—I—*can't* recite——"

" You can sing."

Jennifer's heart stood still.

" You may happen to remember I once heard you sing ' Cherry Ripe '. It was outside a cinema." Lindsay, still looking out of the window, spoke in a cool, detached voice that Jennifer found disarming. " I know you can sing better almost than any other junior in the school——"

" Oh!"

" And so," continued Lindsay, " I shall put you down to sing it again next Wednesday—all right?" She glanced at Jennifer and smiled.

Jennifer, colouring furiously, stared at her with uneasy eyes. There were a dozen things she wanted to say, but she couldn't find words for any of them. Most of all she wished she dare ask if Miss Hazell or the other prefects knew about the cinema queue and if Lindsay herself was very shocked.

Lindsay's next words were only slightly reassuring because Jennifer was too engrossed with her worries to notice the laugh in her eyes.

" I'm glad you seem suitably abashed by your deplorable lapse."

" Oh, I am," whispered Jennifer fervently.

" That's all right, then. Run away now, because I'm busy."

Jennifer obeyed, but not very willingly. The question that had weighed her down since the first day of term, like an enormous haversack fixed to her shoulders, was still unanswered. Had anybody else been told? Was her lapse, as Lindsay called it, piling up interest to be taken into account by Miss Hazell the first time she got into serious trouble? Lindsay was being so nice. If only she could stay with her a little longer she might find courage to ask about these things.

She moved slowly towards the door, but before she had reached it Lindsay, with unerring intuition, answered the question she knew Jennifer was too shy to ask.

" Your guilty secret is safe with me." She was smiling rather sympathetically, and Jennifer felt a surge of relief. In that second the haversack had slipped away, and it was as if she could stand up straight for the first time that term.

" Oh—thank you, Lindsay, I do think you are nice—some day I'll do something lovely to help you," she burst out impulsively. " I know it was a dreadful thing to do——"

" Silly, I should say, rather than dreadful," commented Lindsay.

" Yes, silly. But, Lindsay, I wish I'd known you—you—didn't mean to tell anybody."

" You would have known if you'd asked me,"
Lindsay pointed out indifferently.

" It was nice of you not to tell——"

" Perhaps I didn't think it important enough."

" Oh no, p'raps it wasn't," agreed Jennifer,
feeling very relieved but also rather small.

All the rest of that day the lower fourth were
electrified with astonishment at the change they saw
in Jennifer. She giggled and strutted and talked
a great deal about nothing in particular; almost
as if something lovely had happened to her as they
told each other wonderingly. It had, but knowing
nothing about the haversack they couldn't guess
what the lovely thing was. They were amazed, and
also a little critical. After that shocking exhibition
at the Agony Inter they felt a humble, slightly
ingratiating attitude would have been more becoming to a new girl.

But Jennifer was too happy to mind what they
thought. Her happiness made her reckless and even
her recklessness brought her unexpected rewards.

When a certain history question had gone unanswered almost round the form and extra prep
loomed ahead, Jennifer made a brilliant guess,
which happened to be the right one.

When, during a stealthy forbidden game of
cricket in Rotten Row, the ball hit Mademoiselle's
ankle as she was coming upstairs, it was Jennifer
who ran to apologize in such elegant French that
Mademoiselle actually forgot to inquire what a
lemon was doing on the stairs in the middle of the
afternoon. When, soon after prep, all the lights

went out, plunging the house into darkness and a delicious confusion, Jennifer's voice was loudest in suggesting humorous and impossible causes.

When, before bed, the lower fourth invaded the upper third territory in order to teach their rivals how to behave correctly in future, Jennifer's brilliant ideas for driving the lesson well home dazzled, not only herself, but everyone else in her form.

They could not believe it was Jennifer.

Later while getting ready for bed the strutting and the chattering continued, and long after lights out a torch gleamed uncertainly from Jennifer's cubicle.

Jennifer, having unscrewed John's letter from the ball she had made of it, was scribbling hard on her writing-pad.

" I dare you," wrote Jennifer, " to switch off the lights at the main . . ."

CHAPTER VIII

Thanks to Jennifer

Lindsay was alone in the library collecting material for an essay when the lights went out, and for a few minutes she stayed where she was by the fire, wishing, as she stared at the glowing coal, that she could have an inspiration for coping with what the Head called the silliness in the lower fifth. Probably the Head had no idea what form the silliness was taking, Lindsay decided, but the word accurately summed up their attitude towards most things just now.

There was no real harm in them. They only wanted to prove to themselves and each other how wonderfully sophisticated they had become now that they were seniors. Most likely they kept a hidden store of lipstick and cigarettes too, not because they particularly valued these things, but to show their superiority over the athletic set in the form whose childish interests still lay in the playing-fields and on the river.

Preaching wasn't the slightest good, Lindsay knew, wondering why the lights didn't appear again. Rachel, well coached by Olive and Anita, had already made one speech on the subject of cheap novel reading, and the lower fifth had remained politely unaware that what she was saying could possibly have anything to do with them. An appeal to their common sense would probably only reveal that at the moment they didn't possess any. Their sense of responsibility too was at a pretty low ebb just now. Lindsay sighed. The situation, she considered, called for a more dynamic policy than the present leaders of the school, with their listless, ineffective rule, were capable of following.

Her own methods would have been original rather than conventional, but she knew Miss Hazell did not wish her to act in opposition to the other prefects, only to try and inspire them with a more enterprising sense of leadership.

Lindsay's mouth twisted into a grim smile as she wondered what Rachel and Co. would think if they knew Miss Hazell's opinion of her influence. Although, apparently, they had forgiven her for her lapses earlier in the term, and socially were as eager to be friendly as usual, she knew they had no confidence either in her judgment or her efficiency. And who could blame them? Certainly Lindsay did not. She admitted to herself, as she got up to see if the whole building was in darkness or only the library, that she had lost her feverish interest in ordinary school things. All she wanted now was peace so that she could write until she was dizzy and cramped and wonderfully thrilled —and then she wanted to go to sleep.

The corridor was in darkness too, and although muffled sounds came from the other parts of the house, it was so quiet close at hand that a stealthy movement at her side made Lindsay start uneasily.

" Oh——" she began as a figure, coming out of the shadows into the circle of firelight reflected in the doorway, thrust a parcel into her hands.

" I thought you weren't coming, Miss Blake," said the voice of Violet, one of the housemaids, " and I couldn't have waited for you much longer. I've got the books and the library says there's another fourpence to pay——"

" But I'm not Miss Blake," Lindsay interrupted, and for just a moment there was a startled pause; then apparently Violet decided to brazen things out. " Well, will you give her the parcel, please, miss, and I'll tell her the message in the morning.

Miss Blake said she'd meet me here at eight o'clock, but I can't hang about any longer because my friend is waiting to take me for a nice walk into Horning. There's no funny business, miss," she added anxiously, as she noticed for the first time the gleam of Lindsay's prefect badge in the fire-light. " If you'll just give her the parcel and not say anything about it—I didn't recognize you with your back to the light."

" I'll give her the parcel, but I can't promise to say nothing about it," Lindsay replied, and feeling strangely elated—this appeared to be one of those rare occasions when luck had befriended inability—she went towards the senior common-room. As she opened the door the lights leapt on again to reveal the lower fifth clustered about the fire roasting chestnuts in a noisy, cosy intimacy reminiscent of their unsophisticated fourth-form days.

Lindsay's appearance was hailed with an enthusiasm which made the job she had to do particularly unpleasant.

" Come in and sit down, Lindsay."

" This an honour!"

" There is plenty of room in that chair if Jenny sits on the floor."

" The first batch of chestnuts is almost ready."

" Thanks, but I haven't dropped in for a chat; I've got something for Marjorie," Lindsay answered laconically, and in an uneasy, glassy-eyed silence she lifted the parcel over the circle of heads and placed it on Marjorie Blake's knee.

Marjorie, a fragile person with pale, fluffy hair,

instantly decided to repeat the technique which had been so successful with Rachel. Bland unawareness that rules had been broken was her device, and if Lindsay proved more persistent than Rachel had been, complete inability to understand what she was talking about until she grew tired of explaining. Her friends, Marjorie knew, would back her up; the rest of the form, now looking on with smug amusement, would keep a discreet silence, although no doubt they would make themselves tiresome afterwards with their hearty and pseudo-humorous comments.

She smiled brightly.

"I suppose this came by the evening post? Thanks for bringing it, Lindsay."

"Oh no. Violet has just given it to me," Lindsay answered. "She thought I was you."

"Dear me! The girl must be mad, but all the same I appreciate the compliment." Marjorie gave an affected little shrug. "I still don't see why it shouldn't have come by the evening post. It's probably from home——"

"It certainly might have done," Lindsay agreed, with a nonchalance that made Marjorie's airy manner seem artificial, "except that it isn't stamped and Violet happened to mention she had just fetched it herself from the lending library."

"Really?" Marjorie looked slightly disconcerted. Other culprits exchanged apprehensive glances. How much did Lindsay know, and what, if anything, did she intend to do about it? Her politely interested expression told her intention no

more clearly than it had told Jennifer at the cinema
queue.

" Aren't you going to open your parcel?" Lindsay
inquired, breaking an awkward little silence.

" Do *you* open your parcels in public?"

" I do when their contents are of interest to at
least six other people in the room." Once more
significant glances were exchanged. Lindsay, it
appeared, knew rather more than was comfortable.

Marjorie tried rather feebly to bluff.

" I simply cannot imagine what you mean, or
why you should interest yourself so much in other
people's parcels."

" I'm interested," Lindsay explained in a banter-
ing tone, " because I'm simply dying to know what
type of novelette Violet picks out for you. Pretty
lurid, I should imagine, judging by what I've
noticed of her other tastes. Does she also choose
your cigarettes and—and—other small extrava-
gances?"

" Lindsay, you are simply being objectionable!"

" And you are being remarkably silly!"

" Oh, hear—jolly well hear, hear!" came encouragingly from a hockey enthusiast on the out-
skirts of the circle round the fire.

Marjorie cast a supercilious glance in her direction before turning angrily to Lindsay.

" I'm afraid your two months as a prefect has
rather gone to your head, Lindsay. You used to
be great fun, but now you seem to be almost as
fluffy as Feathers herself."

" Oh, please, not quite," pleaded Lindsay mockingly.

Marjorie shrugged.

" Feathers came drooning in here the other day about forbidden library books, but we soon convinced her we simply didn't know what she was talking about and she fluttered away—looking bedraggled."

" H'm," commented Lindsay. " While you are undoing your parcel, Marjorie, perhaps Viola or Elaine would pop upstairs and fetch your hidden stores of candles."

" Candles?" echoed several artless voices.

Lindsay smiled at them charmingly.

" For reading after lights out," she gently explained.

" You seem to know so much about the subject one might almost suppose you read after lights out yourself," Marjorie sniffed.

" Sweet are the uses of imagination," murmured Lindsay, still gently.

Marjorie, who had been collecting advice from her friends by means of much agitated and expressive eye-play, made a graceful gesture of resignation.

" What are you going to do about this, Lindsay?"

" Oh, nothing at all spectacular—if you are reasonable."

" And suppose we don't happen to agree with you about what is reasonable?"

Lindsay, who was kneeling before the fire, held out her hands to the flames.

"I'm wondering," she said thoughtfully, "if, as you find so much pleasure in reading trash, perhaps it isn't rather selfish to keep it all to yourselves."

"What has that to do with being what you call reasonable?" Marjorie asked, looking uneasy.

"Everything. If it means so much to you all that you won't promise me to give it up—*entirely* —then I suggest you all take turns in reading us some of the more lurid extracts at the Agony Inter on Wednesday—that of course isn't a threat," she added lightly over her shoulder to Marjorie, "it's merely a suggestion."

Marjorie wasn't very sure about this.

"You can't make us read," she attempted feebly.

"I don't expect I shall need to try, because I'm sure you are going to be reasonable." She stood up and her manner became official and determined. "Viola, will you fetch those candles, please, and also any other contraband small luxuries you may have collected? Marjorie, if you will get your pad I'll dictate a letter for you to send to the library. I'll cope with Violet myself in the morning."

Half an hour later Lindsay, feeling rather heady with success, but amused too in a detached way because even such a determined author could still find school interests intriguing, went into the prefects' room, where Rachel and her supporters were waiting for her. When she noticed their grim expressions she realized that her unusual headiness would not last long.

" There has been more trouble in Rotten Row," began Rachel, who was looking particularly battered. She had so much enjoyed the last few weeks of peace in the prefects' room, because Lindsay had taken her responsibilities seriously, and so could be appreciated for herself without any criticism for her slackness as a prefect.

Lindsay flushed guiltily. In the interest of coping with the lower fifth she had forgotten Rotten Row. At that moment all her headiness went, leaving her deflated.

" What happened?" she asked, after waiting for someone to tell her.

" I don't think," Rachel replied stiffly, " that that matters so much as why you were not on duty."

" I was doing something else."

" Finishing a chapter?" Olive suggested with ready malice.

Lindsay appeared not to hear the interruption.

" What has happened in Rotten Row, Rachel? You may as well tell me now as later."

Drearily Rachel sketched the details. The details concerned hidden bedclothes, a battle with brushes and combs for weapons, the arrival of some of the staff, and a long story from the lower fourth about how Lindsay had asked them to keep the upper third in order. Rachel had put both forms into detention to-morrow afternoon, and now Anita was annoyed because junior hockey would be disorganized.

" And if," Rachel ended in a tone of querulous

resignation, " you really asked one set of juniors to be responsible for the behaviour of another, so, I suppose, that you will be free to scribble in peace, your methods, as a prefect, are even more impossible than they seemed to be at first."

Lindsay was looking so unusually embarrassed as she listened to Rachel's harangue that even the loyal Prudence thought she must be guilty.

" But I don't think I did ask them to do that." Although she looked concerned, she was not apparently very certain.

" Then they must have misunderstood you. What were you doing before lights out, Lindsay? I think you must agree I have a right to know." Rachel dropped wearily into a chair; the others remained standing in stern attitudes on the hearthrug.

" I was coping with the lower fifth. I don't think there will be any more trouble with them— not over the lending library anyway."

Perhaps Lindsay's manner was rather too casual. It certainly lacked the humility her judges expected from the prisoner in the dock. Even Rachel's eyes held an angry gleam as once more she fluttered into action.

" If only, Lindsay, you would content yourself with trying to be efficient in your routine work before you dabble in really serious matters, I think you would make life a great deal easier for us all. I really must insist on knowing what you have done. Things are quite bad enough in the lower fifth without being made worse by amateur handling."

4   (G 203)

Smothering a laugh, as she remembered Miss Hazell's more flattering opinion, Lindsay curtly outlined the facts.

"But why didn't you bring us the parcel first?" Anita asked in a bullying voice when the tale was told. "It was such a marvellous opportunity, and we could all have discussed the best thing to do."

"I thought I should manage more efficiently alone," Lindsay replied with perfect truth.

"You *thought*!" Olive's smile was not designed to encourage Lindsay's deplorable complacency.

Even Prudence was looking a little shocked, but she managed to suggest convincingly enough that it was of little importance who had coped with the lower fifth as long as it had been done effectively.

"But that's our point," Mary objected, ready as usual to take the gloomiest view. "Lindsay has probably only made everything much worse. If a prefect can't keep juniors in order, *is* she likely to be able to manage that really subtle affair in the lower fifth?"

"Only as it happens I have managed it," Lindsay insisted quietly.

"Perhaps to say you *think* you have managed would be safer. Our opinion may be very different."

"If," flashed back Lindsay, suddenly furious, "your opinion is as dull and uninspired as everything else about you, it scarcely seems worth considering." She strolled to the door. "Prue, I'm going to make cocoa, will you come?"

"We need Prue here; we have a lot to discuss,"

Rachel answered coldly, as Prue made an eager movement to follow.

" Oh, very well."

" But I don't expect we shall be long, and I'll come as soon as I can," Prue cried, drawn as usual between her duty and her devotion to Lindsay.

" Just as you like, my dear." Lindsay had gone, and Prue was not the only one who felt she had taken something vital and important with her. The room, in spite of its leaping fire, seemed desolate.

For almost the first time at school Lindsay felt lonely as she strolled through the quiet warm corridors to her study. Prudence was a dear; kind and loyal and always the same, but in some odd way inadequate as a friend these days. Their interests were so different now, and although, as prefects, they should still have had the same obligations to bind them, even these they saw in different ways.

Lindsay sighed, walking upstairs with a dragging tread. It was she who had changed, not Prue. She was only completely happy now when she was writing alone in her study. Of course Prue *might* have understood, but she didn't and it wasn't her fault. Prue was certain that if only Lindsay gave up scribbling, life would be lovely again, but Prue was wrong. Ever since her talk with Miss Hazell, after the squirrel incident, she had sacrificed her writing a good deal in order to concentrate on the things for which the Head thought her especially qualified, and she had felt irritable and restless in consequence. She wished she had someone to talk to. Someone who could take her mind off her difficulties. Almost anyone would do.

As she reached her study, which would be lonely and hateful to-night, a hand shot out from behind to grasp her sleeve, and a small, very forlorn voice said breathlessly:

" Lindsay, *please*. I must confess something or the suspense will be too fearful for words."

" Come in," Lindsay said in a tone which showed neither surprise nor the gratitude she felt to Jennifer for being there just then. She pushed open the door. The firelight was making patterns on the ceiling, and outside the window the moon revealed bare trees and a wintry river, which emphasized the cosiness of the little room.

" You should be in bed," Lindsay said, putting the cocoa saucepan on the fire. " What do you want to tell me?"

" Lindsay, it was me who switched off the lights."

" Oh," Lindsay said, and then: " Why?"

" I—I did it for fun." She might have said for a dare, but a sentimental loyalty to John and to things at home prevented her.

" Is that why you sang to the cinema queue?"

" Well, yes—in a sort of way."

" You've got some odd ideas of fun, haven't you?" Lindsay commented, reaching for a tin of cocoa on the cupboard shelf. " What did you mean about the suspense being awful?" she went on, as Jennifer swallowed hard and looked embarrassed.

" Only that worrying and *worrying* about something is so much worse than having it happen."

" Not always," Lindsay said, and added after thinking for a moment: " On the whole you are right, though. Things very seldom turn out to be as dreadful—or if it comes to that as lovely—as we expect they will be. About this light business. It's no good coming to me, you know. Miss Hazell will make the inquiries, if she suspects a rag. You had better go and tell her quickly before she asks who did it."

" What, now—in my dressing-gown?"

Lindsay nodded.

" Unless she has visitors she is always in her study at this time, so that any senior who has a trouble or difficulty may go and talk it over with her. I should tell her what you told me about the suspense being awful; that will explain why you are not in bed."

" And shall I go straight to bed afterwards or would you be interested to hear what she says?" Jennifer asked hopefully.

" I should be rather interested to hear what she says."

Jennifer slipped away; in a very short time she was back looking extremely colourful, but cheerful and very relieved. On the table were two cups and Lindsay was pouring cocoa into both. Obviously she expected a visitor. Jennifer was disappointed. She felt like a cosy grown-up sort of chat about feelings and motives. In fact she felt like talking about herself on as expansive and impressive a scale as possible.

" Well—what did she say?" Lindsay invited companionably.

" Oh, she said she would overlook it this time as I went so soon and confessed, and that no doubt I thought it was a harmless joke, but no joke is harmless which causes inconvenience and discomfort to other people, and my joke did," Jennifer reeled off in one breath. " Did it cause you discomfort or inconvenience, Lindsay?" she asked, hoping to extend the conversation at least until Lindsay's other visitor arrived.

" No, quite the reverse," Lindsay said with a laugh. " Actually you kept your promise of doing something to help me very promptly indeed. Come and drink your cocoa by the fire, Jennifer, and then you must go to bed."

Jennifer's beam reached nearly to her ears.

" Is that for me? I thought perhaps you expected another visitor."

" I don't think she will be allowed to come," Lindsay remarked dryly, as she cut a piece of chocolate cake in half and passed the plate to Jennifer.

Jennifer settled herself in the small armchair opposite Lindsay's big one.

" We've had an awful time with Rachel and the other prefects this evening," she remarked, politely making conversation.

" So I should imagine and it serves you right. It seems quite pathetic that people of your age can't behave sanely for five minutes without supervision, doesn't it?"

" Well, it was because of a sort of campaign we've started to make things easy for you," Jennifer explained carefully, " although I don't think we've helped much so far."

" If to-night is an example you certainly have not, but I don't want to row you about it now. I shall have a few words to say to you all in the morning."

Fortunately the cocoa was too hot to be hurried over, and as Jennifer sat sipping it a lovely conversation started in her head between herself and the fascinating person lounging on the other side of the fireplace. The conversation chiefly concerned sailing boats and regattas, especially the last one when Lindsay had raced her *Whitewings* with such dazzling skill that a long account had appeared in one of the yachting papers. Such a conversation was obviously wasted in her head. It was time it was put into words.

" Is that a picture of *Whitewings*?" she asked, staring reverently at a framed photograph on the mantelpiece.

" Yes, it was taken after the regatta last term."

" Oh. Who is that with you, Lindsay?"

" Rita Grandin. She left afterwards to go to America with her parents. You would have liked Rita. She acted as my crew. Each competitor takes one junior to help her."

Jennifer knew this already. She had heard too of the heartburning, the rising hopes, the suspense, and the wild canvassing that went on among the juniors until the crews, and especially Lindsay's crew, had been chosen. Secretly she could sympathize with the heartburning; her own had started giving trouble already and would be unbearable before next June.

"Was Rita a good sailor?" she asked in a small hopeful voice.

Lindsay laughed and reached for the saucepan to divide what was left of the cocoa. She was grateful to Jennifer with her confessions and her suspense, and her artless, anxious eyes for taking her thoughts away from the row in the prefects' room.

"She knew one end of the boat from the other of course."

"Oh." Jennifer hardly knew even that yet. "Did you teach her to sail, Lindsay?"

"I coached her a little, but she learnt the elements, as you will, out in the tubs on the Windrush. Jennifer, if you've finished your cocoa you must go to bed."

"It was lovely," Jennifer sighed, getting up regretfully to go. "It certainly pays to profit by experience, doesn't it?"

"I'm afraid I don't quite follow you," Lindsay murmured politely.

Jennifer was only too ready to explain.

"Well, if I hadn't so hated the suspense of not knowing whether you were going to tell about the cinema queue I shouldn't have confessed about turning off the lights, and then I shouldn't have had this lovely time in your study. Oh, it certainly pays and I always mean to profit by it in future."

" It certainly is a good idea," Lindsay agreed, and added crushingly for the good of Jennifer's soul: " It might have been better still if you had profited to the extent of not turning off the lights at all."

" Oh well, I more or less had to do that," replied Jennifer, slipping away happily to bed.

Back in the dormitory she was received by much whispered comment and curiosity.

" Where *have* you been?" demanded Pam. " We almost began to think the *Jolly Roger* had captured you."

" I've been having cocoa with Lindsay because I switched off the lights," Jennifer explained sketchily.

" With *Lindsay*!"

" *You* switched off the lights!"

" Well, if Lindsay gives you cocoa for just switching off the lights, what on earth will she give us for having a battle with the upper third and getting the staff up here and all the prefects?"

" A jolly good rowing; she said so," giggled Jennifer, scrambling into bed.

This piece of news was received in a rather gloomy silence which was presently broken sleepily by Pam.

" Did you *really* switch off the lights, Jennifer? Well, you have improved a lot lately. You are *much* nicer than when you first came. I suppose you have caught it from us—niceness like nastiness is very catching."

Sleepy grunts were the only response.

CHAPTER IX

Christmas Shopping—and After

" I've composed the verses," remarked Geraldine very complacently to no one in particular, " and now I'm going to paint a picture to set them off. The picture will be symbolic and will be executed in lapis lazuli on a sepia background."

The lower fourth, busily designing Christmas cards in a snug corner of the studio, were too engrossed with their own ambitious efforts to be interested in other people's, and after a polite pause Geraldine was forced to invite herself to read the verses aloud. This she did in a raspy, sentimental undertone calculated not to reach the ears of the upper third grouped about the dais at the other end of the room.

> " You shall hear how Lindsay Dysart,
> Gallant, tall, and very handsome,
> Lindsay, from the lakes and rivers,
> From the small streams of the Broadlands,
> From the melancholy marshes
> Where the bittern, mawkish, morbid,
> Booms among the reeds and rushes.
> You shall hear how Lindsay triumphed,
> For her greater skill in sailing,
> Far outshone the skill of others,
> Dazzled, blinded all beholders,
> Lindsay's matchless skill in sailing.

There, what do you think of that? And all by itself on the back of the card I'm going to print in large letters: ' Just a tiny token of my regard for you. Signed Geraldine Crator '."

Her friends looked slightly bewildered.

" Is that all?" asked Anthea, squeezing red paint out of a tube.

" Well, it's all I can get on to the card, and surely it's enough?"

" Too much, I should say," Pam agreed emphatically, " especially as it doesn't seem to be about anything. I mean there is no *point* to it."

Geraldine was justly annoyed by this criticism.

" It's as much about anything as most poetry is. The whole point about good poetry is that it leaves practically everything to the imagination. Look at Browning. Look at—look at almost any poet. They just left it to their readers' imaginations to make what they liked of their poems. As long as it *sounds* clever——"

" I think I should call yours reminiscent—as Miss Matthews would say—rather than clever," interrupted Caroline smoothly. " Surely—still quoting Miss Matthews—it bears the hall-mark of another great master?"

" Dear me, who can you mean?" simpered Geraldine, not to be outdone in suavity. As, however, a big copy of Longfellow's " Hiawatha " was at that moment propping up her drawing-board, further discussions seemed unnecessary, and presently Gretchen, swirling her paint-brush madly in her water-jar, approached the subject from a different angle.

" Don't you think that line ' From the small streams of the Broadlands ' is a mistake? It might give people the impression that Lindsay is a fresh-water fish?" she suggested.

" Not anybody whose opinion I should *value* at all," replied Geraldine very grandly indeed.

" Well, I think it's nice," sighed Jennifer, looking with distaste at her own slightly lop-sided robin poking at a sprig of holly. She wished she had thought of such a flattering tribute to Lindsay. " Will you send it to her for Christmas?" she asked enviously.

" Oh no!" Pleased by the unexpected support, Geraldine became expansive. " I shall put it on her mantelpiece for the stocking party. Oh, I forgot, you are so new that you haven't been to a stocking party! It's lovely fun. We all buy each other presents which mustn't cost more than six-pence each, and then the night before the last night of term, we hang up our stockings just as if we were children, and the dorm prefect comes in after lights out and fills them with the things. Then at half-past six next morning the bell goes and we unpack our stockings—last year it was snowing outside—and then we process in our dressing-gowns to the dorm prefect's study with our presents for her, and when we've sung a carol outside the door she flings it open and we all go in and give her our presents and have a sort of feed which she supplies and——"

An excited squeal from the Duckling interrupted Geraldine's eloquence.

" I say, people, do you *realize* something? Lindsay is our dorm prefect this year. It was fun last year even with Olive, but with Lindsay it will simply be heavenly."

Jennifer was glowing with anticipation of the most blissful kind.

" Fancy a stocking party—what a super idea!"

" It's one of the oldest traditions of the school," Caroline told her solemnly. " The rest of the day is pretty good too, because in the afternoon we have the concert and in the evening the Christmas party."

" And when do we buy the presents?" Jennifer asked with shining eyes.

" Each form takes it in turn to go into Horning during the last week of term. That's fun too, because, although there are only very few shops, there are plenty of things to choose from and we always finish up with a good tea at The Coot's Nest."

For a little while they continued their dabbing and splashing in a silence glowing with visions of Christmas. It was broken presently by a cautious whisper from Pam. The upper third had ears like —like—rabbits, and it was important that they should not hear.

" I say, people, what shall we all give Lindsay?" she asked very seriously.

" It mustn't cost more than sixpence each," Caroline reminded her.

The Duckling heaved a sentimental sigh.

" I wish we could think of something worthy of such an absolute angel, because she *is* an angel, even although I don't believe she has quite forgiven us yet for hiding the upper third's bedclothes."

" I'm afraid she hasn't. I've never seen her so angry before, have you?" worried Anthea.

" No, but I'd rather have her angry with me than just ignore me," Pam remarked. " And we really have set the upper third—don't let them hear —a good example since then; in Lindsay's way I mean. There hasn't been a row now for years and years. About her present. What do you think? Shall we club together and buy her something really nice, or each give her a present separately?"

" Oh, separately!" cried everyone, Jennifer especially loudly. She would send home for one of her greatest treasures, a tiny sailing ship enclosed in a green glass bottle. Perhaps Lindsay would stand it on her mantelpiece beside the photograph of *Whitewings*, and perhaps whenever she looked at it she'd think of Jennifer, and perhaps one thought might lead to others equally satisfactory and, well, by next year's regatta anything might happen.

The lower fourth had a lot on their minds as the end of that Christmas term drew near, but most pressing of all was what to do about the owner of the frail pathetic hand.

" We've simply *got* to get her out of the kidnapper's clutches before we break up," Pam asserted in her most emphatic voice at break one morning when, snugly wrapped up in scarves and sweaters, they had gone out into the frosty garden to eat their biscuits and wait for the *Jolly Roger*. It had just gone by with the frail white hand waving at them from the port-hole as pathetically as ever. " Here we are," she went on with a rousing gesture, " making lovely plans for the holidays and getting excited about going shopping this afternoon and yet content to leave that poor creature in the clutches of a rogue. It's surprising really that ordinary people can be so selfish, but I'm more surprised at myself than I am at any of you."

" I thought to-day her hand looked thinner than ever; I expect he starves her," remarked the Duckling in a morbid voice. " I wonder why her people don't hurry up and pay the ransom? Surely it's pretty rancid of them."

" Too poor, I expect."

This was an uncomfortable thought.

" Then why don't they rescue her by force?" suggested Anthea, looking worried.

" Because they don't know where she is, of course," flashed back Pam, ready with an explanation as usual. " You don't suppose when he writes his threatening letters he gives his name, address, and telephone number, do you?"

" N-no, but I should have thought they or the police could have done *something* about it by now."

" The police may be on the watch," put in Caroline, without much conviction.

" Which only makes it all the more clever of

us if we rescue her and they don't," wound up Pam cheerfully.

Jennifer had been fumbling for a different idea as, nibbling petite beurre biscuits, she strolled beside the others over the crisp grass. With the last mouthful the idea came.

"You don't think it would be better if we tried to collect the money—asked for it instead of Christmas presents, for instance, and then sent it to Rose's parents for the ransom—do you? I mean, instead of trying to rescue her," she suggested.

They stared at her blankly. What was she talking about? How could sending money possibly be a better idea than all the excitement of a daring rescue. No. Most emphatically they did not think so. Just giving money to people showed a sad lack of enterprise as everyone with any sense knew.

"No, it isn't a better idea because, you see, it's the *thought* that counts," Pam informed her brilliantly. "Besides, my father is going to give me a bicycle for Christmas. He's awfully thrilled about it. I shouldn't like to disappoint him."

And to everyone's relief Jennifer subsided. She had felt it right to mention her idea, but a Christmas without presents would certainly be very dull, so she soothed her conscience, which was still prodding, with the hope that there would be an opportunity of helping Rose when they went into Horning shopping that afternoon.

It was a lovely day, frosty and exhilarating, with a great red sun hanging over the little woods on the other side of the river. Just a perfect day, in fact, for Christmas shopping and, having listened restlessly to Miss Matthews's instructions about keeping together and not speaking to strangers, they set off purposefully down the drive.

" Isn't it heavenly being all by ourselves—not even a prefect?" the Duckling gushed, as they turned in the direction of the village.

" It's only once a year so we must enjoy ourselves," remarked Pam, " and we must all promise not to watch what the other people are buying because we want the presents to be great surprises."

At Horning the little row of shops stood back from the river on the opposite side of the road from the staith where boats tied up when they stopped at the village. In the summer it was a gay, bustling place always full of holiday people, but now there was an air of belonging-to-itself about it which was by no means desolate. A sound of hammering came from the boat-builder's shed near the staith, a big black wherry was coming up beside it, and from the shops close at hand and from the inn at the curve of the river lights were already blinking cosily.

Having strolled across the grass to look at the wherry, the girls turned back towards the shops, beautifully decked for Christmas with holly and cotton-wool snow.

" Now for the presents!" cried Pam, giving the signal to begin, and clutching their purses they scampered inside.

As the choice of sixpenny articles was rather limited and there was always a risk of any present being duplicated, it was not considered a breach of good manners to make exchanges, as on one occasion when Gretchen found five out of the seven parcels in her bulging stocking to contain china pigs.

After much thought and careful inspection Jennifer bought a packet of toffees wrapped in fancy cellophane paper, a pin-cushion in a tasteful shade of pink, a lucky black cat with an enormous tail, three pencils tied up in red ribbon, a green-covered diary, and a mauve-and-pink Chinese lantern. These she packed carefully into her bag, meaning to decide later how to distribute them.

After shopping came tea at The Coot's Nest, a cosy little place with its glowing fire, bright-green furniture, and sprigs of holly on the tables.

" We each give our own order and pay our own bill," Pam informed Jennifer as they squeezed round a table in the window. " We have to do that because of Gretchen," she added, tactfully lowering her voice. " Do you know last year I found I had paid for five cream buns and only eaten three? I couldn't sleep a wink all night for thinking about it."

Jennifer was in a positive glow of enjoyment —an enjoyment which was emphasized still more when she compared her present happy state with her feelings last time she had had a meal in a restaurant. Then she had been on her way to a new school. The incident at the cinema queue, with all its misery and suspense, was still before her. She hadn't even met Lindsay Dysart. And now look at her. She was one of a group of friendly people. The cinema incident was buried, although possibly not dead, and as for Lindsay—well, no world could help being practically perfect that contained Lindsay Dysart.

A brown mist was creeping over the river when they came out of the tea shop, making the lights, which earlier had only blinked in a cheerful way, now glow a comfortable red. It seemed a pity to have to turn away from them into the frosty lane leading back to school, but no one could think of a good enough excuse for staying any longer in Horning.

"One thing, it's dancing to-night and none of us have got to agonize at the Inter," Pam was reminding them when Caroline suddenly clutched her sleeve.

"What's that?"

Listening with thumping hearts, they heard a familiar sound coming rapidly closer round the bend of the river.

Chug-chug*ger*-chug-chug*ger*.

It was the *Jolly Roger*.

"Quick," hissed Pamela, "don't let him *see* us!"

They dashed across the road into the shadow near the boat sheds where they waited alertly, peering out of their hiding-place to see if the boat was calling at the staith.

"She must—oh, she must!" whispered the Duckling. "I shall die if she doesn't."

"Well, she is," breathed Pam, nearly beside herself with excitement.

Caroline poked her head an inch in front of all the other heads.

" No, she isn't, she's going too fast!"

" She *is*, I tell you. She's coming into Horning."

Other heads poked forward.

" Yes, she is!"

" Pam's right!"

" There she is beyond the wherry."

They clutched each other, their eyes gleaming with all the fervour of the chase.

" And there is the kidnapper!" They were too intrigued almost to breathe.

" Look! He's throwing a rope to that boy with the dog!"

" He's coming ashore!"

" He is—yes, he is!"

" No, he isn't; he has turned back!"

" Only to fetch a basket!"

The *Jolly Roger* rocked as the kidnapper stepped heavily up on to the staith, and the lower fourth drew back into the shadows. Seen for the first time on land, he looked bigger and more savage than ever.

" And Rose will be rescued before Christmas after all," breathed Jennifer. It was going to be all right. Now perhaps her conscience, which was of the kind that must interfere, would leave off reminding her that it was quite time to call in grown-up help for the rescue of the frail pathetic hand.

" If she's on board," murmured Caroline, in the mood to throw cold water.

Automatically all eyes turned to Pamela.

" We must go and find out," Pam said, calm

and determined in the face of this emergency.

" Oh!"

" But suppose he comes back?"

" He's probably only gone to get a drink."

" And he looks most awfully fierce."

Now that the opportunity had come they secretly wished it had not. The kidnapper did look rather fierce. Besides, he might fancy one of them to hold for a ransom, and then there would be two pathetic—although possibly not frail—hands to signal from the port-hole.

Only Pam's enthusiasm seemed still to be intact. She had hurriedly torn up seven pieces of paper, two of which were marked with crosses, and now she was squeezing them together in her hand.

" Each take one," she commanded when they were well shuffled.

They each took one. Their sighs of relief when the crosses were drawn by Pam and Jennifer were cleverly turned into coughs.

" What are we going to do?" whispered Jennifer, who was being pulled in so many ways by her fear of the kidnapper, her relief that Rose's rescue was imminent, and pride at the part she must play in it, that she didn't know whether to be glad or sorry she had drawn a cross. One thing she was sure of, however. If she'd got to invade the *Jolly Roger*, then she would rather have Pam for company than anybody else. Pam would know what to do.

Pam did know what to do.

" We must go and peep into the cabin first and see if Rose is there. If she is there, we must rescue her—you others be ready to help." Pam turned a cold suspicious eye on the rest of the company, who were making spasmodic attempts to appear enthusiastic. " If she isn't there, we'll try to leave her a ray of hope."

" A ray of hope?" Jennifer looked bewildered.

" She means an encouraging note," Caroline translated briskly. " Hurry up; he may come back at any moment. We'll wait for you here."

For so notorious a kidnapper the boat looked depressingly ordinary. It was shabby too, and the odd noise the engine made was obviously caused by old age rather than by anything sinister in its design.

" It's got two little boats tied on the back," Jennifer whispered, following Pam on board.

" Yachts' dinghies," nodded Pam. " I expect he has repaired them and is taking them back to their owners. Don't forget that he masquerades as a shipbuilder. I say, the cabin doors are shut. Do you think we should knock? We don't want to give Rose a shock. People with frail hands often have weak hearts."

Jennifer, in a flutter, nodded and then quickly shook her head. Anything might be in that cabin.

Pam knocked and then opened the door. The cabin was empty. Beyond was a smaller one, separated from the other by swinging doors; that was empty too.

" It looks most horribly ordinary. No chains or handcuffs. Not even a hatchet," grumbled Pam, adding with a flicker of hope: " But of course, he would have to behave like an ordinary shipbuilder or the police would immediately suspect him."

"What shall we do, then?" whispered Jennifer, trying to appear interested, but her only real concern was to find herself safely back on the staith.

"Perhaps we'd better just write a hopeful sort of note for Rose and hide it under the cushions of that bunk——" Pam was beginning, when a sudden lurching of the boat and heavy footsteps outside caused both their hearts to leap into their mouths and stay there. They had sufficient presence of mind, however, to fly for the inner cabin where, crouching in a panic between the bunks, they heard the engine beginning to chug.

Chug-chug*ger*——

If the noise was alarming when they were safely tucked up in bed at school, it was pulverizing now.

Jennifer was on the verge of tears.

"W-we—m-m-must t-tell him to s-stop."

"What, and be kidnapped ourselves? Not much. We'll stay here quietly and wait for an opportunity to escape," whispered Pam in a quivering voice, which contrasted oddly with her stout words.

Jennifer knelt up to peer through the port-hole. Nothing was to be seen but dreary rushes and the muddy edges of fields. Already the village was left behind. Soon they would be passing River Place. Oh, if only, *only* she could wake from this terrible nightmare and find herself safely back there, never, never, *never* again would she grumble about the baked beans for breakfast or Miss Matthews's sarcasm or the absurd amount of poetry one ordinary brain was expected to learn in three-quarters of an hour.

" H-he may be taking us anywhere," she gulped despairingly.

" Think of poor Rose Gubbins," whispered Pam, who, although far from happy, had such faith in her ability to cope with any emergency that she looked upon this present one as a temporary inconvenience rather than a calamity. " Poor Rose must always feel like this," she went on, much moved by her own unselfishness.

" We may always feel like it now as well as Rose," Jennifer whispered, feeling the first tear trickle down her face.

" Well, if we do ever escape we shall get into a horrid row at school," Pam reminded her, with a vague idea of providing a counter-irritant. " The others will have to go back without us, and although they won't tell till they have to, they'll have to tell pretty soon." She actually giggled. " What a flap they'll be in at this moment!"

And Pamela was right. They *were* in a flap. For fully a moment after the *Jolly Roger* had chugged away through the darkening winter afternoon, the group at the boatshed was held motionless by horror. Then Caroline, with the others at her heels, ran uncertainly on to the staith, where they stood in a helpless row staring at the *Jolly Roger* until she was out of sight.

" We—we must go at *once* and tell Miss Hazell," decided Anthea, with a determination in her voice that was new to them all.

" But she'll be in such a rage," faltered the others, equally determined not to tell until it was absolutely necessary.

" But if he's kidnapping them?"

" Oh, *of course*, he isn't yet. They'll hide so that he won't know they are there."

" But he is sure to find them soon and then every moment will count."

" Oh, Anthea, don't be so stupid." Caroline's voice was raspy with anxiety. " Surely we've had enough rows this term, and we've simply got to keep this one from Miss Hazell as long as we can —besides, we've no real proof that that man is a kidnapper," she added, rather surprisingly.

They argued all the way back to school. By the time they reached there, Anthea had been bullied into agreeing not to go to Miss Hazell until it was time to change for dancing. That would give Pam more than an hour to extricate herself—as the Duckling put it—from the coils of the kidnapper. Pam, being Pam, could do a lot in an hour. So they settled down to wait as hopefully as possible.

By half-past six the adventurers had not returned and spirits, in consequence, were very low.

" It's a good thing there is no prep to-night or we couldn't have kept it a secret," remarked Gretchen to Anthea in a throaty mumble, so that the upper third, at the other end of the common-room, should not be able to hear.

" I do hope we are doing the right thing," muttered Anthea, pale with suspense.

At a quarter to seven Pam and Jennifer still had not returned.

" Only fifteen minutes more and then we must go to Miss Hazell," Anthea decided.

At ten to seven they went upstairs to tidy themselves. Nothing annoyed Miss Hazell more than unbrushed hair. At nine minutes to seven a dinghy, being rowed over the water with a splashing technique wonderful to behold, was approaching River Place.

" If only, *only* we are back in time to stop them telling Miss Hazell," Pam was muttering for the twentieth time.

Jennifer, intent on steering, shivered and said nothing. It was incredibly cold on the water, and Pam was making such a noise with her oars that it might almost be supposed the kidnapper would hear.

At five to seven Anthea, Caroline, Geraldine, Gretchen, and the Duckling, with beautifully brushed hair and thumping hearts, were preparing to invade the Head's sitting-room.

At four minutes to seven Pam and Jennifer clambered on shore, set the dinghy adrift, and raced across the lawn towards the house, dragging their hats and coats off as they ran.

" Do you know where Caroline and the others are?" Pam asked a passing junior as they fell in at the garden door.

" I ve just seen them crossing the hall," the junior replied without interest.

They pelted into the hall, across it, out the other

side, and were just in time to see Anthea knock on Miss Hazell's door. By the time Anthea noticed them the Head's voice could already be heard telling her to go in. Making a hopeless gesture with her shoulders she disappeared, leaving Caroline and the others standing helplessly outside.

Pam and Jennifer clutched them apprehensively.

" What is she going to do?"

" She's going to *tell*," Caroline mouthed at them with stealthy gestures.

" But—but—she mustn't; we're back!"

They stood for comfort very close together, listening to the voices which came through the half-open door.

" Yes, Anthea?" Miss Hazell sounded indulgent. Anthea, an easily managed person, was always a favourite with the staff.

" Oh—er—Miss Hazell, please——"

" Well, what is it?"

" Em——"

" Are you in trouble?"

" Oh no—that is—" An inspiration came at the moment it was needed most. " May I telephone my aunt at Norwich, please?"

Miss Hazell glanced at her shrewdly. For the maker of such a simple request she seemed strangely ill at ease. In almost any other junior Miss Hazell would have suspected mischief of one kind or another, but Anthea was above suspicion.

" Is it important?" she asked.

" It is rather, Miss Hazell." Anthea hated untruths, but she could think of no other excuse for knocking at the headmistress's door. Fortunately the others had had sense enough to stay outside.

" Then you may telephone from the office."

" Thank you, Miss Hazell."

She hurried away to meet the wide smiles and dumb-show congratulations of her friends waiting in the hall.

" I've got to phone Auntie," she whispered as they all walked away in great relief. " Goodness knows what I shall say. Don't start telling what happened, Pam, until I come."

" *Rather* not," Pam answered gratefully.

As they changed for dancing up in their dormitory they talked the affair over by inches. Christmas shopping was so remote that it seemed to have happened last year instead of this.

" But however did you escape?" everyone was clamouring to know.

" Well, it wasn't *quite* all because of me," Pam admitted with unusual modesty. " We had some luck as well. You see, the kidnapper left us alone in the boat at Meadow Farm dyke while he went to deliver one of the dinghies, and so of course the moment he had gone we skedaddled into the other dinghy and here we are. We had an awful time wondering if we could get back in time to stop you telling Miss Hazell."

" And didn't you discover anything about Rose?"

" Not a single thing, but we have left her a note and Jennifer's toffees and my box of crayons

all hidden under the cushions of the port-side bunk.
Just above we drew an arrow pointing to where the
things are. She will be sure to notice it, languishing
there in captivity, and we simply had to risk the
kidnapper finding it first."

" What did you write in the note?" Caroline
wanted to know.

" Oh, the note—that was rather good. We told
her to look out for the Sign of the Ginger Biscuit."

" Ginger Biscuit? Whatever was that for?"

" Well, we are generally eating ginger biscuits
when the *Jolly Roger* passes, aren't we?" Pam
retorted, annoyed by even so small a hint of criticism. " I thought we would make a sort of banner
with an enormous biscuit painted on it and hold it
up to-morrow at break. Then she'll know from
what quarter help is coming."

" So will the kidnapper if he happens to have
read the note," Caroline reminded her.

Pam was annoyed, and her annoyance took the
form of extreme dignity.

" If you will kindly use your brain—such as it is
—Caroline, you may happen to remember I admitted we had taken a risk. After all, it is easy
enough to criticize when you are safe on land, but
we had to think all this out with the kidnapper's
fingers practically at our throats, crushing out
life——"

Pam was obviously rattled and a tactful chorus
quickly rose.

" Oh, of course, you were *wonderful*!"

" You must have been scared!"

" The ginger biscuit is a lovely idea."

" Nobody else would have thought of anything half so clever."

" And surely you must have felt terrified in case he came back before you got right away in the dinghy," Geraldine marvelled. " I'll write a poem about it if you like."

They all looked at Jennifer. At the moment no one dare suggest that anything had the power to terrify Pam.

" It was pretty bad, but Pam managed it all— not me," Jennifer said gratefully, as she remembered her own incompetence and quivering fright. " She rows very sort of *strongly* you know, and fortunately the river curves just there—but it was dismal with the water all round."

The suggestion of a simper flickered across Pam's face.

" Well, as a matter of fact," she admitted, " I'm not bad with boats. I expect you'll notice that next summer, Jennifer. I know Lindsay has noticed it, and I *rather* suspect she means to ask me to crew for her at the regatta. I thought she gave me a very significant look the other day when somebody mentioned sailing."

" Oh, did she? I didn't notice." Jennifer's heart fell like a cold stone inside her.

The others, busily scrambling into their evening frocks, made no comment. They were grateful to Pam for her courage and resource, which had certainly saved the form another row. Of course even to suppose that Lindsay had thought of asking her to crew for her when they were all there to be chosen—oh, well, it didn't matter.

If such a pathetic delusion made her happy it did them no harm. Besides, the regatta was still a long way off.

CHAPTER X

The Stocking Party

" It has been a putrid term," Lindsay said to Prudence, who was helping to decorate her study for the stocking party next morning. When it was finished they would take what remained of the holly and tinsel over to west wing and deck Prue's study for the pleasure of the seconds.

" There have been too many rows," agreed Prue, adding cheerfully, for fear Lindsay might imagine she was referring to her slackness: " Nothing serious, of course, except the trouble in the lower fifth, and you coped with that pretty efficiently."

Lindsay grinned as she pushed sprigs of holly behind the mirror over the fireplace.

" They've been walking about on tiptoe as far as I'm concerned ever since. It's a pity Rachel and Co. are not so much impressed by my technique."

Prue, who was kneeling on the table trailing tinsel over the light-shade, sank back on her feet, dropping her arms to her side. It was necessary

to muster all her tact to meet this dangerous subject.

" I think they feel small," she explained in a
careful voice. " You see, they were rather uppity
about your not having any helpful ideas on the
real problems of running the school."

" Uppity seems a masterpiece of under-state-
ment," Lindsay interposed dryly.

" Oh, well, you know what I mean, and then for
you to cope so successfully in that cool way while
they were—they were——"

" Doing my elementary work of keeping order
in Rotten Row?"

" Well, yes. That was rather an unfortunate
business, but all the same, old thing "—Prue gazed
imploringly at Lindsay's unresponsive back—
" they are not seriously offended, and if we all try
to meet each other half-way things will be much
easier next term."

" You really think so?"

" I'm sure of it," Prue asserted fervently,
" because I know they all like you for yourself
just as much as they have always done."

" Do they?"

The sixth, in accordance with the dignity of
their position, were always polite and even super-
ficially friendly to their black sheep, but Lindsay,
more sensitive than she sometimes appeared, could
detect the undercurrent of criticism and restraint
in their attitude, and for the first time at school
felt neglected by her form.

" What?" she inquired experimentally, when

the decorating had continued in silence for a time, " what did you mean by meeting each other half-way next term?"

Prudence, as she had expected, looked both embarrassed and determined.

" I only meant that I'm sure they would all be most awfully pleased if they knew you didn't intend to start any more stories when the one you are working on now is finished."

Lindsay glanced at her with amused indulgence.

" Surely in that case I should be going the whole way? Besides, the one I'm writing now won't be finished for ages. It's going to be a book—60,000 words."

Prue's face clouded.

" What's it about?" she asked mechanically.

" Sailing."

" Oh, I *see*." And now Prue, full of sympathy and understanding, was smiling. " If that is all, you'll be glad to give it up when real sailing begins. I can quite realize that it is comforting to write about a thing when you can't do it for any reason, but when real sailing begins there will be no need to write about it, will there?"

Lindsay, because she would have said too much, passed over Prue's incredible point of view with a lazy shrug.

" Perhaps we ought to go and start your study now," was all she said. " We've done enough in here and we don't want to be late for Rachel's cocoa party."

Prue agreed at once, appreciating what she supposed to be Lindsay's compliance. Lindsay was so sweet. She never resented a hint and was always ready to look at all angles of a difficult subject. Now that she absolutely realized how her writing upset Rachel and Co., she would give up most of it, and there would be peace in the prefect's room next term.

Gratefully Prue seized the change of subject.

" Rachel has got a glorious spread for us," she smiled. " Candied greengages and coffee layer cake, and some little cream puddings in those frilly cardboard dishes."

Lindsay, gathering up armfuls of holly, cheered visibly.

" Oh, has she? Jolly good!" Even such a very frustrated author could still enjoy a spread featuring little cream puddings in cardboard dishes.

She could also enjoy a stocking party. From the moment when a shrill and sentimental rendering of " Silent Night, Holy Night " outside the door announced the arrival of her guests, until the rising-bell broke up the party and, gorged and hilarious, they departed, Lindsay was completely happy. The kids were such fun, she thought, when they were not arguing or showing off or making nuisances of themselves in other ways. And they were so ready to believe she was perfect. With Miss Hazell's few words about leadership fresh in her mind, she determined to be different next term. She'd try to be the kind of person Miss Hazel and Prudence expected her to be and every junior in the place trustfully believed that she was.

When the carol was ended she flung open the door and they all trooped in with their presents —lower fourth and upper third in a wonderful harmony which might, if conditions continued favourable, last out the day.

Pam made a speech, prompted at audible intervals by anyone else who had a helpful idea, and then the presents were given to Lindsay. It was not easy to keep the exclamations of astonishment and delight at the correct level of enthusiasm as the long procession of china animals, pencils, and packets of sweets were displayed, but nobody had any doubt about her pleasure in the sailing boat enclosed in its green glass bottle.

" Jennifer, it's simply perfect, but I don't think you should have given it to me," she said, standing it, as Jennifer had hoped she would do, beside the photograph of *Whitewings*.

Jennifer glowed with pleasure. The others looked annoyed. They wished Lindsay would smile at them in the way she was smiling at Jennifer.

" We were only supposed to spend sixpence," Pam could not help muttering in an audible aside to Caroline.

" Making up to Lindsay," mouthed Caroline disagreeably. They glared across the present-strewn table at Jennifer, who was too happy to care, or even to have any doubts as to whether her choice of a present had been a wise one.

But if the present-giving was a disappointment to some people, the spread which followed was all

that a spread could possibly be at half-past six
on a snowy December morning. Lindsay not only
had a larger allowance than was probably good for
her, but she liked spending it on other people, and
by the time the fruit and the cakes were eaten and
the quite dazzlingly beautiful crackers pulled,
her guests' mood was so sunny that even the originality of Jennifer's present was temporarily forgiven.

After the meal Pam made another speech—a
habit which seemed to be growing on her lately,
her friends noted with dismay—and then when
Lindsay had gravely replied, Geraldine jumped up
and, clipping on her nose the pair of spectacles
she had found in her cracker, started to read the
verses she had composed for Lindsay's card. After
so much delicious food, even Caroline was inclined
to admit they sounded quite professional.

> " You shall hear how Lindsay Dysart,
>   Gallant, tall, and very handsome——"

They glanced proudly from the form poet to the
object of her enthusiasm, whose expression they
found slightly baffling. If Lindsay hadn't looked
so very solemn one might almost have supposed
she was amused.

" Thank you, Geraldine," she said when the poet,
with a graceful bow, had handed her the card
amid an outburst of applause. " I must say I
think your matchless skill in hyperbole quite out-
shines my mighty skill in sailing, but it was very
nice of you to write it, and the colouring of the
card is most original."

She put it on the mantelpiece beside the boat.
Geraldine appeared much pleased with herself.
Jennifer, quite unreasonably, felt disappointed.
The others, lower fourth and upper third, looking
at their ordinary presents piled among the brown
paper and good wishes on the desk, decided something wasn't fair. Nobody quite knew what.

"And now," said Linday, according to custom,
" come and eat chestnuts round the fire—I think
some are ready—and we'll all tell in turns what
we are going to do for Christmas. Jennifer, you
start; you are the newest person here."

Jennifer, taken by surprise, flushed and looked
doubtful, but no one was staring at her; they were
all too busy with their chestnuts, so presently she
began, rather breathlessly, to speak.

" Well, in the New Year we are going to Ireland
to stay with a big family of cousins, which will be
very interesting because we have never been there
before, but for Christmas we always go to my
grandma's. She's got a much nicer house than we
have, with a lake in the grounds, and if the frost
holds we shall skate and we always go out carol
singing with the vicarage children. Last year we
collected twenty-two shillings in aid of the choir
boys' Christmas tree. That's all, I think."

" Very nice too," nodded Lindsay. " You next,
Anthea."

Anthea looked rather depressed.

" My mother and father are in India, you know,
and I always go and stay with my aunt in Norwich.
She's very nice and gives me a lot of presents,

but my cousins are all grown-up and go to dances
and parties and—and—well, it isn't much *fun*
really."

Lindsay smiled in her sympathetic way.

" Wouldn't your aunt let you take a friend
home, if you asked her?"

Anthea's depression deepened.

" She might, but my cousins say one kid is
enough about the house."

" Oh!" Lindsay thought for a moment. " Well,
look here, I shall be in Norwich for part of a week;
perhaps we might go out somewhere together
Give me your telephone number before you go.
Next one—Pam."

Pam, in contrast to the now radiant Anthea,
looked rather blue. The distinction of being
invited to give Lindsay one's telephone number
appealed to her self-importance.

" Lindsay, will you be in Sheringham for part
of a week too?"

" I'm afraid not."

" Oh, well, then—" If a bad-luck tale would not
bring her Anthea's rich rewards, she might as well
turn them all green with envy as she had first
intended. " It's really very lucky for me," she
began, " that my brothers break up after I do,
because Dad has promised to take me to London
to meet their train from Hampshire, and then we
shall buy our Christmas presents and some of our
winter sports equipment and go to a matinee
and spend the night at a hotel—Claridges, I
shouldn't be at all surprised—and then after

Christmas, of course, we are going to Switzerland. I think I may have mentioned that to some of you before." She had—more than once.

" And now it's your turn, Lindsay!" cried many interested voices, for already the snowy dawn was creeping in through the curtains and the rising-bell might go at any minute now.

Lindsay thoughtfully peeled a chestnut.

" I'm afraid my holidays would seem dull to you because I shall be very busy doing something that you wouldn't think interesting, but there will be dances of course, and we always give a party and a Christmas tree to the village children. We generally have people to stay—dull ones some-times, but my brothers may bring some friends from Oxford—and I suppose there will be hunting, and if there is any ice we shall skate."

The juniors listened intrigued. They loved these occasional glimpses into Lindsay's home life, partly because Lindsay was Lindsay, and partly because they suspected that her background was rather sumptuous and glamorous, like something in a film.

" And you'll be in Norwich for part of a week," Anthea reminded her.

" Yes. I shall be staying with an aunt, too, and I expect I'll be just as bored as you are, so we must cheer each other up."

Now it was Anthea's turn to look pleased with herself, and fortunately the rising-bell dispersed a sort of despondency which was beginning to settle on the rest of the party. During the chorus of thanks for a lovely time, Lindsay spoke to Jennifer. " I shall take your boat home with me; it's much too nice to leave behind for four weeks."

Jennifer nodded. She envied her boat. If only she could squeeze herself into the tiny cabin, what fun it would be to go home with Lindsay!

A spirit of revelry was abroad that day. Trunks were packed, desks turned out, and closed for the last time for four long weeks. Rows of chairs had appeared in the hall. The platform was a bower of flowers. Unofficial last-minute rehearsals for the concert were going on wherever the harassed artists could find a quiet corner. The telephone scarcely ceased to peal as parents rang up about times of trains.

Although that morning there was no official break, at twenty-past ten the lower fourth slipped out into the garden, squeezed through the hedge, and arranged themselves in a row on the tow-path, holding aloft a cardboard banner on which was painted an enormous ginger biscuit. Exactly five minutes later, the chugging, which to Pam and Jennifer now sounded more ominous than ever, was heard approaching.

Chug-chug*ger*——

The *Jolly Roger* appeared round the wide curve of the river. It passed, and the watchers on the bank nearly swooned with the violence of their emotions. The frail pathetic hand was waving a small Union Jack. She had found their message. She had gussed where it came from. Almost anything might happen now!

" If only we weren't going home to-morrow,"
mourned Pam.

" *Pam!*"

Pam shrugged.

" Oh, well, you know what I mean. If only we
had done something more definite about Rose
earlier in the term, she might have gone home for
Christmas too."

The others looked uncomfortable.

" It was pretty rancid of us."

" But we *seemed* to do all we could."

" Perhaps the police will rescue her before next
term."

" Oh, surely not!" Pam cleverly turned her
dismay into a scornful laugh.

" Well, if they haven't we will; we *really* will,"
everybody decided, looking cheerful once more.

They hurried indoors to finish their packing. It
was a great shame that Rose must spend her
Christmas with the kidnapper, but since they could
do nothing about it now, except, of course, to tell
the police about her, which, they sternly informed
their consciences, would be absolutely useless—
there was no point in spoiling their own fun with
useless anxiety and self-reproach.

CHAPTER XI

The Loofah

" But whoever heard of a new girl in the sixth?" said Olive Sanders.

" She is certain to upset everything and be horribly critical," said Mary Cooper.

" She may be too winsome for words," said Lindsay with a grin.

Rachel, Prue and Anita, lounging on the study window-seat, said nothing at all, but their grim expressions showed how much they disapproved of new people invading the sixth. A sixth form should be composed of people who had worked their way through the school and—for better or for worse—were soaked in the traditions of the place.

" Anyhow, she won't be allowed to use this study," sighed Mary, drawing what comfort she could from the thought.

Rachel nodded, looking more cheerful.

" Perhaps, after all, she won't make much difference to us. Greta and Vivien and Audrey will look after her."

There followed the usual first day of term business—the lists to be checked and put up on the notice-board, the allocation of the various duties, the discussion about teams and fixtures—and then, just as they had finished and were thinking pleasantly of tea, a knock sounded on the door. It was a frivolous kind of knock, as if the person on the other side were playing a tune.

" Is there anybody at home?" The voice, besides being a new one, was frivolous too, and before Rachel could answer, its owner had flung open the door with a flourish and strolled into the room. " How do you do?" she smiled. " Matron told me to come along and introduce myself. I'm Lois Turner."

"Oh, how do you do?" They shook hands with the new girl a little stiffly. She was a tall, immaculate person, with neat, undistinguished features and blond hair very fashionably arranged.

" Isn't anyone looking after you?" Olive asked, when Rachel had completed the introductions and they were standing in an aimless circle in the middle of the room.

Lois smiled readily.

" Oh, I can look after myself, thanks. Mind if I sit down?"

She sank, with another smile, into the chair Lindsay offered and glanced approvingly about the room.

" Rather nice for a school, isn't it? And what a heavenly view from the window. I shall just love to curl up on that window-seat and dream my days away."

The prefects exchanged glances. Presumptuous was the only word for Lois.

" This is the prefects' study," Olive explained. " Just for the use of prefects, you know. The rest of the sixth have a sitting-room of their own. I hope you will find it comfortable."

" Oh, I dare say it will be all right. As a matter of fact I peeped in on my way here, but I prefer the view from this window, and I do think one's surroundings are most awfully important, don't you? I'm afraid that is rather a fad of mine. I absorb my surroundings like an enormous loofah and then "—she shrugged eloquently—" when I squeeze myself, *out* they all come."

" Squeeze yourself?" echoed her audience, looking politely bewildered.

For the first time since her arrival Lois seemed a little uncertain.

" Oh, that's just a private joke I have with myself—nothing important. Were you having a discussion? I hope I haven't interrupted. I'll just curl up quietly on the window-seat while you carry on."

Rachel gave her a stiff little smile.

" I'm afraid prefects' meetings are held in private," she said. " In any case we've finished for to-day, and it is nearly tea-time. Perhaps you would like to come with me now and I'll show you the way to the dining-room?"

" And surely Vivien and the others will have arrived by this time; they are not generally as late as this," Olive hinted in a significant aside.

" Yes, well, if they have, we can introduce Lois to them," Rachel answered, leading the way.

" What games do you play?" Anita, in her official capacity, asked the new girl as they went downstairs together.

Lois looked unenthusiastic.

" Oh, I'm quite keen on tennis and play a pretty useful game, but as far as any other is concerned "—she shrugged again, spreading her hands in a fastidious gesture—" I hate getting all hot and hysterical, especially in the mud, don't you?"

" I'm afraid I don't know what you mean; I've never had hysterics," Anita answered with a deliberate repressiveness which she was afraid was lost on the new girl, who was swinging along beside her, apparently enjoying the many interesting glances she met in the corridors.

" This is the sixth form table," Rachel explained as they entered the dining-room—a low, attractive place with its panelled walls, blue-clothed tables, and vases of cape gooseberries—" but as Greta and the others have not arrived yet you had better sit with us at the prefects' table."

Lois agreed, while noticing the welcoming grins and shrill scraps of holiday news which greeted Lindsay from the junior tables. A red-haired child with a lot of freckles made herself conspicuous by running out of her place to meet her, but was quickly drawn back by the shocked comments of her companions.

Lois noticed other things: Rachel's nervousness as she said grace; the odd mixture of self-assertiveness and indecision which seemed characteristic of Anita and Olive; the special smile which the pretty dark girl they called Prudence kept for Lindsay; Lindsay herself, more distinguished and certainly more self-assured than the others. She noticed the dainty china, the well-served food. She appreciated the air of graciousness and abundance which lingered about the place, and she wondered how long she would be able to conceal the fact that her own background had been neither gracious nor abundant until her father had that unexpected luck in business which made him a rich man.

Until then they had lived in a grey, shabby street which, to her secret amazement, had always contented her mother and sisters. In those days there had been washing-up to do and uninspiring, economical shopping; preparation in the noisy sitting-room, her books pushed to one end of the table, which always seemed to be laid for a late-comer's meal; the wireless jangling, her little sisters arguing, the older sister running up frocks on the machine, or draping hurriedly washed garments in front of the fire. Lois unconsciously set her mouth in a grim, determined line. No, the girls of River Place must never guess. They were sure to be snobs who would despise her for her ordinary beginning. She flung back her head ready to resent their snobbishness and to meet it with aggression, not realizing that both the concealment and the aggression showed a snobbishness in herself quite as despicable as that she was preparing to resist.

Lindsay was speaking to her across the table as she handed bread and butter.

" We get a lot of sailing here. Do you care about it?"

Lois looked straight into the other girl's face,

and something she saw there, a certain sympathy and encouragement or possibly just an unusual charm of expression, made her say almost meekly:

" I've never done any sailing, but I'm sure I should love it, and I'd certainly like to learn."

" I'll teach you when we start again," Lindsay offered impulsively, and no one at the table was more surprised than she was herself.

Lois looked delighted.

" She is exactly *right*," she thought. " I must have her for my friend."

That evening when Lindsay, simply aching with good resolutions for the new term, had dropped in on lower four to make sure they were putting themselves quietly to bed, Lois sauntered up and thrust her head round the door.

" Hullo," she smiled, " I thought I'd find you here."

Lindsay's answering smile was very cool. The juniors stared at the tall new girl belligerently. Lindsay was being an absolute angel and they were so enjoying telling her all about themselves.

" Do you want me, Lois? I'm just coming."

Disapproving sniffs drifted over the curtain rails.

" Oh, Lindsay, don't go yet!"

" Lindsay, I haven't finished telling you about how I was rescued from the middle of the pond!"

" You can tell me to-morrow," Lindsay promised amiably. " Lights out will be going in a minute now. Good night." And she came out into the corridor where Lois, working hard to assume that effortless air of distinction she admired in her so much, was waiting.

" Do you want me, Lois?" Lindsay asked again.

" Only to have a chat."

" Oh! I thought perhaps it was something important. Surely a chat could have waited until I'd finished with the kids?"

Lois flushed very slightly, resenting Lindsay's tone, but she was careful not to sound annoyed when she spoke.

" It must be pretty marvellous to be so popular, isn't it?"

Lindsay agreed at once, but indifferently.

" It takes up a good deal of time, and time is precious at River Place," she said.

" But you *need* not let it."

" Need not?"

" I mean, you would be just as popular if you didn't waste time over the kids."

" I suppose so."

" Then why bother about them?"

Lindsay paused before she answered, disliking Lois suddenly and unexpectedly.

" Oh, shall we call it just a whim?" She had no intention, she told herself, of getting up a piharangue on the subject of Popularity: its Problems and Responsibilities. If this impossible person did not understand about these things without being told, she must have come from a pretty queer sort of school.

Lois tactfully said no more. Lindsay, she thought, seemed quite unaccountably up-stage about her poor little attempt to be flattering and sympathetic. Hers would probably not be an easy friendship to capture—things so really worth having seldom were, but she generally managed to get what she wanted in the end. Meanwhile, she must apparently be very meek; almost as if she were quite an ordinary new girl.

"Let's go down to the library," Lindsay was saying. "It's usually more or less deserted at this time."

"Oh, but need we?" Lois looked both disappointed and determined. "I thought perhaps we could curl up really snugly in your study."

"I'm afraid not." There were two reasons why this suggestion was not practicable and fortunately one could be more casually mentioned than the other. "Only prefects have visiting privileges. Let's go down to the library; it's quite cosy there."

"I suppose," Lois said enterprisingly, "you prefects are expected to be rather priggish—it wouldn't be your own fault, of course, I don't mean that——"

Lindsay turned back at the top of the stairs.

"How sickening! Do we give that impression?"

"Oh, I don't know, and it would be quite unconscious if you did," Lois informed her in an encouraging tone. "Please don't think I'm criticizing. Only to visit in your study, if *you* don't mind, I mean, seems such a little thing to want. I feel rather lost to-night and Vivien and the others are so busy unpacking and gossiping

about their own affairs." She smiled rather diffi-
dently, and because of something in that smile it
occurred to Lindsay that she was being boorish
to a new girl.

" Come in then and I'll make cocoa," she offered,
opening the door and hoping Lois would not notice
the spread of writing materials, the dictionaries,
and the manuscript of her new story on the table.
" I'm afraid the place is in a marvellous mess, but
I haven't finished unpacking."

" I think it's lovely and I do envy you," Lois
said, settling herself in a chair by the fire as contentedly as a pale-haired well-fed cat. " I had no
idea school studies could be half so jolly."

" But surely you've been to school before?"
Lindsay asked, busy with milk and cocoa.

Too late, Lois noticed her slip. She had, however, provided herself with plenty of ready-made
answers to fit even the most awkward questions.

" Well, no—as a matter of fact I haven't. My
people are frightfully old-fashioned and preferred
governesses, you know, but as soon as I got old
enough, I started to plague their lives out of them
to send me to school. I won at last—when it was
almost too late—and "—she shrugged expressively
—" here I am."

" Oh, I see," Lindsay murmured, supposing that
she did see. And now Lois's presumptious little
ways were explained. She hadn't understood what
was expected of a new girl—even a new girl in the
sixth.

They drank their cocoa companionably, eating

shortbread out of a tin on the floor. Lindsay chatted of sailing, hockey, and other school interests. Lois contributed a few careful items about her home and family, and began to like Lindsay for herself. Lindsay, she suspected, was only being polite. Even her conceit boggled at the hope of making much impression so soon on this popular and important person—but she'd get her. She'd make her glad to forget all that rot about visiting privileges. With Lindsay for her friend and the run of this delicious little study . . .

" May I look at your pictures?" Lois asked when the cocoa was finished.

" Of course. Do." Lindsay glanced uneasily at the muddle on the table, wondering if it would be less noticeable to leave it there or to put it away, but before she could decide, Lois, prowling round the room, had noticed it too.

"Oh, I say, what luck! Can we take typing here?"

" Nobody does, but I dare say you could as an extra."

" Then what is this?" Lois picked up the pile of manuscript and held it out to Lindsay.

" It's part of a story I'm writing."

" A story—oh, Lindsay, do you really write?"

" Yes."

" What an extraordinary coincidence!"

" Why a coincidence?" Lindsay asked indifferently.

" Only because I write myself. In fact, I'm working on a full-length book."

Lindsay smiled at her with shining eyes.

" Then it is a coincidence—a pretty good one. I'm glad you've come. Nobody else here cares a fig about writing."

" But surely Rachel and the others are interested in what you write, even if they don't care about it themselves?" Lois suggested adroitly.

" Gracious, no!"

" Oh, well—" Lois's shrug made large allowance for other people's peculiarities. With this un-expected plum in her hands she could afford to be generous—besides, she was already learning that Lindsay would not tolerate from an outsider like herself even a hint of criticism about either the customs or the people of River Place.

They sat down again, this time on the table with the manuscript spread out between them. Then they started to talk, and were still talking, *talking* when Prudence came in for a good-night chat with Lindsay.

Lois tactfully slipped outside, leaving the friends together.

" I shall get her now," Lois told herself, swinging away to bed.

CHAPTER XII

Neither Frail nor Pathetic

The lower fourth were full of good resolutions for the new term too, but their good resolutions—which was so fortunate—all happened to concern the things they particularly wanted to do.

First on the list came the Frail Pathetic Hand.
It was essential, Pam assured her friends, borrowing her form-mistress's voice, to proceed in this
matter with both caution and dispatch, or poor
Rose Gubbins would soon be wondering if she was
ever going to be rescued at all.

" Well, if you ask me, she must be rather an
optimist not to have started wondering long before
this," commented Caroline. " It isn't as if anybody
in this form—except me—*does* anything except
talk."

" Oh, and what have you done, pray?" rapped
back Pam, quick to resent any slur on their
efficiency.

" Well, I don't know, but anything that *is* done,
I do."

" Dear me! Most interesting I must say, seeing
that nothing of any use *has* been done about it
yet."

" That's what I'm saying," Caroline explained
patiently.

" *And*," continued Pam, now well in the grip
of her argument, " what about me and Jennifer
risking getting kidnapped ourselves and possibly
even murdered? I suppose you are going to tell us
next, that being carried off on the *Jolly Roger* and
leaving those signs and messages for Rose wasn't
doing her any good?"

" Yes, what about that?" echoed Jennifer,
thinking hard about something else, but hoping
to appear interested.

" I don't suppose it was much use. We've

probably only raised her hopes for nothing. I thought her hand looked frailer than ever this morning," Caroline was answering in a gloomy voice when Gretchen, full of news, appeared in the common-room doorway.

" I say, the upper third have got a secret society."

The lower fourth declined to be impressed.

" Really? How utterly mid-Victorian."

" Too tepid for words."

" How do you know, Gretchen?"

" Well—" Munching hard, Gretchen came into the room. " I'd just looked into the dining-room to see if the tea tables had been cleared, because I thought a little extra sustenance might help me to tackle that shocking French poem we've got for prep, and as there was no one there, but a new maid with carroty hair exactly like Jennifer's——"

Jennifer bristled.

" I beg your pardon, the colour of my hair is burnished amber."

"—carroty hair exactly like Jennifer's," continued Gretchen, taking another bite. " I just gave her a sweet smile and removed half a slab of sultana cake from the hatch. She looked rather surprised, but she was too new to say anything, and then I slipped into the cupboard in the senior cloakroom to eat it. I hadn't been there long when it was inadvertently brought to my notice that a very secret meeting was taking place just round the corner in the ' showers '. I didn't *exactly* listen, of course, but I couldn't help hearing that they

were distributing badges and that it is something
to do with the suppression of somebody, and they
are going to have a meeting to-night after lights
out. Then," wound up Gretchen regretfully, " just
as I was thinking perhaps I ought to go away, they
went away themselves and I came here to tell you.
There, what do you think of that?" She swallowed
the last mouthful and looked beamingly round for
some appreciation.

The lower fourth, while expertly sifting the news
to find the necessary ingredients for a rag, continued to appear unimpressed.

" Well, as I said before," commented Caroline,
" I think secret societies are pathetically first-
formish if not absolutely mid-Victorian."

"And I repeat, ' they are simply too tepid for
words '," added the Duckling.

" Still," the casualness of Geraldine's tone was
not really convincing, " I think perhaps we ought
to find out more about it. I mean, a secret society
can be an absolute hotbed of—of—perfidy and
fraud. Look at the gunpowder plot—and I
wouldn't call the upper third any *more* moral than
Guy Fawkes, would you?"

" I certainly would not, and of course Lindsay
did ask us to keep an eye on the upper third for
her," glibly asserted Pam, who was firmly of the
opinion that if only one kept on saying a thing
loudly enough and often enough people in time
would begin to believe it.

" I don't think Lindsay likes us any more now
Lois has come," pouted the Duckling, staring out

of the window into the rainy darkness. " She only looks in for a moment before lights out now, and won't even stay and talk, because she says she's busy—pretty tepid, if you ask me."

" Yes, and I think Lois is horrid. She called me a ' scrap ' last night and Lindsay laughed. Me a *scrap*!" Gretchen drew herself up indignantly.

" Well, I suppose an elephant is a scrap to a dinosaur," Anthea pointed out consolingly, " but I agree; Lois isn't nice enough to be real friends with Lindsay. Lindsay is so frightfully super, and in private life, you know, she is even nicer than she is at school."

The others at once looked alert and slightly sentimental. They were never tired of hearing how splendidly Lindsay had kept her promise to cheer Anthea's dull holidays, and how she had looked while doing it and what she had worn and what she had said, and the frightfully super way in which she had said it. For this peep into a side of Lindsay's life, unconnected with school and therefore denied the others, quiet, easy-going Anthea had become head-line news until something more important came along. Only Jennifer tried not to listen. She wanted to be Anthea so much that it was like a pain.

" And now," bustled Pam, when Anthea had obligingly described the afternoon at the theatre for the seventh time, " what are we going to do about the upper third's meeting to-night?   I honestly think we ought to attend it—strictly incognito, of course."

" We've got to find out where they are holding it first," Caroline reminded her.

Pam assumed an air of exaggerated restraint.

" Well, naturally we shan't attend a meeting if we don't know where it is being held; that, I should have thought, was obvious even to a first-form brain."

" Caroline means ought we to find out where it is *first*," Anthea put in helpfully.

Pam looked wildly round for help.

" Of *course* we've got to find out where they're holding it; don't all keep on talking bunk in such a clever way. If we start lurking directly after lights out we'll soon find out where they are. It is sure to be one of the attics. We shall have to be jolly careful, though. We don't want to get into a row with Lindsay."

" Oh, she'll be too busy shut up in her study with Lois to bother about us," Geraldine remarked comfortably.

On second thoughts Pam, although relieved by the reminder, preferred to take a more elevated point of view.

" As a matter of fact it won't matter if she does catch us. We're doing it for her benefit. We're only doing it to prevent her having a lot of trouble later on with the upper third."

" Oh, rather—of course we are," a virtuous chorus agreed. All the same, it was rather comfortable to know that Lindsay would be too busy with Lois to interrupt their activities for her benefit.

In spite, however, of Pam's optimism the upper

third had chosen their meeting-place cleverly, and after half an hour of stealthy searching, the lower fourth, swaddled in sweaters, scarves and blazers against the bitter January night, retired baffled to an attic staircase to decide what to do next.

" You may happen to remember I *said* we ought to find out first where they were going to hold it," grumbled Caroline, who was feeling particularly dismal because she suspected a tooth of beginning to ache.

" Well, you said Peru was in Arabia at geography this morning, and, you see, you were wrong," Pam reminded her unkindly.

Caroline gave her a very acid look which unfortunately missed its mark in the darkness.

" That was simply a slip of the tongue. Surely you recognize a slip of the tongue when you hear one?"

" Not when it has slipped across an ocean and a couple of continents, I don't——" Pam was beginning when Anthea interrupted her, leaning mysteriously down from the top stair.

" Do you all hear a funny sort of sniffing noise?" she whispered.

They listened alertly. They could hear a funny noise. And it was a sort of sniffing sound. Almost as if someone was crying. It came from the luggage room at the foot of the stairs. In the very dim light shining up from the corridor below they went to investigate.

The sniffing stopped as they pushed open the door and a husky voice asked:

" What do you want?"

In the stream of light from Gretchen's torch they saw with surprise the new red-haired maid sitting on a trunk, wiping her eyes with her apron.

" What's the matter; are you in trouble?" Anthea asked softly.

" No, thank you," the husky voice replied. " I felt a bit funny, that's all—homesick, you know. I only came last night."

They clustered about her in a sympathetic circle.

" Where is your home?" Jennifer asked, for something polite to say.

" I come from Yarmouth."

Instantly they were on the track. Their noses down, their ears alert. The frail pathetic hand had come from Yarmouth.

" I say," Pam burst out excitedly, " do you know many people in Yarmouth?"

" Quite a few," Rose nodded.

" You don't happen to know a Rose Cow of Gubbins Street?"

The new maid gave a croaky laugh.

" No, but I know a Rose Gubbins of Cow Street all right."

Terrific sensation.

" Oh, that's what I meant," cried Pam. " We know her, too—at least we don't exactly *know* her; we've never spoken to her, but——"

" Well, you're speaking to her now," the new maid answered almost cheerfully, and her astonished audience nearly toppled over backwards in the stress of their emotion.

When sufficient breath had been recovered a storm of questions descended on Rose, who was giggling now instead of crying.

" But—but how can you be——"

" Surely you passed this morning on the *Jolly Roger*?"

" How did you escape?"

" Did you escape or did he let you go?"

" You waved to us only this morning—or—or—didn't you?"

The mention of waving made them look at her hands. She had strong, red hands, which were certainly neither frail nor pathetic, and for the first time they were forced to admit that they had never had any proof, apart from their overwhelming conviction, that the frail pathetic really was Rose Gubbins. Still, there must be a satisfactory explanation if only they could find it. Nobody could bear to part with an interest that had become as much a part of school life as dancing on Wednesday evening, or Friday's fish pie.

Pam concealed her bewilderment under a sternly efficient air.

" Rose, have you ever been kidnapped?" she demanded.

" No."

The lower fourth exchanged despairing glances.

" But, Rose, Doris told us—she was a dormitory maid last term, you know."

" *Do* you know Doris?" Caroline interposed briskly.

Rose nodded.

" She lives in our street. It was her mother got me the job here."

" Well, Doris told us that a Rose Gubbins had disappeared, and it was thought she had been kidnapped, and just about that time we saw very suspicious signs on board the *Jolly Roger*, and of course we put two and two together."

Rose was giggling again. They had certainly cheered her up.

" Oh, that! I did disappear for a bit. As a matter of fact I stowed away on a fishing smack for a lark."

" But Doris said it was all in the papers."

" So it was," nodded Rose, looking important. " A reporter came round to see Mum. He seemed to think I'd been kidnapped. It was all in the papers when I was found too. Didn't Doris tell you that?"

" No, I suppose she forgot."

They felt limp and dazed with disappointment.

" Then *who* is the frail pathetic?" weakly demanded Pam of no one in particular.

" And will she pass in the *Jolly Roger* on Friday as usual?" asked the Duckling. It seemed impossible—absolutely and completely impossible— to believe that she was quite unconnected with their astonishing discovery.

Rose shrugged and stood up.

" I shouldn't know."

" We were trying to do something to help her, you know."

" Well, you've done something to help me

instead," smiled Rose. " I feel a lot better now. Hadn't you all better go back to bed soon? You don't want to get into trouble with that matron. She looks a bit of a tartar if you ask me."

They agreed, feeling smaller than they had ever felt before. They were cold too, and there really seemed nothing left to do but to follow Rose Gubbins's advice. *Rose Gubbins*. That sensational name that had tamely turned out to belong to the new maid with ugly red hands and flaming red hair.

On Friday morning they raced down to the river. The *Jolly Roger* passed, and there was the hand, waving out of the port-hole as pathetically as ever.

They waved back rather dubiously until it was out of sight, and then Pam, who had been thinking hard, turned to face her companions.

" Well, if you ask me, there is *still* something jolly fishy about the *Jolly Roger*," she observed, in a tone which dared her audience to disagree. " I mean, who *is* the frail pathetic anyway, and what is she doing in that boat?"

They sadly shook their heads.

" We must find out," asserted Pam.

" And what do we do in the meantime?" asked Caroline.

" In the meantime we go on cheering her up in every way we can. If you ask me, that hand looks more frail and pathetic than ever this morning."

" She wasn't waving the flag either," Jennifer pointed out hopefully.

" Probably too weak to hold it. I expect he starves her. I expect——"

" But who can she *be*?" demanded several voices impatiently.

" Haven't I just told you we've got to find out? Come on, people, there is the bell."

Pam stalked ahead determinedly. The frail pathetic had been an absorbing interest too long to be relinquished without a struggle.

At the garden door she stopped for a final word before the tedium started of a double period of French.

" Really the whole thing is getting more exciting than ever," she assured her irresolute friends over her shoulder, " because before, we did know the name of the frail pathetic——"

" Or thought we did," interrupted Caroline.

" And now," continued Pam blandly, " we don't even know that, so it makes our job tons more exciting and—and—*onerous*, if any lady present has heard the word before."

CHAPTER XIII

Influence

The residents of Rotten Row were not the only people affected by Lindsay's new friendship. Her friends in the sixth were astonished and dismayed. What, they wondered, *could* she see in Lois? How could the cool, fastidious Lindsay admire a person whose chief characteristics, in their opinion, were presumption and conceit. Her odious triumph at having annexed the most popular person at River Place could be better understood than forgiven.

They were bound to admit, of course, that they had often criticized Lindsay's slackness; they still did, and they certainly resented her air of casual efficiency when there seemed nothing in fact to support it, but now that her visits to the prefects' room were only business affairs, the prefects' room seemed desolate.

As for Prue, her dismay and self-reproach had made her as prickly as a hedgehog, and woe betide anyone who approached with attempts at consolation. If only, she wished a dozen times a day, she had tried harder to understand the change in Lindsay. If *only* she could have shared her new interest as determinedly as Lois was doing. What a fool she had been! She had felt so proud of her tact when she had hinted about the reduced books on Smith's bookstall, and now she realized that Lindsay had never once confided in her since.

It was not that Lindsay didn't appear as friendly as ever when they met, but they met so seldom. And it did not occur to Prue, being Prue, to fight to win back Lindsay's friendship. The shock of losing her so unexpectedly to Lois deprived her of her spirit. Yet if she had tried she might have been successful, for although Lindsay was certainly yielding to Lois's influence, the process was much more gradual than anyone supposed. Only Lois knew how slight at first was her hold on her new friend.

Lindsay's standards were not her own, and she was shrewd enough to realize that Lindsay was contemptuous of her attitude towards many things, even although she needed her. The books they were writing was the only vital link between them, and Lois with determination and resource made the link a little stronger every day. Still, she was not always wise. There was the affair in the library.

Lois hated working in the library. It was not only that she was exposed to every sort of interruption, but it annoyed her to think that Lindsay, who was two months younger, should possess a snug little study in which to work in peace while she had no more privacy than a fourth-form child. Besides, as she often remarked to Lindsay, it was so much more inspiring for them to work together. Lindsay agreed, and one night brought her writing things down to the library; but it was not a success. The lower fifth happened to choose that evening to look for a play for their end of term show, and Lindsay was appealed to so often for advice, that neither she nor Lois could concentrate, and both were irritable in consequence.

" I suppose you are so stuffy about inviting me to your study because it is against your principles to encourage an innocent little new girl to break rules," she remarked mockingly, as they were on their way to bed.

" No," Lindsay said. " I should be breaking rules myself."

" And you don't feel up to trying a new experience at your age?"

Lindsay grinned.

" If you must be so fussy, why not ask permission for me to work with you?" pursued Lois, determined not to fail this time.

Lindsay went into the little room that was the cause of so much argument and started to put away her things.

Lois stopped with painstaking self-denial in the doorway.

" I haven't asked permission because I know it would be refused," Lindsay explained, beginning to wonder if it were worth while bothering to hold out any longer. " Miss Hazell is most awfully strict about study privileges—don't ask me why— she won't even let Vivien do her prep in Mary's study and they have been friends for years."

" Oh, then we won't mention it," Lois agreed quickly. " We'll manage without."

" Manage?" repeated Lindsay.

" If," Lois said, " you would come out here we might be able to clear this affair up, but it is a little difficult to talk confidentially when one is standing in the corridor shouting at a person several yards away."

Lindsay laughed at her, wrinkling up her nose in the way that not only every junior in the place but Lois herself found irresistible.

" Oh, come in, then, you ass."

Lois came in purring as usual when pleased like a contented cat.

" You care so much for little things, don't you?"
she remarked, dropping into an armchair and
stretching her legs luxuriously to the fire.

Lindsay came out of the shadows and stood
looking down at her, one elbow propped on the
mantelpiece.

" You may as well come to the point," she
drawled.

Lois was only too ready.

" I mean, you really think it more important to
fuss about obeying a silly little school rule—which,
by the way, in this case is purely tyrannical—
than that the book I am writing should be spoiled,
and my career as an author—er—jeopardized
because there is absolutely nowhere else in this
building where I can work in peace? You are not
selfish, Lindsay, I don't mean that, but surely this
is a case of putting wrong things first?"

Lindsay stared into the fire. " You are not
selfish," Lois had said, but now that selfishness
had been mentioned she wondered if it was partly
that which had made her so determined to keep
Lois out of her study. And then surely Lois was
right? Some of the school rules were rather tyrannical. They must certainly seem so to Lois, who
had no solid background of school life behind her.
But even so Lois, at her age, should understand
something of what lay behind the rules and traditions of River Place—surely it was odd that she
didn't?

" You see," she began, after a long pause, " I'm
supposed to keep some sort of order here in Rotten

Row, and how the dickens can I enforce the rule
unless I keep them myself?"

This sort of problem, however, presented no
difficulty to Lois.

" The kids won't know you are breaking them,"
she pointed out easily. " Anyhow, I think there
is altogether too much supervision here. Why
shouldn't the poor little brats have a little fun?"

" Lois, I wish you wouldn't say things like
that."

" Like what?" asked Lois in honest bewilderment.

Lindsay, wondering if she could even explain
without sounding a prig, decided she couldn't, and
remained silent.

" What have I said now?" Lois persisted.

" Well, surely the principle is the same whether
the kids know or not?"

" Oh, *that*!" Lois spread her hands in airy agree-
ment.

Presently she got up to go.

" I knew of course that you were most *pulver-
izingly* good," she remarked on her way to the
door. " Much too good for little me. I'm afraid
I'm one of the ordinary sort of people who think
doing a good turn more important than all that
fuss about principles. But you're right of course,
absolutely right, and it must be a great satisfaction
to you." She shrugged, smiling charmingly in the
firelight. " I like you so much, Lindsay, and I
thought we'd have glorious times together because
we have a great interest in common, but I'm not

a half and half sort of person. I must be a real
friend or no friend at all. Don't bother any more
about the study. Good night; perhaps we'll have
another chat some time."

" Good night," Lindsay said, hating her; but
she couldn't do without her now and she knew
that Lois had won.

The new arrangement of sharing her study with
Lois soon became such a success that sometimes
Lindsay wondered how she had ever started
writing at all without Lois's constant encouragement and inspiration. But there were difficulties
at first.

Lindsay, still full of the new term's good resolutions, insisted upon devoting the first half-hour of
their precious work time to the juniors under her
supervision. She had a habit, which Lois objected
to because she found it unsettling, of popping in
and out of the study before junior lights out
sounded, for a chat or sometimes a lecture in one
or other of the dormitories. Sometimes a junior
would come to the study with a trouble, and then
Lois, inwardly fuming, would be expected to leave
her life work to fetch a book she didn't need from
the library, or be reminded that Vivien or Greta
wanted a chat with her about Saturday's debate.

" Do you realize that all this fussing with the
bothering little brats leaves us only half an hour of
uninterrupted work time?" she demanded on one
occasion, speaking pleasantly as she almost always
did, but with an undercurrent of criticism and
contempt in her tone.

"Oh, Lois, don't call them brats," Lindsay pleaded. "Jennifer is a jolly little kid, only she seems rather miserable this term. She's got a perfectly gorgeous voice for her age too. I've put her down for the Agony Inter on Wednesday, so you'll hear her sing."

"I don't want to hear her sing," Lois snapped, her annoyance getting the better for a moment of her usual discretion. "The fact of the matter is she's got a crush on you as every kid in the place has, and you simply encourage it."

"If you think that, perhaps you had better take your work away," Lindsay said, in a voice that cracked with cold.

"Just what I intend to do, thanks. Ta-ta," Lois smiled, making a swaggering exit.

Lindsay, feeling miserable when she had gone, was brusque and hard with the juniors that evening. Not that there was any truth in Lois's thrust of course—or was there just enough to make it annoying?

"That Lois is making Lindsay horrid," Pam muttered through the darkness in the dormitory when the prefect had closed the door, leaving behind her a crop of order marks and some pretty pointed comments about silliness.

Sniffs of resentment hovered over the other beds. Lois was so unpopular now in Rotten Row that she was never referred to without the scathing prefix "That". In the sixth she was known, contemptuously, as the Loofah.

Jennifer's sigh was almost a groan. She had

come back to school, her common sense drugged by her foolish dreams about Lindsay, only to find her completely absorbed in a new senior who condescended to the juniors, making feeble jokes at their expense almost as if they were four-year-olds. " I hate her, the horrid show-off," mouthed Jennifer into her pillow, clenching her hands under the blankets. " Her eyes are too small and her mouth is too small, and she's got a mean little mind. I'd love to pay her out in some way, and if she's going to spoil Lindsay nothing would be too bad to do to her."

On the following evening Lois appeared in the study, diffident and full of charming apologies. Lindsay welcomed her warmly; the chapter, which last night would not move, started to write itself, and for the first time that term she did not visit Rotten Row. Lois was so friendly, and so eager to put things right, it would simply have been boorish not to meet her half-way.

After that there generally seemed something important to keep Lindsay shut up in the study during the half-hour before lights out. They would be in the middle of an engrossing discussion about a title or a chapter heading, or Lois would beg her to listen to a description that wouldn't go right or to give her advice about some point that was holding up her story. Lindsay almost always yielded, particularly as Rotten Row had taken a fancy to behave in a most saintly manner. This was in itself, of course, another proof of Lois's wisdom, and one she did not forget to mention.

" You see, as I told you, there is no need to fuss about the children. If you show them that you trust them they will always play up," gravely asserted Lois, who believed in giving her friends what she thought they wanted.

Lindsay grinned at her across the book-strewn table.

" Oh, I know that is supposed to work in theory," she drawled, " but not invariably so in practice —especially when kids are used to constant supervision, or are rather young."

" Well, obviously Rotten Row are not too young. Aren't they proving it?" Lois retorted triumphantly. " Why, there hasn't been any trouble of any sort for a fortnight," which was true.

But sometimes Lois was neither wise nor discreet and then she showed a pettiness so completely unconscious that Lindsay was puzzled. She would appear absurdly jealous of Lindsay's contacts with other people, especially of the odd minutes she spared for Prue. She would be almost vulgarly curious about Lindsay's home life while showing intense reserve concerning her own. Sometimes a chance remark of Lindsay's would make her unaccountably angry in a curious brittle way, as once when the boat in the green bottle was mentioned, and Lindsay told her Jennifer had given it to her at Christmas.

" I simply cannot imagine what you see in that child," she rapped out. " I think she's a cheeky little minx who wants sitting on hard."

" I've never found her cheeky." Lindsay dusted

the old green bottle with her handkerchief, and put it back on the shelf.

" Well, she has cheeked me more than once; in fact, this morning for a couple of pins I would have run her into you."

Lindsay lazily changed the subject. She had noticed that Lois was sometimes overbearing with the children and she had noticed, too, that Jennifer seemed especially to dislike her.

One evening Lois, in her sunniest mood, asked Lindsay for her photograph, and a few days later brought her an expensive studio portrait of herself.

" I thought you might like to have it," she offered, with a diffident smile.

Lindsay was amused but pleased. It seemed unnecessary to exchange photographs with a person one saw practically all day long, but sometimes Lois seemed almost pathetically anxious to show Lindsay how much she admired her.

" It's very good of you. I'll put it on the mantelpiece," Lindsay said.

" No, I will. Don't get up." Lois complacently propped the photograph up in front of Jennifer's boat.

These affectionate moods, Lindsay noticed, were gradually taking the place of the critical ones; almost always now the atmosphere in the study was peaceful. It was glowing too with the thrill of creative work, so that the books they were writing leapt ahead.

As was only to be expected, such a flagrant breach

of study rules was not overlooked in the prefects' room, and Rachel, well coached as usual by Olive, tackled Lindsay seriously about it. Lindsay was charming but unrepentant.

" It is only for an hour each evening," she shrugged, " and there really is nowhere else that Lois can work in peace. You must admit, Rachel, that some of the rules are rank tyranny. We're not children now. My mother was married at my age."

" Then she married unusually young," Rachel commented stiffly. " But you know as well as I do, Lindsay, that that is not the point. The rules *are* there, and although, as prefects, we are not bound by most of them, I do feel, and you felt until Lois—until this term—that we should respect them."

" Yes, you are right, I do agree; but surely there is room for discrimination? I mean "—she shrugged with an ironic little smile that Rachel did not care for—" it really all depends on whether you consider blind obedience a higher law than— well—than kindness or unselfishness."

" Why not ask Miss Hazell's permission and then everything would be all right?" Rachel persisted, ignoring Lindsay's challenge.

Lindsay looked at her impatiently.

" Because, my dear old Feathers, the Nutkin would certainly refuse, as Lois is so new. You know how strict she is about study privileges, and neither Lois nor I care to take the risk. Don't look so glum, my dear. You must admit that this is

the only complaint you have about me this term.
I haven't cut a single committee, and Rotten Row
is rapidly moving up into the halo class."

" They certainly have improved," Rachel admitted grudgingly. " They seem better in every
way this term. How have you managed it?"

" Oh, I have my methods," smiled Lindsay,
meaning nothing in particular, and she sauntered
away to find Prue. It had occurred to her with
something of a shock that Prue had not called in
to say good night for quite a long time. She was
more shocked still when she realized that she had
no idea how long it was since Prue had left off
coming. She would go and rout her out for a walk,
she decided; it would never do for poor old Prue
to feel neglected. Prue was a dear. Much nicer
in every way than Lois, but in some odd way Lois
was becoming so completely absorbing that her
niceness—or lack of it—simply did not matter.

From a landing window she saw Prudence
mooching about in the garden in the pale February
sunshine, and she sauntered out to join her.
Prudence looked pleased, but she seemed unresponsive, as they talked rather carefully about hockey
fixtures and some tiny primroses they found under
the trees of Willow Dyke, until it was time to go
in to tea. For quite five minutes after the meal
began Lindsay's conscience prodded her. Prue was
depressed. She was depressed because she felt
neglected, and no wonder. She must be kinder
to Prue in future. She would see more of her. She
certainly had had no intention of casting off an

old friend for a brand-new one. Perhaps she and Prue and Lois could make a threesome, and if Lois objected—as she certainly would do—she must put up with it.

Lois seemed to have an almost uncanny knack of sensing Lindsay's frequent bouts of conscience and of opposing them with some fresh inspiration about their work. Her latest and most dazzling inspiration she was keeping for a special emergency, which came on a black streaming evening in February.

They had settled down companionably with their notebooks, dictionaries, and other oddments spread over the table between them, when a frightened tap was heard on the door, and before Lindsay could reply Pat's anxious face was pushed into the room.

" Oh, Lindsay, please come. Sybil has hurt her wrist and she won't stop crying."

Lindsay, hurrying away with Pat, found Sybil in a heap on the floor, clutching her arm and sobbing unrestrainedly, while her companions stood in a frightened group asking if it hurt much.

" She was practising somersaults on the curtain rail," Pat explained to Lindsay, when Sybil had been sent to the san and placed in nurse's care. " We were all doing it a little. It's the first time we have done anything bad for ages."

" Yes, it is, but we liked it better when you came to see us, Lindsay," agreed several eager voices.

" Better than what?" Lindsay asked sharply.

Looking abashed, they eyed each other in doubt about the answer.

" She means we like you to come and—tuck us up, Lindsay," Pat hurriedly explained.

" You're a lot of babies, aren't you?" Lindsay commented with a mocking glance, but her voice was gentle. " Next you'll be wanting me to kiss you good night, I shouldn't be surprised."

Squeals of delight greeted this proposal.

" Of course we'd love you to kiss us good night."

" It's not our fault you don't, is it?"

" Why don't you kiss us good night, Lindsay?"

Lindsay smiled as she picked a dressing-gown up from the floor and straightened the sheet under Pat's chin.

" Because I shouldn't dream of encouraging you to be so babyish. Now go to sleep, and if there are any more parlour gymnastics on the curtain rails you will all get into trouble. Good night."

" Good night."

" Will you come and see us to-morrow?"

" We do miss you, Lindsay."

" *Do* come to-morrow, Lindsay."

" Yes, probably I will."

She closed the door and hurried back to the busily scribbling Lois.

" Anything much?" Lois looked up to ask.

" Sybil has sprained her wrist fooling about on her curtain rail. Look here, Lois, I shan't slack any more where the kids are concerned, but that need not disturb you. I won't come into the study at all until after junior lights out."

Lois appeared particularly understanding.

" Of course, old thing, you must do what you think best—it's a pity though. I've got a letter here I want to discuss with you. I was rather excited about it, but it won't do any good now. If you don't get your full hour you'll never have time to finish your book by the spring, and I should hate to send mine in without yours."

" A letter? Who from?" asked Lindsay, starting to fill her fountain pen.

" It's from a publisher—Knoxton Jervis."

" Knoxton Jervis? But, my dear, they publish lovely things. Whatever is it about?" Lindsay's eyes were shining.

" They are willing to consider our books if we care to submit them in the spring."

Lindsay simply could not put all her pleasure and excitement into words. Instead she snatched the notepaper, with its splendid scarlet heading, and read it over and over until the letters danced before her eyes.

" Oh, Lois, how lovely!" she cried at last. "And they are in New York and Bombay as well as London. Fancy a firm like that bothering with us."

Lois carelessly flicked a cotton off her sleeve.

" Oh, well, of course I showed by my letter that I knew what I was doing."

" You certainly must have done." Then her imagination danced ahead. " Lois, fancy, when we get the author's copies! I can just *smell* them, can't you? And the lovely creaky way new books open!"

Lois smiled at her. This flushed, excited person was more like Jennifer than the nonchalant Lindsay she knew.

" But you'll never finish yours by the spring—say by early April—unless you work pretty hard, will you?" she hinted in a casual tone.

" I must finish it, and I will," Lindsay decided. " Lois, how marvellous of you to write to Knoxton Jervis. I should never have dared to send anything to a publisher for years."

" Don't let's talk," Lois begged, starting to scribble again.

" Rather not." Lindsay, suddenly full of business, joined her at the table.

CHAPTER XIV

Really, Jennifer!

It was matron who noticed how much more money than usual the upper third had to spend at the tuck stall. She questioned them closely, found them guarded and unresponsive, and was on her way to consult their form mistress when she met the head girl. Having a rather short-sighted respect for her capabilities, she mentioned the matter to her instead.

As usual Rachel's first anxiety when faced with a problem of this sort was to guard herself and the prefects against any charge of inefficiency, so now she begged matron not to mention it to Miss

Beaumont until she had made some inquiries.

" One of them may have had a birthday present," she suggested hopefully.

" Money presents are supposed to be handed over to me," matron replied, looking grim. " Besides, one of the children actually admitted that a senior had given them a prize for being good."

" A prize for being good?" Rachel turned pale with the shock of an ugly suspicion. She remembered the saintly behaviour of Rotten Row during the last few weeks. She remembered Lindsay's casual remark about having her own methods of keeping order. Lindsay must have been bribing the children to be quiet—*Lindsay*!

Immediately she tried to hide her misgivings under a particularly confident smile.

" Well, thanks for telling me, Matron," she said. " I'm sure we shall be able to clear things up, and I do like to manage without troubling the staff whenever possible."

" Then I'll leave it to you," matron replied cheerfully. " In the meantime I shall stop the upper third from spending any money at all at the tuck shop."

Later that day Rachel arrived at the prefects' meeting she had called with querulous puckers across her forehead and a hopelessly martyred air, even more pronounced than usual.

" I have questioned every senior in the place," she said, dropping into her chair at the head of the table, " and most particularly Lois, and they all deny ever having bribed a junior to do anything whatever."

"Have you mentioned it to Lindsay?" Olive asked, after a significant pause.

"Certainly not. Lindsay isn't an ordinary senior, but I have sent her a formal note asking her to attend this meeting."

"You mean, as the prisoner in the dock?" Prudence asked, ominously calm.

"No, not exactly; but I shall certainly expect her to answer some questions. Oh, Lindsay, here you are. Something rather unpleasant has happened and I wondered if you could help."

Lindsay looked surprised.

"Are we having a court? Who are you hauling up?" she asked, with a glance at the formal party round the table. Generally prefects' meetings were conducted in easy-chairs in front of the fire.

Rachel looked embarrassed.

"No, it isn't a court as—as—I think we are the only people concerned. Lindsay, I want to ask you some—well—some rather unpleasant questions."

"Do," Lindsay invited encouragingly, as Rachel paused, looking uncertain. "May I sit down?"

"Lindsay, did you offer the children in Rotten Row money to leave you in peace while you finished your book?"

"No."

"You—you didn't buy them a feed and carelessly give them the impression that it was because they had been good?"

" No."

Lindsay had not sat down, and now, her hands in her blazer pockets, she leaned back against the table as if suddenly she felt tired. Her eyes glinted oddly as she glanced sideways over her shoulder at the people in the chairs, waiting for one of them to speak. The others, staring at her, waited for Rachel.

" I see. Well, thank you, Lindsay." The head girl spoke with an obvious effort. " You didn't mean anything, then, that day when you told me you had your methods of keeping the children in order?"

There was a perceptible heightening of the tension. Eyebrows shot up inquiringly. Meaning glances were exchanged across the table. The prefects had not heard of special methods before.

" Did I say that?"

" Yes, don't you remember? It was when I tackled you about sharing your study with Lois. You—didn't mean anything special by it?"

" I certainly did not mean what you appear to think I meant."

" I see," Rachel murmured, again looking irresolute. Lindsay had denied any knowledge of the bribing, and it was, of course, impossible to disbelieve her. Lindsay was also a prefect and so could not be dismissed in a summary way from a prefects' meeting; and yet there was so much to discuss about the affair and it would be easier if Lindsay were not there.

Lindsay, knowing her Rachel, was both touched and amused by her obvious distress.

" If you don't want to ask me any more questions perhaps you'll excuse me. I'm rather busy just now," she said with a tact for which Rachel almost forgave her everything—even for being the most impossible prefect the school had ever possessed.

" Thank you, Lindsay," she said gratefully, forgetting that it was Lindsay who was supposed to have asked the favour.

The moment she had gone, everyone started to speak at once.

" I told you Lindsay wouldn't dream of bribing the children and you see I was right." That was Prue.

" Lindsay seemed rather queer. I wonder if after all Lois did it, and Lindsay suspects?" That was Mary.

" But why should Lois bother? *She's* not responsible for their behaviour." That was Anita.

" Well, I should ask her to resign." That was Olive, summing up.

They discussed the subject endlessly; round and round the table went their depressed questions, their answers and their weary surmising.

" We certainly can't ask Lindsay to resign now or it will look as if we don't believe her." Rachel, unexpectedly firm about this, pointed out more than once.

Olive waved her hands impatiently.

" Oh, surely not? This simply comes as a climax to her general inefficiency. If she had kept an eye on Rotten Row, she would have found out the trouble before matron did and stopped it. I don't say Lindsay actually bribed the kids," she went on, without a shred of conviction in her tone " but I do say so much slackness in a prefect is a bad example to the school. It isn't only where Rotten Row is concerned. She hardly ever turns up to extra hockey practice—Anita will tell you that—she ignores practically all the societies although she has condescended to pay her subs, and last Wednesday she went as far as to forget to put up the list for the Agony Inter."

It was all too true. Even Prue could only mutter something about Lois as an excuse. But, in spite of the blackness of Lindsay's record, Rachel, who could be obstinate, refused to take any drastic measures that afternoon.

" I'm sure it wouldn't be right now, but the next time there is any sort of trouble due to her slackness we'll ask her to resign," she promised as the tea bell rang and they started to collect their papers.

As they were leaving the room, Mary, impulsive for once, squeezed Prue's arm.

" Don't look so wretched, my dear. If only you *expected* unpleasant things to happen you'd feel quite cheerful when they did. Come and have tea with me; I've a Fuller's cake from home."

The tea bell reminded Lindsay in her study that Prue had not been to tea with her for ages. If she flew downstairs she might be in time to catch her leaving the meeting. She flew, the room was empty, but the door of the cupboard seemed to be behaving in an odd way. Crossing the room, she pulled it wide open and found Jennifer, pink and dishevelled, emerging on all fours.

Lindsay looked at her, and Jennifer, still on the floor, squirmed before her cool gaze.

" How long have you been in the cupboard, Jennifer?"

" Most of the afternoon," Jennifer gulped.

" Please stand up." Jennifer, cramped and uncomfortable, obeyed with difficulty. " What were you doing there?"

" I was listening to the prefects' meeting."

At the complete unexpectedness of the confession Lindsay's voice lost some of its contempt.

" But, Jennifer—why?"

" I wanted to hear what they said about you— and I did," Jennifer answered stubbornly.

Lindsay's first reaction was simply one of fury that a junior, any junior, should have overheard so private—and certainly so damaging—a discussion about herself. She could with pleasure have crushed Jennifer unmercifully with a few well-chosen words, and only restrained herself because she noticed a sort of dogged satisfaction about Jennifer, almost as if she had accomplished an important duty, which intrigued her in spite of her anger.

" You had better come up to my study," was all she said, and Jennifer followed without a word.

Lois was lounging in the study, where a tea-table was laid for three and the firelight danced cheerfully about the ceiling. Lindsay glanced at her meaningly. As usual she had arrived to tea sooner than was expected, which was a nuisance.

Lois was so dense about taking a hint. Still, she would have to clear out for a time while Jennifer was coped with unless—as the kettle was already boiling—Jennifer had tea there too and the inquiry was held afterwards. Obviously it was no use inviting Prue now. She would have started tea already in her own or someone else's study.

Lois ignored the meaning glance, if indeed she noticed it.

" Well, Threepenny?" she remarked deplorably to Jennifer.

Jennifer scowled until her brows met, and she wondered dispassionately if her face, creased up as it was like a concertina, would ever straighten out again.

" What mischief have you been up to now?" pursued Lois, with nauseating condescension, for Lindsay's sternness and Jennifer's flaming cheeks told their own story.

Jennifer looked wildly round for help, or failing that, for something to throw at Lois's neat and patronizing face. She hated Lois. It was all her fault that Lindsay was in trouble with the other prefects. And it would be all Lois's fault if they asked her to resign. Lois was always with Lindsay now—walking beside her in the garden; sprawling in front of her fire. Lois was simply everywhere. Why, goodness! help! There she was on the mantelpiece grinning from an enormous photograph and—and Lindsay had *actually* used her boat to prop it up in a prominent position. Only the tip of the bottle could be seen. Jennifer could have howled with rage and jealousy.

Lois, in spite of the thunderous glances, continued to smile in her condescending way. Lindsay was getting the caddy out of the cupboard. She had decided to give Jennifer tea, as she had missed the school one, and hold the inquiry afterwards. Already her anger was cooling rapidly enough for her to feel critical of Lois's manner, and to wish she would realize how the juniors hated being patronized—Jennifer especially.

In surprise she heard Jennifer speaking rudely from the other side of the room.

"As you don't seem to *like* my boat, I may as well take it back."

"Do, if you like," Lindsay agreed indifferently.

Jennifer snatched up the photograph, intending to toss it on to the nearest chair, but on a sudden impulse she flung it into the fire. As the flames clutched at the corners, turning them brown, Lois sprang up.

"Jennifer, really this is rather too much. Fancy getting into such a rage just because my photograph happened to be standing in front of your silly little boat!" She looked for support to the silent prefect, whose expression just then was grave but unreadable.

"Lindsay, I've often told you what a cheeky little thing she is and now perhaps you'll——"

"It isn't and I'm not," Jennifer roared, quite beside herself with jealous fury. "And if you've told Lindsay, you horrid sneak, that I'm cheeky, I can tell her something much worse about you and I will too. It was you who promised us all a lot of money if we didn't make a noise—and—and—it isn't fair—you told Rachel a fib about it, and some of the prefects still think it was Lindsay. You're mean and you're a cheat and everybody hates you." Picking up the bottle she threw it straight at Lois, who dodged aside so that it fell harmlessly to the floor. As Jennifer, in dismay at what she had done, heard the glass break, Lindsay caught her by the shoulders and ran her into the cupboard.

For a few seconds Jennifer kicked and shouted, then remembering suddenly that if she made so much noise she wouldn't be able to hear what Lindsay was saying to Lois, she subsided in a tired little heap on the floor. She still couldn't hear, but she felt too worn out to fight any more.

" Funny," Jennifer thought, soon almost herself again, because the absolute blackness acted as a cold douche. " I've never been shut up in a cupboard before to-day, and now I've spent the whole afternoon in two of them."

When Lindsay let her out a short time later, Lois had gone, and her precious boat was back in its old place on the mantelpiece, sailing more gallantly than ever without its green glass bottle.

Lindsay, stretched out in her big armchair, looked at her thoughtfully.

" Jennifer, I simply don't know what to do about all this. What on earth has happened to you? First the cupboard and now Lois's photograph."

" I know—it is sort of bad," Jennifer agreed, standing helpfully on the hearthrug. In fact, never before in all her life had she behaved so badly, and never before had she felt so queerly satisfied.

" If I give you tea here while I'm thinking, you won't imagine it's a reward for good behaviour, will you?"

" No," Jennifer promised readily, and at Lindsay's invitation made a very good tea indeed. She had got rid of most of the fury against Lois, which had been worrying her for days. She had told Lindsay the real truth about the bribing—and for two bullseyes she would tell Rachel too—and although Lindsay, of all people, had caught her hiding most despicably in a cupboard, she felt happy for the first time for weeks. She was happy for another reason too. Now that she knew for sure that Lindsay would be asked to resign if there was another big row, she would plan ways of preventing rows. She might even, if only she could find the courage, warn Lindsay that Rachel intended asking her to resign.

It was Lindsay who presently broke the long silence.

" Jennifer, what gave you the idea of hiding in a cupboard and deliberately listening to a private meeting?" she asked, waving aside the cake Jennifer was politely pressing on her.

" It just came into my head when I knew there was going to be a prefects' meeting about the trouble the upper third were in with matron."

" But why, Jennifer? What business was it of yours?"

" I told you; I wanted to hear what they said about you so that I could help you."

The blandness of Jennifer's attitude baffled Lindsay. She seemed so honestly sure that she had done the right thing that it was impossible to treat her as she would have treated any other junior caught in such an appalling piece of eavesdropping. Thoughtfully she refilled the tea-pot from the kettle on the hearth, while the culprit munched shortbread contentedly.

" I simply can't imagine how you thought anything justified your behaving so meanly," she said presently, in a tone which made Jennifer quail for a moment. " Besides, what good could it possibly do me, or anyone else, for you to know what the prefects said?"

" It may do a lot of good," Jennifer answered darkly. " I mean, I heard Rachel say that Lois had absolutely denied offering us money to leave you in peace."

Lindsay's expression hardened. " I don't want to know what Rachel said about Lois or me or anyone else," she cautioned her self-denyingly. " The least you can do to make up for behaving so badly is to promise not to repeat what you heard to anyone."

" But, Lindsay, *please*—I want to warn you about something."

" Thanks, but there's no need. Rachel will tell me anything I ought to know. You've already made one wild and probably quite unfair assertion about Lois and the bribing."

" Oh, but I didn't overhear that," Jennifer interrupted eagerly. " In fact, Rachel told the others that Lois had denied that she did it." (She would get that in again, anyway.) " I knew already because she promised us money as well as the upper third, and we won it the first week. That's why matron didn't find out before, because we kept our two pounds instead of spending it at the tuck stall."

" Two pounds!" Lindsay echoed involuntarily. She had had a terrible shock about Lois—so great a shock that it was impossible yet to realize it fully. She pushed it resolutely to the back of her mind. Somehow she would have to cope with that later, but in the meantime she must decide what to do about Jennifer.

" You see," Jennifer was explaining, leaning forward earnestly in her chair on the other side of the fireplace, " we saved our prize for something more important than sweets for ourselves."

Lindsay buried her face in her hands, pressing her fingers up into her hair.

" Jennifer, I really think we have all gone mad this term. Whatever were you and Pam and Caroline thinking about to accept money for such a thing; even if it was offered to you by—by a senior?"

Jennifer was ready as usual with an explanation. " It was partly that Lois turned it into a competition, and, of course, we wanted to beat the upper third, and partly we needed the money for something—a sort of charity really. We haven't spent a penny on ourselves. Pam said that would make it all right and Caroline and I thought so too."

" If you had come and asked me I would have helped you with your charity, as you call it," Lindsay said. " I will still if you tell me what it is, but you must give Lois back her prize." She was grateful to Jennifer for supplying that word— it was so much less damaging to Lois.

" I think if you gave us your autograph it would be enough," Jennifer answered, after thinking for a moment. They were receiving regular messages from the frail pathetic by the thrilling means of sealed bottles, and although she seemed reticent about who she was and what she was doing on the *Jolly Roger*, they still had hopes of rescuing her. The last bottle to be dropped stealthily from the port-hole and helped on its journey to the tow-path by a long-handled dusting brush had contained inquiries about the person like a princess who sailed a little boat so beautifully. In the juniors' opinion the description could apply to no one but Lindsay.

Unfortunately for Jennifer, Lindsay passed over her reference to an autograph and returned to the much more unpleasant subject of the eaves-dropping.

" Must we always make a thorough search of the room now before a prefects' meeting in case you are lurking in some odd corner, or up the chimney?" she asked ruthlessly.

Jennifer had the grace to look uncomfortable.

" No. I *promise* I won't be there. It really was the only thing for me to do this once, Lindsay. It —it was *right* for me. You know you once said in the dorm that something inside us always tells us what is right and wrong. Well, it told me this was right, and you wouldn't want me to go against my conscience, would you?"

" Not if you are certain you weren't bullying your conscience," Lindsay smiled at her, remembering the quotation she loved about the drummer, which had even impressed Rachel and Co. Jennifer must be stepping to some new and outlandish swing rhythm. Perhaps she heard a saxophonist instead of a drummer, but, whatever the music, she believed Jennifer was sure she had done the right thing and she respected her conviction.

" About Lois's photograph," Lindsay said presently.

Jennifer coloured guiltily.

" I'm sorry about the photograph—if you liked it."

" I liked it very much, but that doesn't matter because Lois will give me another one. You must apologize to her for behaving so rudely and for losing your temper. You might have blinded her when you threw that bottle."

" Oh—I don't want to apologize!" Jennifer exclaimed dismally, but she got up immediately to go and obey. Looking back quite dispassionately at her afternoon's work, she had to admit that Lindsay had treated her with amazing indulgence.

" Aren't you going to take your boat?" Lindsay asked as she reached the door.

" Not if you really want it to prop Lois's photograph against," Jennifer answered sincerely, trying to make amends.

" I do want it, but not as a prop," Lindsay said with a smile. " Don't be more of a little lunatic than you can help, will you? Good night."

CHAPTER XV

Getting Round Lindsay

The lower fourth were crouching behind the hedge by the tow-path waiting for the *Jolly Roger* to pass. They were expecting an unusually interesting note to arrive by bottle that morning, because, fastened round their last gift of sweets, had been a long list of questions they particularly wanted answered. Who was she? How old was she? How long had she been a prisoner on the *Jolly Roger*? Why didn't she ever show them her face? She could see them; why not let them see her?

Although the frail pathetic had been the first to establish direct contact, she remained annoyingly reticent about herself and her life on board the *Jolly Roger*. This, the lower fourth gleefully put down to fear that her letters should fall into the kidnapper's hands. That she was too weak to hold a pen for more than a few seconds at a time was a popular and more romantic theory but one that did not invite close inspection. It was not that she wrote so little; rather that what she wrote was so little to the point. She had not asked for either food or help in her first letter, but she had begged them to write to her because she was so miserable. She had given them instructions, too, about posting their letters. They were to be put in the bottle in which she sent hers and hidden in the hollow trunk of a certain old willow tree in the river bank just beyond the playing-field. She would arrange secretly to have the bottle collected, she promised, and this she managed to do, although, lie in wait as the lower fourth might and frequently did, they never discovered who collected it. She told them she was called Mavis, but ignored their inquiries about her surname.

The sweets had been Anthea's idea, and when funds were low they made parcels of cake or anything else suitable that could be smuggled from the dining-room. Also they painstakingly answered her questions about unimportant details of their school life, although her interest in such dull things as how far they had got in geometry, when they had their hair washed, and what they had eaten for dinner puzzled them from someone in her perilous position.

"It is a shame that we had to give our prize money back to Lois," Caroline was grumbling as they waited. "Although Lindsay usually seems so easy-going, she can be tougher than all the other prefects put together, don't you think?"

"What I simply can't understand," grumbled Pam for the tenth time, "is how Lindsay knew we were in it too. Matron couldn't have told her because, crude, conceited and annoying as the upper third are, they would never have given us away."

Jennifer, making a little posy of some primroses she had found on the bank, said not a word. She was always cautiously silent when this dangerous subject was broached, but she felt hot and prickly about the ears with suspense for fear they found out she had hidden in a cupboard and then confessed to Lindsay that her form, too, had accepted money from Lois. Two lapses from the school code which, not surprisingly, would have been neither understood nor forgiven.

Lindsay had been marvellously tactful the other night in the dormitory when she had questioned them about what she called the prize money. She had been scathing, too, but in the culprits' opinion, rather sweet considering everything. Only Jennifer knew with what skill and discretion she had handled a tricky affair.

"I'm surprised we didn't get into more of a row," muttered Pam to no one in particular. "Matron is so fussy about juniors not having any more to spend than their potty little allowance."

Caroline stretched a cramped leg out behind her. "What I'm wondering is, if Lindsay knew it was her precious Lois who started the whole thing."

"Well, I saw Lois coming away from the prefects' room looking sort of *huddled*," the Duckling remarked darkly.

" Huddled?" everyone echoed, looking alert, but as just then, in the distance, they heard the first sounds of the *Jolly Roger's* approach, she was not pressed to explain her meaning.

Round the curve of the river chugged the *Jolly Roger*. Out of the usual port-hole appeared the bottle. The bottle was stealthily dropped, the white hand fluttered feebly in greeting and then was gone.

" It really is remarkable that the kidnapper *never* notices the splash," Geraldine cried, as they dragged their long brush through the hedge, and with it coaxed the bobbing green bottle ashore. It had had farther to come than usual to-day, and they waited, jigging with impatience, while Pam uncorked it and took out the letter. The bell would ring for French at any moment now, and they must know which of their questions she had answered. As usual she had not answered any, but this time she did make a roundabout reference to them in her customary intense flowery style.

" Your letters and gifts cheer a soul wearying of captivity," she wrote. " Ask no more. I dare not trust my thoughts and experiences to paper. Some day of days, some dawning yet to be, we may meet face to face, although not on these earthly shores. In that day all shall be revealed. The treacle tart was lovely. I ate it in my poor straw bed and blessed you. Farewell. The road winds uphill all the way but the banks are spread with primroses."

The lower fourth stared at each other in anxious bewilderment.

" She's even more miserable than she seemed at first," murmured someone.

" Yes, she's *terrified* of the kidnapper," pointed out someone else.

" I suppose we are the primroses on life's uphill road. I think she writes rather beautifully," murmured the Duckling, looking complacent.

" M'm, except that she's inclined to take other people's ideas and alter them a bit," pronounced the poet, Geraldine, who was an adept at this popular form of self-expression herself.

" Here is something else." Gretchen pulled a second twisted note from the wet bottle. " ' P.S. In haste and secrecy,' " she read. " ' Could you leave a strong coil of rope at the tree? I shall need it at dawn to-morrow. Perhaps it would be safer to put it there after dark as it won't go in the bottle. Someone might see it and steal it. N.B. Be sure to send a rope that will stand much strain!' "

" She's going to try and escape; we must help her all we can," cried Pamela, summing up.

Gretchen was struck by a splendid idea.

" I say, all of you, do listen. I vote we take it to the tree after lights out, and wait and see who fetches it. It's ages since we did anything bad— well, really bad," she added, as a small concession to recent activities, " and I shall burst if we don't have some fun soon."

The others were enraptured with the suggestion; only Jennifer turned pink with dismay.

" Oh, need we?" she cried impulsively, without stopping to be tactful. " Let's leave it there this afternoon; we can easily poke it out of sight. It doesn't matter to us who fetches it. I'm sure we have had quite enough rows for one term."

They stared at her, too surprised to be really annoyed. What could have come over Jennifer? Jennifer, who had plunged the whole school into delicious confusion by switching off the lights? Pam was the first to think of a suitable rebuff.

" I'm afraid I can't quite see what business it is of a new girl's to decide when we've had enough rows," she observed stiffly.

Jennifer quaked.

" Besides," put in Gretchen, " there won't be a row if we are careful not to be caught—and we shall be very careful."

" Oh, never mind about Jennifer. I vote we do what you say," Pam said impatiently as the bell rang, and they all moved towards the house. " It's absolutely time we found out for certain who collects the letters and things, and we are bound to if we wait all night."

Jennifer followed at a little distance. Her form's annoyance now would be nothing, she knew, compared with their fury later on, for she was determined to prevent their breaking bounds after lights out. Perhaps then they would refuse to speak to her at all. Probably she would never have a partner for anything again, but the prospect of being a martyr for Lindsay's sake was thrilling —as long as Lindsay knew.

Lindsay happened to be too engrossed with her own affairs, however, to have any sympathy left for even the most high-minded of martyrs. She had tackled Lois about bribing the juniors and Lois had attempted to bluff.

" You see, I don't happen to consider a prize at all the same thing as a bribe," she retorted with a gay indifference, copied not very successfully from Lindsay's own. " Besides, why should you be so sure I did it?"

" Surely that shouldn't be a very great mystery when every child in Rotten Row knows?" Lindsay reminded her.

Lois, staring blankly out of the window, made no reply. She was hastily mustering her forces in the face of a desperate emergency.

" You also told Rachel a lie," Lindsay continued, in a most chilling tone. " She told me that you had denied bribing the children and quite naturally she thought I'd done it."

Lois's angry embarrassment showed in a flaming patch of colour on each cheek, but she managed to control it sufficiently to answer in an airy, scoffing way.

" I have already given you my reason for that. I don't happen to consider offering the kids a prize at all the same same thing as bribing them."

" And that, in the circumstances, is, of course, pure quibbling," Lindsay commented with infinite contempt.

Quite suddenly Lois saw a friendship which she valued crumbling to pieces while she stood looking on, and she determined to save it at almost any cost if she could. It was not only that she was growing as genuinely fond of Lindsay as she was capable of being with anybody apart from herself, but she loved the distinction the friendship gave her. It was true the prefects remained aloof, but the rest of the sixth and both the fifth forms treated her, as Lindsay's chosen friend, with a deference she could not have expected on her own account.

She decided to take a big risk. If she failed her position would be more uncomfortable than ever, but she did not intend to fail. In a diffident, rather appealing way, she began talking about her home life—its makeshifts, its dullness, its lack of privacy. She spoke of her ambitions. How she had longed for a real school life, for games, and stimulating companionship instead of those lessons in a poky room with a frusty and permanently tired governess.

" But surely you could have gone to a day school?" Lindsay asked, trying to understand what all this had to do with Lois's deceit.

" I could have done, but as I was dreadfully delicate as a child my mother paid a sort of governess—she couldn't afford a good one—to teach me. Then when I was stronger I was much too old to get into any but the expensive private schools, so I just stayed on with Miss Rich. I hated it," Lois confessed, shuddering at the memory. " The house was too small for us all, and we generally had to share clothes, and we never had a fire in our bedroom unless we were practically dying. ' Doing Without ' was a sort of family slogan. I don't know why I'm telling you all this. I suppose so that perhaps you would try to understand why I'm not like you and Prue, and make allowances."

" I'm sorry," Lindsay said, joining her at the window in the old friendly way. It did not occur to either of them that Lois was not necessarily to be pitied or excused simply because she happened to be discontented with a comfortable, kind, and fairly average home life.

" And then," Lois went on, satisfied with the impression she had made, " I took a job in a book shop soon after I was sixteen—that is where I got the idea of writing myself—and I stayed there until father had a simply amazing piece of good luck in business, when we moved into a really nice house and I begged him to let me come here just for a year." She shrugged. " That is all, I think— nothing very interesting, I know, but I do want to enjoy my one short year. I can't tell you how much I want to enjoy it."

" It would be sickening for you if you didn't," Lindsay agreed gently, thinking of the seven gay, adventurous years at River Place which lay behind her.

" And so," Lois resumed, after an effective little pause, " I wonder if you could forgive this lapse?" She smiled rather winningly up at Lindsay. " I see now how dreadful it must have looked to you. I admire the lofty attitude of yours most awfully, although I don't think I shall ever achieve it, but after all it was for your benefit that I tried to keep the children quiet. I'm not responsible for their behaviour."

Lindsay smiled in the old charming way. The shock had been a bad one, but now Lois had made her understand how an unsympathetic background could explain away her failings. Besides, she wanted to forgive her. The study without Lois would be desolate.

" I know that you did it for me," she murmured, " and it was kind of you to bother."

" Oh, that—" Lois dismissed Lindsay's gratitude with a superb gesture. " I'm just as keen for your book to be a success as I am for my own. More keen really, because I'm so grateful to you for the super time you are giving me. I'm most awfully fond of you, Lindsay."

Instinctively Lindsay withdrew behind the guard she always put up between herself and anyone who showed signs of becoming demonstrative. She was grateful to Lois for her inspiring companionship. If through Lois her book was published, nothing would be too good for her, but she could not pour out her gratitude in extravagant words as Lois would do when in the mood.

Instead, she said, staring thoughtfully out of the window:

" Lois, I suppose you intend to tell Rachel that —you did offer those prizes?"

Lois had hoped that in the delight of mending their friendship Lindsay would have overlooked such a trivial point, but she neatly concealed her dismay.

" Did Rachel believe you when you said you were not responsible?" she asked cautiously.

" Well, naturally."

Lois nodded and got up, managing to give the impression that she was going at once to the head girl's study. She did not go, however, until after hockey when, having considered carefully, she decided that too many people knew she was the culprit to make concealment safe any longer. Lindsay would be sure to find out she had not confessed. It was sickening that honesty in this case should happen to be the best policy.

Later that day Rachel, in the privacy of the prefects' room, had an announcement to make.

" The Loofah was responsible for the trouble in Rotten Row. She offered the children money—to make things easy for Lindsay, so she says."

The prefects were shocked, but not disappointed, and as Lindsay was not there, being busy in her study starting a much closer friendship with Lois, they were free to express their opinions. They did so unsparingly.

" Well, really! Fancy Lindsay of all people making a friend of a person like that!"

" Even her tastes seem to have deteriorated lately."

" Surely she will drop Lois now?"

Prue gave a great sigh.

" They have a great interest in common and—and—I'm afraid Lois is rather clever at getting round Lindsay."

Rachel showed only relief that the matter had been satisfactorily cleared up without calling in the help of the staff.

" I must go at once and tell matron," she said.
" I do hope she will be satisfied, without too many
details. I don't mind admitting I let fly at Lois
and she seemed pretty shattered."

Olive, who had been remarkably silent, now
found something to say.

" I don't know whether you have noticed," she
began, leaning eagerly forward in her chair, " that
Lindsay has been at the root of every scrap of
bother we have had this term. Even Lois admits
that she did it for Lindsay's benefit and there is
no reason why we shouldn't believe her. *Lois* is
not responsible for keeping order in Rotten Row.
Now I put it to you all, absolutely seriously, that
it is our duty to ask Lindsay to resign."

Mary and Anita looked irresolute; Prue burst
into angry words which Rachel, with unusual
dignity, restrained before starting to make a formal
reply.

" I think we must all agree with you up to a
point, Olive, but I'm not sure that this is the
moment to ask Lindsay to resign. If there is any
more trouble——"

Olive gave a scoffing laugh.

" There *will* be more trouble. Of course there
will, so we might just as well do it at once and get
it over."

" If there is any more trouble for which Lindsay
is responsible," Rachel quietly resumed, ignoring
the interruption, " I suggest we ask her to resign.
This time Lindsay was not directly responsible—
after all, Lindsay is Lindsay and I would rather not

decide in a hurry to do something we may all regret later. Do you others agree?"

They nodded. Some of the nods were rather dubious. It was true Lindsay had caused them a great deal of trouble that term, but, as Rachel had reminded them, Lindsay *was* Lindsay.

CHAPTER XVI

"A Pretty Rancid Plight"

It was fortunate from Jennifer's point of view that her form should have decided to combine the all-night rope adventure with the suppression of the upper third's secret society. Not that there would have been much point in suppressing the society—a harmless, sluggish affair—if they had not discovered that its chief purpose, apart from its use as an excuse to behave mysteriously, was for the suppression of themselves.

" It isn't that the poor little creatures can do us any harm," Pam remarked compassionately as they made their plans for the evening, " but I feel for the sake of the school's reputation it should not be allowed to continue."

Everybody agreed with solemn enthusiasm. Pam, it appeared, had taken the suggestion right off the tip of their tongues.

" And so," Pam continued, having noticed with surprise that Jennifer looked especially pleased, " as I happen to know they are having a meeting to-

night in the trunk attic immediately after lights out,
I suggest we go up there and assert ourselves in
some impressive way, and then when we've coped
with them we'll take the frail pathetic's rope and
some food to sustain ourselves out to the willow
tree and lie in wait for her messenger."

Again they all agreed. Only Caroline made one
small objection.

" If they are holding their meeting immediately
after lights out, it means we shall have to go up and
stow ourselves away in the attic *before* lights out.
Suppose Lindsay looks and finds the room empty?"
she pointed out in her competent way.

" Yes, and supposing she doesn't?" scoffed Pam.
" Lindsay hasn't been near us for ages. She isn't
likely to come to-night."

And certainly it did not seem likely. Even
Jennifer, busy with her secret plans, was willing to
risk being caught to-night if, for Lindsay's sake,
she could not only prevent all similar expeditions
in future, but also the far greater crime of breaking
out of the house after dark.

" Then we're all agreed to carry on?" questioned
Pam royally.

They were all agreed.

It seemed a very long day, especially to Jennifer,
who spent most of her spare time in prowling about
the attic and the attic stairs. At one time, if anyone had been near enough, the sound of stealthy
hammering could have been heard. At another,
Jennifer, balanced precariously on an upturned
suitcase, removed the bulb from the light at the

foot of the attic stairs. It was on the way down-stairs after this last manœuvre that she stopped at a landing window-seat to reread the letter that had arrived from John that morning.

" I dare you——" began John.

Jennifer grinned to herself as she folded it and slipped it away. It would be fun, and it would serve the horrid things right, she decided. Besides, she would have to do it some time or John would be one point ahead and that must never happen. Perhaps if her scheme went well to-night she'd give herself a little treat. She would certainly deserve it. Then for a time she forgot the dare in waiting anxiously for the evening.

It seemed odd to the lower fourth, crouching behind trunks in the darkness beyond the ring of torchlight in the centre of the attic, that the upper third should each bring with her a pillow-case and two pairs of stockings knotted together. Some kind of fancy dress, they supposed, and extremely silly they would look to their hidden audience play-ing at ghosts when they should have been in bed.

It was awkward too that they should have chosen after hardly a minute's thought to sit on the trunks behind which the conspirators were hiding —awkward and odd, as there were plenty of other trunks in every other corner of the attic. The lower fourth could see their victims' shapes, stiff and upright, a mysterious silent group with Pat in the centre, revolving slowly, her big torch held high over her head like a lighthouse. Part of the ceremony, they supposed, and remarkably silly it looked.

They were expecting Pamela to give the signal to attack at any moment now. They knew she was only waiting for the upper third to settle down and start their meeting. Then what a surprise they would have! But it was a nuisance it was quite so dark beyond the small revolving circle of light Pat made with her torch. It was absolutely necessary that they should all attack together when the time came, and it would not be easy to catch Pam's sign in the darkness. It was pretty cramping too behind those trunks. Goodness only knew what would happen if they were all casualties through pins and needles by the time Pam's signal came.

Pam herself was watching warily and also a little anxiously. Whatever sort of a secret meeting was this? No speeches, no plans, no food. Only this nerve-racking silence, and that one torch revolving so absurdly. Surely it was almost time for Pat to feel giddy and fall over? Pamela was just as cramped as her followers and she dare not move for fear June Berry, sitting squarely on the trunk in front of her, might notice and turn round. If only Pat would switch off that torch.

Suddenly Pat switched it off, but before Pam could spring up to attack June, light from another torch much closer and gleaming straight into her eyes immobilized her. Before she could move to escape, a pillow-case had been pulled over her head, and she found herself lying stretched out on the floor, her hands and feet firmly secured by stockings knotted together. Muffled squeals from all over the attic proved that she was not the only victim, even before Pat, in a triumphant whisper, started to make a speech.

The speech was brief but ruthlessly to the point. The lower fourth had simply got what they deserved, Pat pointed out, for attempting to gate-crash into a secret meeting. She proposed now to leave them where they were all night in order to teach them how to behave in a more cultured way in future, while she and her friends would hold their meeting in a place unmolested by skunks, guinea pigs, small cats, and other annoyances.

The lower fourth, helpless and defeated, writhed with humiliation under the pillow-slips. Who would have supposed that an expedition started from purely unselfish motives could have ended so disastrously?

" And if you make so much noise," Pat added, to stem the flow of abuse coming up from the floor, " you will have the prefects here in no time. Not that we shall care. We are going now. Have you each secured your man?" she demanded sternly of her followers. " Then follow me."

They followed her as far as the door. No doubt they would have followed her farther still had not the door been securely fastened on the outside. In dismay Pat rattled the handle. As there was no keyhole it was obvious that the door could not be locked. What, then, had happened? Everyone in turn wriggled the handle.

" Can I be of any help?" came a sprightly voice from outside.

Aghast, the upper third stopped their frantic assault on the handle while the lower fourth listened alertly under the pillow-cases.

It was Jennifer, who must have slipped away in the darkness when they first arrived at the attic. She had certainly started from Rotten Row with the expedition.

Pat immediately decided to bluff things out.

" Oh, hullo, Jennifer; glad you are there. Just give this door a push, will you? It seems to be stuck."

" No, it seems to be bolted," Jennifer answered brightly.

" Bolted?—Oh!"

There was a grim pause. Happy giggles came from under the pillow-cases.

Pat shivered slightly.

" Well, open it anyway, will you, Jennifer, please?" she pleaded, simply aching with politeness. " It's—er—pretty cold in here."

" It will be colder still round about dawn to-morrow," came a cheerful reminder from the other side of the door.

The upper third, knowing they had been tricked and feeling helpless because of the unexpectedness of it all, eyed each other doubtfully. They had laid their trap for the lower fourth so skilfully from the very first moment when they had made sure that Pamela had overheard what she was meant to overhear—their whispered arrangements for the secret meeting that evening. Could the locked door mean that lower fourth had set a counter-trap? No, it could not. Their fury when they were made prisoners was too real to be faked. Jennifer must be working on her own.

Pat, having silently asked for and been given her friends' views of the disaster by means of nods, shrugs, and wide mouthings, changed her tactics.

" Why won't you open the door, Jennifer?" she asked almost meekly.

" Why should I? You are all so fond of breaking the lights-out rules; it's not my business to spoil your fun."

" But you *are* spoiling our fun," someone pointed out unwisely, and faint, gloating noises came once again from under the pillow-slips.

" Have you got Pamela and Co. in there?" Jennifer asked, apparently much surprised, after a nerve-racking pause for all the prisoners in the attic, while she wriggled the bolt to and fro on the other side of the door, purely for her own amusement. Where, by the way, had the bolt come from? They were certain it was not there yesterday.

" We have got them here," Pat agreed grimly.

" Would that be Pamela and Co. making those funny snorting sounds?" Jennifer went on, politely interested.

It would be Pamela and Co.

Jennifer giggled.

" Why are you snorting, Pam? Is someone sitting on you?"

Suddenly it occurred to Pat that they had all listened to Jennifer showing off quite long enough.

She placed her mouth firmly against the door.

"Look here, Jennifer, if you don't let us out at once I shall go straight to Lindsay and tell her that you won't let us go quietly to bed—" although how she was to get to the prefect she was not very certain.

Apparently Jennifer had thought of the difficulty too.

"Would you like me to bring Lindsay up here?"

Roars of disapproval from the party by the door, and some loud discouraging noises from under the pillow-cases, indicated that for the first time that term the lower fourth and the upper third had found something to agree about.

"All right, then, if I can't help you I may as well go to bed. Good night, dear friends." And there was the sound of footsteps rather obviously descending the stairs. Panic in the attic was too general for anyone to notice the footsteps had not gone very far.

"Jennifer, come back!"

"Jennifer, don't go!"

"What do you want us to *do*, Jennifer?"

Jennifer came back immediately.

"I want you to disband your secret society—you can't possibly suppress us; you've just about as much hope as a beetle trying to tread on an elephant, and also I want you to swear that you won't leave your dorm without permission ever again while Lindsay is a prefect."

The upper third, their torches gleaming distractedly all over the place, discussed the terms in violent whispers. More peculiar noises were coming from the wriggling bodies inside the pillow-cases, whether of amusement or encouragement it was difficult to decide.

" And suppose we refuse?" demanded Pat, making a feeble last stand.

" I shall go and fetch Miss Hazell."

" Rot, you wouldn't be so mean."

" Wouldn't I? You don't know me."

" Well, none of us will ever speak to you again as long as we live."

" Three rousing cheers. That's even better luck than I'd hoped for."

The upper third gave in.

" Oh, all *right*, Jennifer Windgate, but don't imagine you've gone up in our opinion. You're right down in the dregs."

" Do you promise what I said?"

" Yes. Open the door."

" But I haven't finished yet. I want to speak to Pam."

" How did you know Pam is here, by the way?"

" I saw her come in with the others. Pam, what's the matter—what are you doing?"

At a nod from Pat, June released her prisoner and Pam bounced to the door.

" Jennifer, thank goodness you're there. These absolute infants have been playing at robbers and bandits all the evening. They've tied us up in pillow-cases and—is that *you* giggling, Jennifer?"

" I just—sort of coughed," Jennifer explained hurriedly. " Do you want to be let out?"

" Do we want to be let *out*?" Pam could hardly believe her ears.

" Because," Jennifer continued smoothly, " you must all make the same promise as the upper third."

" None of our lot can speak; they are all tied up," Pam answered to gain time.

The door was rattled from the outside in a cautious but peremptory manner.

" Pat."

" Yes?"

" Release the lower fourth immediately."

" Oh, all *right*."

Presently, after some stealthy scuffling on both sides, the prisoners were released.

" Now do you all promise not to leave the dorm before or after lights out, and most particularly not to go down to the willow tree to-night?"

" What about the rope for—for—you know who?" Pam asked meekly.

" I took it myself this afternoon and stuffed it inside the tree."

" Oh!" There seemed nothing else to say.

" Then do you promise?"

" Do we?" Pam, conscious of the amused grins of the enemy, turned with dignity to her stiff and uncomfortable companions.

Gloomy nods were the only response.

" All right; we promise."

At last the bolt was drawn back and the defeated revellers crept outside. The upper third were openly furious with Jennifer but her own form showed more restraint in their comments. After all, as the Duckling pointed out, she had saved them from a pretty rancid plight.

They had been in bed ten minutes before they realized that once again Jennifer had slipped away in the darkness. Nobody could imagine what she was doing, and when she returned a giggle was her only response to their indignant questions.

"You have been doing exactly what you made us promise not to do—leaving the dorm after lights out," Pam informed her stormily. "You mustn't have one law for yourself and another for everybody else, you know," she added, remembering a useful snatch of conversation she had overheard in the prefects' room.

Jennifer, who had been feeling very pleased with herself—she had not only saved the risk of trouble for Lindsay to-night, but she had effectively stopped all future expeditions of the same kind—suddenly bounced out of bed, where she had just settled down very snugly with the blankets drawn up to her nose.

"I—I—didn't think. I—I—forgot. Quick, I must go and undo it."

"Undo what?" asked everybody, sitting up preparing for some fun.

"Oh, nothing—that is—oh, nothing!"

She was flinging on her dressing-gown and fumbling for her slippers. Her plans for saving Lindsay from trouble had worked out so well that success had turned her head a little, and carrying out John's dare had seemed nothing more than a postscript to a thoroughly good evening. Now at

Pam's words she had realized what a fool she had been. If Rachel discovered the—discovered what Jennifer had just done, she would certainly hold an inquiry and then everything might come out. The meeting in the attic, Lindsay's slackness—everything. Oh, why hadn't she remembered this before? She was sick of John and his dares.

She rushed to the door. As she did so a muffled crash followed by the sound of startled voices came up from the prefects' room below.

Jennifer stood still.

"What on earth are the pre's up to now?" Caroline whispered, much mystified.

Nobody knew.

"Aren't you going to undo whatever it was you meant to undo?" Pam asked Jennifer, who, still clutching the door handle, was straining to hear what had happened in the room underneath. "Jennifer, why don't you answer? Aren't you going to undo——"

"It's no good now," Jennifer gulped, creeping back to bed.

CHAPTER XVII

Worse and Worse

"The lower fourth are to go to the prefects' room before prayers."

Vivien put her head round the dormitory door while the morning race against the breakfast bell was in progress.

The race petered out.

" Is it a row, Vivien?" Pam asked anxiously.

" It is, my child," Vivien nodded, " and I think it would be only kind to warn you that our head girl is in a dangerous mood," she added, before strolling away.

" I believe it's all your fault, Jennifer," Caroline grumbled, " for doing whatever it was you did after we were all in bed."

" That crash, you know," the Duckling reminded her.

Jennifer could not reply. If she had moved her face in any way she would have burst into tears.

The atmosphere in the prefects' room was rigid with formality. The prefects sat in a half circle at the far end of the table, their fountain pens and a large, and somehow intimidating, sheet of paper spread before them. If notes on that scale were to be taken, even the most delicate finessing—at which most of the lower fourth were expert—might be more disastrous than a plain answer.

All the prefects were there. Rachel harassed but obviously very angry. Mary depressed. Prudence anxious. Olive and Anita full of business, and Lindsay wearing a quite unreadable expression as she watched the juniors file in and nervously arrange themselves at the other end of the table. The sunshine outside and birds singing only emphasized the arctic conditions of the atmosphere inside the room. Some brown splashes on the walls near the door were obviously fresh and might have been cocoa. Rachel straightened her shoulders and started to speak.

" First I want to know how many of you left your dormitory after the bedder bell last night. I see, you all did." She made a note on her paper. " Now, Pamela, you hold the proud position of form captain, I believe; perhaps you will explain why you considered it necessary to break one of the strictest rules of the school."

Flushing, Pam shifted her weight from one leg to the other. Rachel wasn't much of a hand at sarcasm but she didn't care for that " proud ". It almost seemed like a hint that Rachel thought her a feeble sort of captain, and if Rachel, with her fluff-and-feather standards, thought so, whatever would Lindsay's opinion be? She wished too she could guess how much Rachel already knew. Surely it was unfair to anyone to be expected to make a statement who had no idea how much her judge already knew?

" Well—" she began cautiously, but before she could continue, Jennifer had pushed forward.

" Rachel, I can explain—I did it—er—er—don't ask a lot of questions that—that don't matter— you—don't want to waste time asking a lot of questions that don't really matter—that you may regret."

Rachel looked surprised. Anita and Olive exchanged sympathetic glances—really, the *appalling* audacity of the modern child! Lindsay was decorating the edges of her paper with flags and appeared not to notice the interruption.

" Jennifer, you must please allow me to make what investigations I consider necessary. Please do not interrupt again," Rachel replied in a tone of ponderous displeasure. " Pamela, we are waiting for you to answer my questions."

And Pamela was forced to obey.

" But still I see no reason for your going to the attic at all—what was it?" Rachel persisted, when Pam had rambled round the subject for some time without once leaving the edge of it.

" Well—er—you see—that is——"

It was impossible to continue without bringing in the upper third. Fortunately Rachel at last realized this, or possibly the note which Lindsay scribbled and passed to her contained a reminder.

" I know the upper third were there, if that will help your explanations, and I intend to cope with them later," Rachel said. " Hurry up, Pamela, we have a lot to get through before prayers."

" We went to smash up their secret society," Pam answered immediately.

" I see, and you had no other reason for going to the attic? Jennifer, if you won't leave off trying to interfere you will find yourself in serious trouble."

" No, there was no other reason," Pam answered. After all, the attic had nothing to do with their intentions to spend most of the night on the tow-path and, thanks to Jennifer, who was behaving so queerly, there was no need to mention that since obviously Rachel couldn't know.

And then came the question Jennifer had been

dreading, because more than any other it would implicate Lindsay.

" What time did you go to the attic? Was it before or after lights out?"

" It was before lights out."

The other prefects appeared to be too busy taking notes even to glance at Lindsay, but she could feel their growing antagonism, and almost see a ring of ghostly fingers pointing at her accusingly. Why the dickens need this have happened on the very day her book was finished? she asked herself unavailingly. Once her book was off her hands she had intended—in a rather belated attempt to justify Miss Hazell's faith in her—to devote all her time, brains, ideas, everything to the school. There was to be no more rule-breaking on the juniors' part or slackness on her own. If only they had waited to start their rag until to-night, when she would have been on duty! Jennifer, that little ass who had given the show away and who couldn't even contrive a booby trap efficiently, deserved to be boiled in oil. She was furious with Jennifer, then accidentally she met her eyes—agonised was the only word to describe their expression—and touched, in spite of her annoyance, she smiled at her reassuringly.

" And now," Rachel was continuing, when the scurry of note-making had ceased, " I want to know which of you was so incredibly foolish as to set a booby trap in here last night? You did it, Jennifer? Why?"

" I did it for fun," whispered Jennifer, still

staring at Lindsay, and seeing her expression change to a harder more critical one.

Rachel looked very stern.

" That is no excuse whatever, Jennifer. You have been here two terms now and I think it is time you learnt we have no use at River Place for that kind of fun. Mary was coming into the room with a tray of cups filled with hot cocoa. She narrowly escaped being badly scalded when your hockey boots fell on top of her. Also some expensive china belonging to Lindsay Dysart was smashed and the cocoa spilt has seeped through the floor and made a brown patch on the dining-room ceiling. I am quite disgusted by your absurd behaviour. You will play no games for the rest of this week and you must speak to Lindsay about giving up some of your pocket-money next term to help replace her china. You others will miss games to-day and to-morrow. Pamela, come to my study after dinner, please, and I will give you some work to do. The behaviour of you people in Rotten Row has been appalling this term, and I suppose if Jennifer's silly trick had not given you all away, these nightly excursions would have continued indefinitely. That is all I have to say. You may go."

And feeling incredibly deflated the lower fourth went without a word.

When the door had closed on the juniors Lindsay smiled invitingly at Rachel.

" And now you've finished pitching into the children I know it's my turn," she encouraged her.

Rachel was polishing the finger-nails of one hand on the palm of the other. The moment she had been dreading for weeks had come. She must ask Lindsay to resign. Before, however, she could find the most tactful words to use, Olive, determined to give the head girl no excuse for avoiding this splendid opportunity, had thrust herself forward.

" Then you admit the responsibility, Lindsay?"

Lindsay glanced at her indifferently.

" Yes—if it concerns you at all. Actually I was speaking to Rachel."

Olive appeared not to notice the snub.

" It is sweet of you to be so reasonable. I know we all appreciate it because it makes what we have got to do so much more easy," she resumed in an oily voice. " You see, we have been wondering for some time now—as your interests are so obviously centred on yourself rather than on school affairs—whether you would prefer to resign. If so——"

" If so?" Lindsay repeated coolly, but her heart was beating fast.

" If so, we shan't persuade you to change your mind," rapped out Olive, furious because as usual Lindsay's manner had made her feel uncouth.

Prudence leaned forward angrily.

" You may not try to persuade her, Olive, but I most certainly shall," she cried.

And:

" Olive, will you kindly allow me to manage this?" came sharply from Rachel.

Olive looked at the head girl sulkily.

"Your way would probably be not to manage at all, and you know we've agreed that if there was any more trouble in Rotten Row Lindsay should be asked to resign."

"Olive, *please*——" Rachel glanced quickly at Lindsay, who was looking on in an amused but also rather critical way which successfully hid her anxiety.

"Lindsay," Rachel asked, unmoved by Olive's furious glances, "was there any special reason why you couldn't keep an eye on Rotten Row last night?"

"No," Lindsay answered coolly, "not a special reason to you. It was very special to me as I was finishing my book."

Merely to speak of her book made her heart glow; the others passed it over as if it were hardly a matter to be mentioned in polite society, and the blankness of their expressions seemed to congeal across their faces.

"Then if it hadn't been for that idiotic child and her booby-trap you would not have known about last night?"

"No," admitted Lindsay.

"They may in fact have been playing in the attic every night for weeks past?"

"Possibly."

"Would you prefer to resign, Lindsay?"

Lindsay's eyes gleamed oddly.

"Do you want me to resign?"

"We think it would be better for the school if you did," Rachel said bravely.

"For the school?" Lindsay remembered what Miss Hazell had said about her special powers of leadership. Oh, it was sickening that this should have happened now. It was her own fault, of course; Rachel had been patient. But she hated to resign—how she hated it!

"Very well," she agreed at once, trying not to see Olive's poorly concealed satisfaction.

"Then perhaps you'll speak to Miss Hazell?" Rachel suggested stiffly.

Lindsay stood up.

"I'll go now."

Prue could keep silent no longer.

"Oh, Lindsay, don't go. We'll manage somehow —we'll all think of something; and whatever excuse will you make to Miss Hazell?"

Lindsay smiled at her gratefully.

"I shall have to tell her the truth, I suppose. She may understand. Perhaps she's even got a drummer of her own."

She went away, closing the door as softly as if she expected they would soon be asleep.

They listened restlessly to her footsteps running downstairs.

"Really that drummer of hers seems to have gone to her head," said Olive.

"She is definitely in the wrong, and yet somehow she makes us feel guilty," said Mary.

"It's rather a relief to know there will be no more of these fusses," said Anita.

"Perhaps Miss Hazell won't let her resign," said Prudence, none too hopefully.

That evening in hall Miss Hazell, without comment, announced Lindsay's resignation, and desolation swept like a locust plague through the lower school. They couldn't believe it was true. Rotten Row, who suspected Jennifer's booby-trap, not to mention their own adventures in the attic, must somehow have caused the disaster, were particularly miserable. As for Jennifer, who knew the truth which the others only suspected, she was quite beside herself with remorse. Her only consolation was that with a heart smashed clean through the middle there would not be much longer to live.

Perhaps when she was dead Lindsay, bringing her a beautiful harp (or anchor) of violets, would regret her anger with the pathetic well-meaning junior who, by means of a pair of hockey boots perched on a door, had caused her downfall. Perhaps even, in token of forgiveness, Lindsay might offer a hockey boot made entirely of flowers. That would be too, too moving; but what a pity it had to be a hockey boot. If only Jennifer had thought she would have used something more romantic for her booby-trap. But if only she had thought she would not have set that booby-trap at all.

As she curled up in bed, hating Olive, who was striding about the dormitory being horribly stern about untidy cubicles and talking in bed, it occurred to her that she had no idea how angry Lindsay was with her. At the same moment she decided that she wouldn't sleep a wink until she knew. She

would go now to Lindsay's study—Miss Hazell had
allowed her to keep it until the end of the term—
and find out. With a sudden quite unreasoning
thrill of happiness she believed she was going to
put everything right. The broken cups would make
a good excuse. Rachel had said she must pay for
them, and she would pretend at first she had come
to ask how much they cost.

When the dormitory had been dark for a little
while, Jennifer got up and crept outside, ignoring
the drowsy comments from the other beds.

Lois was standing in the study doorway, smiling
over her shoulder at someone inside.

" My dear," she said lightly, as Jennifer waited
in the shadows beside matron's cupboard, " don't
worry about me. I shall manage without the study
if you can, and anyhow I'm glad that you'll be one
of us now and not perched away up there on
Olympus."

Jennifer heard Lindsay laugh rather dubiously
and then, when Lois had gone away, she ran and
tapped on the door. At the sound of Lindsay's
voice telling her to come in, her optimism over-
flowed into wide smiles. Everything was going to
be lovely. Why, she might even be able to hint how
clever she had been in forcing those promises
from Rotten Row.

Lindsay was standing on the hearthrug where
Lois had left her, staring at the fire.

" Well, Jennifer?" she said, not encouragingly.

" It was about the cups," said Jennifer.

" What about them?"

" Rachel said I—I—was to replace them." The optimism was ebbing; Lindsay looked so unapproachable.

" You couldn't possibly replace them," Lindsay said, " besides, there is no need. I don't want your pocket-money. Run away to bed and forget about it. I'm too tired to talk now." She knew she was in a vile temper and she really had no desire to vent it out on Jennifer.

But Jennifer unwisely stayed where she was. She must put things right or she wouldn't sleep a single wink.

" Lindsay, I'm terribly sorry about the booby-trap. I have tried so hard to help you, and when I think it's all my fault that you've resigned——"

" Don't be so absurd, Jennifer. How can it be your fault?"

" Not my fault? But I thought——"

" You think too much of yourself altogether; that's your chief trouble, my child," Lindsay murmured, dropping into a chair and folding her arms behind her head.

" Then wasn't it my fault? Didn't the booby-trap make any difference—sort of bring it to a head, I mean?"

" If it did I'm not going to discuss it with you now; you take yourself too seriously, you know. Try to remember you are quite an ordinary junior, no better and certainly no worse than any of the others."

Jennifer stared at her; her eyes were enormous and her mouth was slowly dropping open. Lindsay, who was generally honest with herself, admitted that she was behaving fiendishly, but she was too wrought up to care.

"And why be so intense about everything?" she continued since, after a long silence, Jennifer was still there. "Pam and Gretchen and the Duckling are much more sensible people. I should try to be more like them."

"More like them?" gasped Jennifer. "Then, do you think they are nicer than me?"

"They are easier to get on with."

"Oh!" Jennifer had a peculiar feeling that she was up to her neck in water, and that if she asked another question she would be completely submerged. All the same, she had to ask it. "Do you like them better than me?"

"I like them better just now because they are not boring me to death, but usually"—Lindsay very slightly relented—"I like you all exactly the same. Good night, Jennifer. There is no need to come to my study any more. Olive is your prefect now." She leaned back and took a book from the shelf behind her. "You must go to her with all your fusses and worries."

"I don't want ever to go near Olive," Jennifer blurted out.

"Perhaps that is fortunate for Olive," Lindsay commented, hating herself.

Jennifer limped away. It wasn't that Lindsay was angry with her. She was something much worse. She was completely indifferent. Jennifer was just a junior, no better than any other junior.

It was improbable, she thought gratefully, that anyone so miserable could survive the night.

CHAPTER XVIII

The Kidnapper

There was almond blossom in the studio and daffodils in the dining-room and a special yellowness in the sunshine which meant that spring had really come. The nearness of the holidays made the sunshine and the flowers seem even more lovely because everyone was excited and ready to be pleased.

Lindsay and Lois dispatched their books to the publisher in great secrecy for fear, as Lindsay pointed out, that the publisher chucked them straight back again, and then turned with tremendous urgency to the end-of-term gaieties for amusement.

There had been much discussion in the sixth-form sitting-room among Vivien and Co. as to what Lindsay, now no longer a prefect and a privileged study-owner, intended to do. Would she and her new friend remain a little aloof as, in the past, she and Prudence had usually done, or would she invite Vivien, Greta and Audrey to make a set? Lindsay had always been the most prominent member of her form, and on the rare occasions when she and Prue had joined any special clique, that clique automatically took precedence of any other. Now they were delighted to find that Lindsay seemed inclined to throw in her lot with them. And not only that; she was prepared to enjoy herself with an almost fourth-form exuberance. That Lindsay had a special reason for this departure from custom and that Lois was the reason, no one, except possibly Prue, moping in the prefects' room, guessed. Lois in her young days had missed the fun of school life, and Lindsay, brimming with gratitude towards her, was determined to make it up to her now. She wanted to cram into Lois's few short terms all the special kind of happiness she had herself known for years. Her book was finished and, thanks to Lois, actually in a publisher's hands. The world outside was full of primroses. *Whitewings* was on the river again. It was fairly easy to forget that Miss Hazell was deeply disappointed in her, that Prudence, whom she never meant to hurt, looked sad these days, and that she—through incompetence—had lost her prefect's badge.

Fortunately for the lower fourth they too had something to take their minds off the dreadful calamity of Lindsay's resignation — the Frail Pathetic. She hadn't passed once since the day when Jennifer had hidden the coil of rope in the willow tree. The *Jolly Roger*, yes. But no hand had appeared at the open port-hole and no answer had come to their many urgent notes; nor indeed were the notes even collected from the old tree. She had evidently escaped at last. Thank goodness, as Pam remarked more than once, beaming encouragement on Jennifer, who was always depressed these days, thank *goodness* they had not failed her S.O.S. for a strong coil of rope.

The form had decided to forgive Jennifer for her astonishing lapse over the booby-trap, partly because she was so repentant herself, and partly —they had to be fair—because she had saved them from a very much worse row. If they had had to confess to spending the night on the tow-path as well as to all their other activities that unfortunate evening, Rachel would certainly have reported them to Miss Hazell, and what on earth would have happened then? Shudders were the only reliable answer. That Jennifer's booby-trap was in some odd way mixed up with Lindsay's resignation they certainly suspected but—still being fair—they could find no actual proof of this, and so Jennifer was given the benefit of the doubt.

" If only the frail pathetic had come to us for sanctuary," the Duckling sighed, as they discussed her disappearance over their morning biscuits. " It seems funny to think we know that hand with such awful intimacy and have never seen its face."

" Now and for ever she has faded from our eyes," Geraldine sighed, wondering if that would make a good opening line for her " Ode In Memoriam ". Sighs—Dies—Cries. There were plenty of useful rhymes. " M'm, I'm afraid we shan't hear from her again," she added absently.

There, however, Geraldine was wrong. One morning as the bell rang for break a maid came to the form-room with a message. Miss Hazell wished to see lower four in her sitting-room immediately. Hurriedly pulling their ties and combing their hair with their fingers, they sped on anxious feet to the sitting-room and there, right in the middle of Miss Hazell's elegant hearthrug, stood the kidnapper. He wore a civilized navy-blue suit and his shoes shone. Stiff with astonishment, they stared at him from the doorway.

" Come in, girls," Miss Hazell invited affably. " Mr. Grierson has something he wishes to tell you."

They came in as best they could, since all their limbs had apparently ceased to function, a thousand questions tumbling about their minds.

However did Miss Hazell know the kidnapper? Was she—masquerading as a headmistress—secretly in league with him? Were they all to be handed over to him now and held in captivity while enormous ransoms were demanded from their sorrowing parents? Had he found out that they had helped his victim to escape, and was he going to kidnap one of them instead? The Duckling moved back a step, all ready to run.

" Good morning, ladies." The kidnapper bowed in the politest possible way. " I have a message for you from Mavis." (Sensation.) " She asked me to thank you for your letters and to beg you to go on writing to her now that she is in hospital."

" In—in—hospital?" They gaped at him idiotically, while Miss Hazell made a grim mental note that something very drastic must be done about their manners.

The kidnapper smiled at Miss Hazell.

" Should I be trespassing too much on your kindness if I repeat the whole story?"

" Please do."

They listened, their astonishment changing at first to disappointment and then to a sense of baffled anger and dismay.

Mavis was his daughter—his *daughter*! She had something the matter with her back, and three times each week he took her into Potter Heigham for massage. She was not allowed to sit up, but had caught sight of the girls playing in the garden and, never having been to school, had amused herself by weaving all sorts of romances about them. Then one day the girls had made her a friendly gesture—whether because he was tactful or because he did not know exactly what the gesture was, he did not mention the note and parcels left under the cushions of the port bunk—and Mavis had been very eager to respond. He—the kidnapper himself!—had suggested floating her letters ashore in a bottle, and he had also collected some of their answers from the willow tree. Here alarm and despondency became so acute in his audience that it was positively painful to hold the necessary expressions of interest and delight on their faces any longer. What about the rope? Had he found the rope? Apparently he had not. Mavis, a good strategist, had obviously provided herself with more than one collector.

For some time, the kidnapper continued, looking very grave, Mavis had believed that too much fuss

was being made about her weak back, and that
she would be able to run and play as other girls
did if only she were allowed. One night she pro-
cured a rope; she refused to say where it came
from—much amazed and innocent eye-play from
the lower fourth at this satisfactory piece of news
—and with the rope she had tried to climb down
from her bedroom window. She had fallen and
broken her leg and was now in hospital longing for
their letters. That was the story of the frail
pathetic. That was the solution of a mystery
bursting, so they had supposed, with kidnappers,
hostages, ransoms, and starving captives. A silly
girl with a weak back, a romantic disposition, and
a doting father. It was enough to make an angel
weary of well-doing, and how much more so the
lower fourth?

"May I promise Mavis that you will continue
to write to her?" the kidnapper asked, smiling at
the well-doers, but with a question in his voice for
Miss Hazell.

"Certainly you may. The girls will be delighted
to do what little they can to make your daughter
happy," Miss Hazell promised graciously.

Feeling faintly ridiculous, the lower fourth continued to wear their guileless, gratified smiles until
they were safely outside. Only then did they relax
and only then did Pamela allow herself a comment.

"Well, thank goodness we didn't give up our
Christmas presents as well as all those sweets. We
may be asses but, thanks as usual to me, we're
not *silly* asses."

On the last day of term Jennifer's chief concern was how to contrive a private word with Lindsay. Since that unfortunate conversation in the study Lindsay had been amiable when they met but quite impersonal and always other people had been there. Now Jennifer felt she could not bear to go home until she had made one more attempt to put things right. Although experience should have taught her that Lindsay was often impatient and not always kind, Jennifer obstinately clung to the belief that if only she could *explain*—— So after breakfast she very cleverly tripped herself up and fell in a heap on the floor just as Lindsay was leaving the dining-room.

Lindsay ran into her.

" Sorry, Jennifer. Not hurt?" she murmured absently, and turned back into the room in answer to a call from Lois.

Quivering with self-pity, Jennifer allowed herself to be dragged to her feet by Caroline and Pam.

At eleven o'clock a meal of sandwiches and cocoa was served to the people who had not left by the early train. Jennifer, too sick with suspense to eat anything, watched Lindsay come in with Prudence and Rachel. She wore her travelling suit but no hat; evidently she was not leaving, as so many were, immediately after the meal.

" Cars are here for Miss Anderson, Miss Grenfell, Miss Thompson," a maid presently announced from the corridor.

Prudence and Rachel hurried away, leaving Lindsay alone at the table reading a letter. Now here at last was Jennifer's opportunity. She half rose, but having no excuse to speak to Lindsay, she suddenly felt too shy to cross the room. Lindsay was folding up her letter, patting away a yawn, glancing at her watch. Soon she would be going. Frantically Jennifer grabbed a knife and deliberately cut her finger. The knife went in deeper than she had meant.

" Ouch!" cried Jennifer, really frightened as the blood spurted out.

Lindsay came over to her, glanced at the finger, twisted her own handkerchief tightly round it, and then beckoned to Vivien, who was standing in the doorway.

" I say, you're not leaving until after dinner, are you? Be an angel and take Jennifer to matron. I've got stacks to clear out of the study."

" I don't want to go to matron," Jennifer roared in a fury.

Lindsay, going back to fetch her letter, was already thinking of more important things. " I'm afraid you've got to. Don't be tiresome, Jennifer."

There was an hour to wait until Jennifer's coach left for the station, and when matron had bandaged her finger she went down to the dismantled dormitory. All her crowd had gone on the ten o'clock train from Wroxham except Anthea, who for the moment was nowhere to be seen. In the study at the end of the corridor she could hear Lois helping Lindsay to finish her packing. No point in trying to get hold of Lindsay while Lois was there, so she might as well go and find Anthea, who was travelling with her as far as Norwich.

She sauntered downstairs and out into the garden. It was very quiet there and very sunny. A sailing boat was passing the end of Willow Dyke, tacking gently downstream. By this time next term she would have learned to sail, but somehow all the thrill had gone since obviously Lindsay would not allow her to crew for her at the regatta. She picked some primroses growing close to the water, pushed them through a buttonhole, and then sauntered back to the house. Miss Beaumont was coming along the passage.

" Oh, Jennifer, you are not in a hurry? Then just run up to Lindsay's study for me and ask her what she has done with the list of new library books. I shall be in the staff-room."

Jennifer, scarcely able to believe her good luck, bounded away. The house seemed very quiet now, except for an occasional burst of chatter as she flew past an open door, but outside in the drive cars were coming and going as they had done all the morning. She raced down Rotten Row and tapped at the study door. When no answer came she put her head inside. The room was empty, with a determined sort of emptiness which left no doubt in Jennifer's mind that Lindsay had gone for good. She stared about her unavailingly while the holidays loomed endlessly ahead. She wouldn't see Lindsay again for nearly a month.

Anthea came running down the corridor.

" Oh, there you are, Jennifer. I've been looking

for you everywhere. What's the matter? Did you want Lindsay?"

" Oh—only a message from Miss Beaumont." In a panic she felt her eyes pricking and rushed over to the window.

"Lindsay has just gone," Anthea said. " I watched her from the landing window. What a lovely car! Quite the nicest in the school, I should think. Lois went with her." Anthea chattered on and on and *on*, poking about the little room which next term would be Olive's. " Why, Jennifer, there's your little boat. Oh, what a shame! Somebody has broken the bottle." She picked it up from the top of a pile of books and brought it to Jennifer.

Jennifer rather overdid her unconcern.

" Oh yes, of course—er—well I'm blessed! I'd quite forgotten I'd given it to her. I suppose I may as well take it away as she's left it here."

Anthea smiled in her friendly way.

" I should. You don't want that horrid Olive to have it," she agreed, all unsuspecting that for the second time that term Jennifer's too-brittle heart had snapped clean in half.

CHAPTER XIX

It Pays to be Practical

" But fancy Lindsay actually getting that book of hers accepted by a publisher!" said Rachel.

" She must feel absolutely triumphant," said Anita.

" I think it has made us all look slightly idiotic because we didn't take her scribbling more seriously," said Mary with a sigh.

Prudence gave a gloating little laugh. Olive muttered something about influence. Vivien, the new prefect, wondered if Lindsay considered the price she had paid for her book too high.

" You mean her resignation?" Rachel asked.

Vivien, kneeling on the window-seat, nodded. " After all, you can write books until you are eighty but you can only be a prefect for such a little while."

" Quite," Olive bounced into the conversation. " And Lindsay wanted to do both at once—burn her candle at both ends. She always has done that, and I suppose she never will learn that a candle doesn't last long that way."

" No, but while it does last it gives a lovely light," Prudence murmured.

As usual Olive ignored the interruption.

" Don't you think we have talked about Lindsay long enough? Surely it's Rachel's turn now. She drops an absolute bombshell about leaving at half-term and our only response is to talk about Lindsay."

Guiltily they accepted the reproof. " Before this term is over one of us will be head girl," was the thought at the back of all their minds as they questioned Rachel about her parents' unexpected business call to Canada and their decision that she should go with them.

Outside the prefects' room the school was re-assembling for the summer term. Cars in the drive again, trunks in the dormitories. Squeals of admiration for the new apparatus in the gym. Feet on the stairs, voices in the corridors. Holiday news shouted from one open window to another.

Lindsay stood at the window of her cubicle in the bedroom she would share with Lois, Audrey and Greta. It had the same view as her old study, which was something to be grateful for, but it was on the floor above. Although she knew how much she would miss her study, she was tingling with well-being and a heady sort of exhilaration. She was an author! Whatever happened now in this narrow, distorted school world nothing could alter that. Oh, it was going to be a gorgeous term. She was no longer a prefect, of course, but it was good to think she would be able to work on her second book without that awful load of responsibility which had so hampered her first. Then there were so many other things to look forward to. Lazy summer afternoons on the river with Lois and Prue. Tennis. The thrill of racing *Whitewings* at the regatta. What, by the way, was that odd child, Jennifer, doing in the garden? Surely that was the third time she had zigzagged down the whole length of the lawn? Now she was coming back along the path by Willow Dyke, lurching from side to side. She really was as mad as a coot, but not without interest on that account.

Lindsay left the window and started to arrange her cubicle. She was glad matron had given her the one next to Lois. They would plan about their books together in whispers before the rising-bell, on mornings when the sun and the birds outside made it impossible to sleep. But it was sickening that Lois wouldn't be back for ten days—longer if she caught measles from her wretched little sister. She took a pile of books over to the shelf by the window. Jennifer was still there prancing about the lawn, and she wondered vaguely where Pam and Co. were, and why Jennifer wasn't unpacking.

As was only to be expected, Jennifer's antics were not escaping comment in Rotten Row; nothing, however unimportant, ever escaped comment in Rotten Row.

" She simply raced through her unpacking and went away without a word," Caroline was informing the company with relish, " and now look at her. Going on like a teetotum in a tornado."

They piled themselves on to the window-sills.

" Jennifer—*Jennifer*!" Jennifer jumped round, realized, apparently for the first time, that she had an audience, waved bashfully, and ran indoors.

" What *were* you doing, Jennifer?" Pam demanded as she arrived pink and breathless in the doorway. " Behaving like a lunatic—or anybody in the upper third you care to mention."

" Oh—nothing much," Jennifer stammered.

" Well, stay here now and help us. We've got to decide how to celebrate Lindsay being an author. *Privately* as well as publicly," she added with a slow, very significant wink.

" How about an ovation?" the Duckling suggested, with a confused idea that she was being original.

" No, I know, let's invite her to a dorm feed." Gretchen, smacking her lips in anticipation, stopped on her way to the cupboard, her arms full of clothes.

Pam scornfully dismissed both suggestions.

" Rot—she wouldn't come."

" She's not a prefect now."

" No, but she still wouldn't come. Anyhow, you know quite well we'd never have the nerve to ask her."

" How about approaching me about embodying our humble congratulations in verse and then having it framed?" came with a pleasing diffidence from the Poet.

" M'm. Not a bad idea."

" You might get Wordsworth or Shakespeare to help you this time—they are a little more formal in style than Longfellow."

" Then if that is settled, what about our private celebration?" someone asked.

" Well——" An inspiration descended on Pam worthy of her at her very best. " I know. A midnight picnic on the *Junk*, only we must wait for the full moon."

This absolutely super idea, as they all agreed, reminded Anthea of an even more super piece of news.

" I say, what do you think? Lindsay is going to skipper one of the training boats *regularly* on Tuesday afternoons. I heard Anita tell Olive at dinner."

" Oh!" Their faces were fixed with the intensity of their longing. How could each manage so that she was on Lindsay's boat?

Pam broke a strained and speculative silence.

" Of course, Lindsay will only take people who know a good deal already. She never wastes her time on beginners. Now Anthea and Caroline and I have had three summers of sailing."

Jennifer could contain her feelings no longer.

" Well, I should think she would take the beginners—you know, to give them a good foundation, as Maddy always says about French."

Their scoffing laughter soon enlightened her ignorance.

" Fancy expecting anyone who can sail as well as Lindsay to waste her time over beginners! Miss Sedley always takes the beginners round and round the island."

" Oh, I see. I didn't think." Jennifer looked confused and was glad when the tea-bell rang and they all went hungrily downstairs.

Jennifer had come back to school with the firm

resolve to be practical. She had read a school story during the holidays in which the heroine, Imogen Willoughby-Devereux (Muggy to her friends), had been so, well, so almost dazzlingly practical, that even the headmistress always asked her advice in coping with the quite extraordinary number of crises which faced her school. Not only that! Imogen, by never fussing or fuming, or being what Lindsay called intense, got everything she wanted with astonishing ease. So Jennifer had come back to school determined to be practical; to be cool, casual and, in particular, never, never to do anything *impulsively* again. For instance there was the crewing for Lindsay at the regatta. Jennifer was being exceedingly practical about that. Obviously, she had bullied herself into realizing, there was only one reason why Lindsay should ask her to do it. She must be more useful to her than any other junior, and that meant she must be the best sailor in the lower school. The others were all ahead—some, as Pam had pointed out, as much as three long sailing terms—but even such an obstacle did not deter Jennifer. In the holidays she had bought or borrowed every book she could find about sailing. She knew what a cleat was; a sheet; a topping lift. She knew how to start and stop a boat in theory and in any sort of wind. She thought she knew as much as all the writers together about tacking and saving a gybe.

And then, too, she had her plan. In spite of her form's hilarious comment she meant to continue with that, only it might be as well to use the side

garden, because only the studio and the form-
rooms and the staff bedrooms overlooked the side
garden and her antics would be unobserved.

So, after tea, she slipped out into the side garden.
Half an hour later Lindsay, strolling lazily on to
the lawn, found her making determined sorties on
one of the lilac bushes just bursting into bloom.
Lindsay felt concerned. She liked Jennifer in spite
of her capacity for making scenes.

" Jennifer!" she called sharply.

Jennifer turned, saw Lindsay, coloured extra-
vagantly, but managed to restrain the urge to
rush at her talking wildly. Always so cool and
poised herself, Lindsay hated intense people who
fumed and fussed and made scenes. Lindsay would
have invited Muggy Willoughby-Devereux to crew
for her on the spot.

" What are you doing?"

Jennifer thought she saw an opportunity and
made a grab at it. Muggy was an adept at grabbing
an opportunity.

" I was practising being a sailing boat."

" Oh."

" And working out what the different winds
would do to me."

Lindsay glanced at her keenly.

" Do you know what the different winds would
do to you?"

" Oh yes—I know." Jennifer's confidence was
Muggy's rather than her own. " I've read ten
books about sailing in the holidays and learnt three
chapters by heart. I know what the throat hal-

yard is and the boom and the topping lift, and I've practised tacking and running free and stopping when there's a following wind."

" H'm." Lindsay was gathering some pieces of lilac for her cubicle.

" But there is one thing I don't know that I'd like to ask you about," Jennifer continued earnestly. " What is luffing up to a roller, Lindsay?"

" Well, you know what a roller is, don't you?" Lindsay asked companionably over her shoulder. " It's a big wave; you won't have to cope with that sort of thing on rivers. Luffing is simply turning a boat into the wind to stop her. It means putting the helm down."

Jennifer looked intelligent.

" Oh, I see. Yes, of course. What do you put the helm down *through*, Lindsay? Would it be the bottom of the boat?"

" No," Lindsay said, " it wouldn't. Look here, Jennifer, I'm sailing *Winkin'* on Tuesday afternoons. You had better come along and see what the winds do to her."

Jennifer's face split into an enormous grin. She wanted to hug Lindsay, to turn a back somersault into the lilac bush. She wanted to shout and sing, but Muggy nudged her just in time and instead she recited carefully:

" Oh, thank you, Lindsay. I had better make a note of it and then I shan't forget. Tuesday, I think you said?"

Lindsay laughed as if suddenly something had amused her.

" You're doing very nicely so far, Jennifer. Mind you keep it up. Are you very keen about sailing, by the way?"

" Keen?" Jennifer's eyes shone. " It's the great passion of my life. It's my Alpha and my Omega. It's my most—oh—it isn't bad," suddenly remembering.

CHAPTER XX

Picnics in the Moonlight

When, after ten days, Lois came back she still had heard no decision from the publisher about her book, but that merely encouraged her complacency.

" It's so much *deeper* than yours, isn't it, honey?" she said to Lindsay. " More for them to *digest*, I mean. They may be a week or two yet, so I vote we celebrate your success to-night; just a little private celebration. As a matter of fact, I've got a super idea."

She outlined it enthusiastically.

Lindsay listened with a humorous glint in her eyes.

" My dear; it's an inspiration worthy of Pam Cameron, but we don't happen to be fourth-form children."

" No," Lois answered tartly, " I agree with you. We are not even ordinary sixth-formers. We are authors; hardly the sort of people to be bound by a lot of childish rules. You are not a prefect now——"

" Too, *too* true."

"—and so I simply can't see what your objection is to having a midnight picnic on *Whitewings*. There's a heavenly moon, and it would be lovely sailing by moonlight. Don't be a prig, Lindsay."

Lindsay paused before she answered in a slow, amused voice:

" We may be authors, but that doesn't make breaking bounds and midnight feeds anything but completely childish."

Lois looked annoyed.

" It must be wonderful to be as good as you are, Lindsay, but it has the effect of making me feel horribly inferior. Are you afraid of being caught, by the way?"

" Are you?"

" Well—oh, of course I am—and you know it."

They both laughed.

" Can't you think of a different kind of celebration?" Lindsay asked lazily. " Something a trifle more dignified."

" But I don't want to be dignified for once; I want to enjoy myself. I've never been to a midnight feed in my life. Naturally you are bored with them. I suppose you have had dozens since you were a scrap in the first form."

" Not more than nine or ten, I should say," Lindsay murmured.

" Nine or ten! And I have never been to one in my life. Lindsay, don't from your splendid banquets grudge me my few poor crumbs," Lois implored, waving her arms theatrically, but still more than a little in earnest.

Lindsay wavered. It was an appeal that never failed to move her; that and the one concerning their books, of which Lois made a much more subtle use.

" It must be only you and me, then."

" Of course."

" And we had better sail down towards Thurne-mouth. Even at midnight someone might see us out on Windrush and would guess we were connected with the school."

" I don't care where we sail as long as we are together in *Whitewings*, with the moonlight on the water and a thermos of cocoa and plenty to eat. Lindsay, don't you think it will be tremendous fun?"

" Rather."

" And it isn't as if you are a prefect any longer," Lois reminded her, with an attempt at consolation, for fear Lindsay's conscience still troubled her.

The flicker of Lindsay's annoyance came and went.

" Lois, must you keep saying that? I'm not likely to forget."

Pam leaned up on one elbow and peered at her watch in the moonlight filling the room.

" Ssh! Are you all awake?" she whispered, and drowsy grunts came from the other beds. " Well, buck up then, because it's nearly twelve now and we really ought to be on the *Junk* by half-past."

Bedclothes heaved as sleepy figures scrambled out from underneath. This was the worst part of a midnight feed: the best part was gloating about it afterwards.

Nothing had gone wrong with their thoughtful plans. The food was ready packed in two baskets. A third basket contained a couple of very old storm lamps and a bottle of paraffin. Their coats, sweaters and wellingtons lay ready. Even the garden door had been carelessly left unbolted, they discovered when they crept downstairs, and this was better luck than they had hoped for.

Once out in the garden they left off shivering, and their spirits, which had not been co-operating so far, leapt with excitement. People stopped telling each other what fun it was and started to enjoy themselves. It was such a lovely night. The moon looked enormous in the empty sky and the wind smelled of lilac and river mud, always a heady combination.

They squeezed through the garden hedge, out into the road, climbed a stile, skipped over the fields to Windrush Broad and were soon piling into a tubby old rowing boat, which was so old that nobody ever thought of putting it into the boat-house at night.

" Surely that's a sail out there on the river by Plug's Farm Dyke," whispered Anthea, as Pam and Caroline shipped the oars and they all clambered on board the house-boat.

They stood in a row on the narrow deck peering at it through the trees.

" It looks like a fairy galleon in the moonlight,"
the Duckling remarked in a soulful voice.

" There's a lovely wind; they *are* having fun,
whoever they are," Jennifer murmured. She had
sailed twice now with Lindsay on *Winkin'* and had
learned enough to realize how little she knew, or
ever would know, as it sometimes seemed in
moments of special inefficiency.

" M'm. Well, they won't come in here; this is a
private broad. Come on, people, I vote we go
inside and eat," suggested Pam, leading the way.
" Have you fastened the dinghy?" she remembered
to call back to Gretchen, as they all pushed into
the big centre cabin.

" Highwayman's knot," Gretchen nodded absently, thinking as usual of food, and afraid of being
left behind.

The cabin, a dismal place, piled high with dis-
used equipment, smelt of rotting wood, mildew and
dust, but when Geraldine had persuaded the storm
lamps to burn and the feast was spread out on a
table made of wooden crates, it certainly looked
more cheerful. The smell, they all agreed, with its
suggestion of smugglers and pirates and the bad
old days, only made everything nice and exciting.

" Lindsay's book is about smugglers—modern
smugglers in private yachts," Anthea informed the
company as they munched shortbread biscuits
piled with tinned cream. They stopped munching
as simultaneously as if they had been switched off.

" Who told you?" demanded Caroline.

" Lindsay did. I asked her. They smuggle wine and silk from France."

" Gosh! I say "—a most intriguing idea occurred to Pam—" I wonder if her people do it? They've got a lovely sea-going yacht, you know. There was a picture of it over the fireplace in her study."

Anthea was shocked.

" Of course not. Don't be silly. As if Lindsay's people would be smugglers!"

" It would be a very refined kind of smuggling," Pam pointed out with dignity. " And, anyway, I bet they do—else how would she have known to write about it?"

This question was so full of romance while it remained unanswered that nobody attempted to answer it, and Pam started to serve her contribution to the feast—gateau nuit à la framboise, which turned out to be raspberry jam spread on gingerbread.

" There are bullseyes to follow," she said in a hurry, to forestall any adverse comment. " Now how about drinking Lind—Our Absent Author's Health?"

They were in the middle of their third toast— Our Absent Author's Prosperity—when Gretchen, half rising with a dramatic flourish, pushed over the storm lamp with her elbow. The storm lamp, perched on the top of a great pile of broken oars, wooden boxes and other rubbish, fell down through the middle. They heard the glass shatter and saw the first twist of smoke. They stared at it blankly.

They had set something on fire in the middle of the night while breaking the strictest rule of the school—this couldn't have happened to them. But it had.

" Quick! A pail of water!" Caroline cried in a strangled voice. There wasn't a pail, however, there were only empty fruit tins.

Scrambling over the table, Pam pushed Caroline aside. " No good putting water on oil. We must smother it. Quick, Jennifer, Gretchen, help me to pull these boxes and things away and then we'll throw our coats on top."

Flames were leaping now and the smoke was spreading. Pam and Caroline, who were nearest the fire, felt their eyes begin to prick. A strip of burning carpet, relic of the days when the *Junk* was a splendid house-boat, had carried the flames to a heap of old magazines in another corner. Dragging, pulling, getting in each other's way; racing backwards and forwards with tins of water and spilling more than they carried, they were all in too great a panic even to notice this new danger until the pile was blazing. Nobody, not even Pam, remembered to put out the other storm lamp or throw the bottle of paraffin overboard. Soon the fire had reached these too, and the *Junk* was burning royally.

" We must go—we can't save it. Gosh, what a row!" Pam gulped through the smoke.

They tumbled thankfully out into the moonlight, their eyes streaming, their faces streaked and grimed.

" Quick, the dinghy; it's spreading so fast we must get out."

But the dinghy had drifted off and was nosing the reeds which fringed the island a hundred yards away. Gretchen had not fastened it securely after all.

Crowding on to the diving-board they looked at it helplessly, too stricken to notice between the trees the tip of a sail racing towards them out on the river.

" We must swim," Pam decided as the roof fell in with a terrifying rush of flames, sending a shower of sparks out over the water.

" But we can't all swim," the Duckling moaned, making no effort to control her tears.

" And the water's deep here," Caroline reminded her. " Surely, *surely* someone will notice the fire soon and come and help us. Pam, wait a moment, don't go yet."

But already Pam had plunged in and was swimming strongly towards the dinghy.

The others, scorched by the flames behind them, shivering with fear, wet clothes, and a growing dread of the row that must inevitably follow their rescue, clutched each other and waited. Pam wouldn't be long now; swimming at that rate she'd soon be safely back with the dinghy. Then as the door behind them burst open, the flames rushed out. By the time they had sprung round to look and, terrified by what they saw, had crowded closer to the edge of the diving-board, Pam was nowhere to be seen. It was Geraldine who remembered the reeds. Swimming was forbidden in the strip of water between the *Junk* and the island.

"Gosh!" Caroline burst out and dived overboard.

"I'll go too," Anthea was beginning, but Gretchen held her back.

"No, look here, we'll all have to go in a minute; you had better stay and help me with Jennifer and the Duckling and Geraldine; they can't swim."

It was only then, at the very worst moment of all, they noticed the sailing boat coming towards them across the broad. But for the water leaping apart under her bows she might have been flying, and even at that dreadful time Jennifer found herself wondering what it must feel like to be able to sail like that. As they shouted with impatience and relief the *Junk* listed heavily, sending sparks flying up to play over them like fireworks.

"Don't get into the water; you're safer where you are," a voice shouted from under the flying sail. "I shall be in time."

"Lindsay—Lindsay—quick!" they screamed. No one was surprised. It seemed only natural that Lindsay should be there to rescue them. And then after a moment's relief there was panic again.

"Jennifer, your hair!"

Jennifer clutched at it. It couldn't be her hair that was smelling so queerly. Such a dreadful thing couldn't happen to her; but she knew it was hers when it burned her hands.

After that she remembered very little of what happened. Everything was hazy with the horrid stifling haziness of a nightmare. She knew that *Whitewings* reached the flaming wreck. She heard Lindsay's terse voice giving orders to the others as she ran towards her. " Get in, all of you, and push off. . . . Lower sail, Anthea, or you may capsize. . . ." Then she felt Lindsay's arm about her, pushing her—actually pushing her overboard. She tried to struggle, but it was no good and she found herself in the water with Lindsay beside her, grabbing her before she went under again. After that the haze grew thicker, but she knew she was on the island, and presently there were torches flashing and men's voices and the sound of boats on the water. She knew that Anthea was kneeling beside her, trying to whisper through chattering teeth: " It's only your back hair, Jennifer. Lindsay got it out in time; the front will be all right." But she didn't care about her hair, she felt too tired. She heard someone crying. She heard Lindsay's name mentioned often, but Lindsay herself did not seem to be there. She saw the burning wreck making a background which reminded her of the robbers' cave she had once seen in a pantomime. Then she was in a boat again and her head was aching so that she felt she must fight the fiend who was holding her. Then she was being carried into the house. Then she was in bed, with matron, remarkable in a green dressing-gown, towering beside her; towering till she reached the ceiling.

CHAPTER XXI

Running Away

Jennifer and Pamela were having breakfast in bed, a delicious, leisurely nine o'clock breakfast, when Anthea came into the san.

Their squeals of welcome made her jump.

" Anthea, you absolute angel! Come and tell us everything."

They had only been separated from their friends for one day, but it seemed like a year, at a time when the school was seething with the great *Junk* rag. A rag important enough to be described with growing pride and suitable trimmings to every new girl for terms to come. Just now, however, although so enthralling, it was viewed from a different angle. Apprehension concealed any pride of achievement, and nobody bothered yet about trimmings since everybody else knew as much as she did.

" I've brought your letters," said Anthea, tossing them on to the beds. " Miss Matthews said I could. And I may stay for a quarter of an hour. Goodness, my goodness, it's awful downstairs, not knowing what Miss Hazell will do, you know! But it's exciting too, and you should see the *Junk*! It's a wonder we weren't all burned alive or drowned or something."

" Is Miss Hazell *foaming* with fury?" Jennifer

asked, not even bothering to open her letter. Nothing from home could be half as interesting as Anthea's gossip.

Anthea shrugged.

" Nobody knows, but she must be, I suppose."

" Perhaps she's so delighted to have us all still with her that she'll forgive us on the spot," suggested Pam, always hopeful.

" She certainly doesn't look as delighted as all that," Anthea answered, putting an end to that pleasant dream.

" Oh! Is Lindsay better?"

" Yes, she was at breakfast this morning, but her hands are bandaged. Everyone thinks she's an absolute heroine." Anthea looked sentimental. " You and Caroline were brave too, Pam." She went on in a more business-like tone. " Miss Matthew said so in English yesterday. She said you showed courage and resource—but it was nothing like Lindsay's of course."

" Rather not," Pam agreed willingly. Naturally ordinary people could not reach those dizzy heights on which Lindsay moved as a matter of course. She was quite ready to admit that she had not remembered the danger of reeds when she started off to fetch the dinghy, and although Caroline had bravely come to search for her, it was Lindsay who had rescued her, in spite of hands burned from coping with Jennifer's hair.

" You—don't think we'll be expelled?" Jennifer forced herself to ask the question, dreading the answer.

" Nobody can tell. We've got to go to the sitting-room after prep to-night. We shall know then."

" Oh!" Apprehension loomed more darkly.

Pamela hurried to change the painful subject.

" Anthea, wasn't it a miracle that Lindsay came when she did? But what was she *doing* in *White-wings* in the middle of the night? She didn't come from the boat-house, Jennifer says; she came in from the river. That must have been her sail we saw through the trees."

Anthea, thinking of something else, lightly dismissed the matter.

" She must have had permiss; she wouldn't have gone without. Turn round, Jennifer, I want to see your hair. Gosh! It's sort of thin on top, isn't it?"

" Oh, don't bother now; it will grow." Pam interrupted in her most casual tone before Jennifer could gloomily agree. " Go on, Anthea. Tell us some more."

Strolling about the room, Anthea glanced at the breakfast trays.

" I say, you've had fruit on your shredded wheat and poached eggs. Lucky pigs! We had porridge and baked beans."

Pam wriggled with impatience.

" Who cares *what* you had? Tell us some more about everything, Anthea."

" Well, there isn't much to tell that you don't know. The doctor from Horning came in his motor boat and gave you artificial respiration on the island, Pam, and looked after Lindsay and Jennifer, and then we were all taken off. Lois apparently gave the alarm at school about the *Junk* being on fire. I don't know how she found out. The flames *could* be seen from school, but only the staff-rooms face that way."

" Has Lindsay said anything about it?"

" Well, not to any of us. I suppose she has to her friends."

Jennifer looked disappointed, but the disappointment turned to glowing smiles when suddenly Anthea remembered something.

" Oh yes, she did ask me, as I came up here, if I knew whether your lovely hair had been quite ruined."

" *Lovely?* Anthea, did she really say lovely?"

Anthea thought for a moment.

" Yes, I'm sure she did, because I remember I was so surprised."

Pam sniffed as she folded her table napkin.

" She didn't happen to inquire, I suppose, if my beauteous face had been quite ruined with being under the dinghy for about a week?"

" No, she didn't mention you, but somehow I got an impression that she thought it a great pity Jennifer's hair had been burnt and not one of ours."

Pam rose in her wrath.

" Well, really, Anthea Ward, if that is your idea of a suitable topic for a sick-room you had better go away."

" It is time to do that, anyway," came nurse's voice from the doorway. " And you people may get up. The doctor doesn't want you to do any

9 (G 203)

work to-day, but there is no reason why you should not go downstairs."

They bounced out of bed and rushed to the window.

" Now we shall have to go with the others to the sitting-room after prep," Pam remarked, suddenly remembering.

Jennifer pressed her nose against the pane.

" Look, there's Lindsay down there on the bridge. Lois too, worse luck. They're talking awfully solemnly. I wonder if they are quarrelling."

They were not quarrelling—Lindsay was too tired and Lois too wily for that—but their friendship, which had never had a particularly solid basis, was in greater peril than either realized.

When Lindsay, weak and dazed, had been brought back from the island, the first person she noticed was Lois, in a dressing-gown and bedroom slippers, quite as if she had never left the house that night at all. Lindsay was puzzled. She had put her ashore to run for help before racing back across the broad to the burning junk. Why, then, had not Lois returned to help with the rescue work after giving the alarm, and why when the whole house was in an uproar had she bothered to change her clothes? Both questions Lois was answering now, on the bridge, in a way which astonished Lindsay.

" Just a spot of tact and forethought, my dear. There was I, complete with dressing-gown and bedroom slippers and hair all rough. Nobody dreamed I'd been out at all. They thought I'd seen the flames from the house."

" But, Lois!"

Lois leaned over to pat her shoulder reassuringly.
" Don't look so worried, Lindsay, I didn't forget
you. I mentioned just casually to one or two of
the staff that when I woke and told you the *Junk*
was on fire you raced ahead in case there were any
kids on board, suggested you'd probably get
Whitewings out and all the rest of it."

Lindsay looked at her with lazy amusement.

" *Don't* be an ass, Lois," she begged wearily.

" An ass? What do you mean?"

" Well, this is serious. There is no time for
fooling. When we tell the Nutkin about our little
jaunt——"

" *Tell* the *Nutkin*? Have you gone crazy,
Lindsay? Of course we shan't tell the Nutkin.
We've got a cast-iron alibi—thanks to me—and
aren't we popular? I gave the alarm. You are the
giddy heroine dashing to the rescue. Nobody
dreams we were out at all, if only we keep quiet."

" But we can't keep quiet."

" Of course we can; surely even you can see
nothing wrong in that. Different if the Nutkin
asked us if we were out and we told a deliberate
lie about it. But she won't ask. I saw to that.
Didn't you wonder yesterday why she didn't
mention it to you?"

" I did, rather, but I thought it might be because
I was in bed." Lindsay leaned her arms on the
wooden rail and stared down into the water. " She
only stayed a few minutes—just a sick-room
visit."

Lois went to lean persuasively on the rail beside her.

"Lindsay, you're not going to be a fool about this?"

"I think you're the fool—really, Lois."

"But, Lindsay, we shall get into a frightful row for absolutely nothing. Why, she might even stop you racing *Whitewings* at the regatta."

"Oh, gosh!"

"There, you see, you're relenting already."

"I'm not relenting," Lindsay said. "I simply can't believe you are serious."

Lois's lips met in a hard narrow line, but when she spoke she managed to keep the anger out of her voice.

"It's all very well, honey, for people to have principles and even to act on them sometimes. As you know, I do admire you most awfully for yours, but I don't quite see why I should be dragged into a row simply because you let your principles get out of hand. If you really must confess——"

"I really must."

"—there is no need to bring me into it."

"No," Lindsay agreed, in a voice which troubled Lois.

For a moment Lois wavered. Should she go and own up too? It was sickening to think she might lose some of her influence over Lindsay through this paltry affair; but when Lindsay, giving her time, had moved her arms from the rail, stretched, yawned, and said: "I may as well go and see the Nutkin now," she let her go alone.

Lindsay walked slowly into the house. Lois was
a rotter, but she was a rotter whose friendship she
found it impossible to do without. Besides, she
had so much to be grateful for. Lois, quite miraculously, had turned her from a struggling amateur
into a professional author. Lindsay had received a
cheque only that morning in advance of royalties
on her book, and Lois had been as thrilled as she
was. Lois wanted to do the right thing. She wasn't
responsible for her upbringing. In time if Lindsay
were only patient she'd understand what really
mattered.

She knocked on the sitting-room door and, with
a heart thumping as it had not thumped since
junior days—and not often then—went in.

Miss Hazell received her very graciously. She
was drinking coffee and insisted on Lindsay taking
some too. When she had heard the story of the
midnight picnic on *Whitewings*, she showed neither
anger nor surprise.

" I thought it probable that you were already
out on the river, and I made no inquiries as I
knew you would tell me," she said gravely. " I am
sorry that you allowed yourself this—lapse, Lindsay, but it can, of course, make no difference to
my real opinion of you. You are not a child, and
there is no point in my pretending to be either
greatly distressed or astonished. I know that you
have never been exactly a model of law and order,
and I know too that you can be trusted always to
behave honourably, even when nobody would
know, which is the only real test. I had intended

to offer you the Headgirlship when Rachel leaves at half term, and what you have just told me will not alter my decision."

Lindsay flushed, pushed aside her empty coffee-cup, looked straight at the headmistress, and said nothing.

"There will, of course, be certain conditions," Miss Hazell continued quietly. "I shall ask you to make a very real sacrifice. You know, I expect, what it is?"

"Yes."

"Would you be prepared to accept the Head-girlship on those terms?"

"Miss Hazell, I couldn't give up writing entirely."

"Not even for one year?"

"A year?" It seemed a century.

"You have the rest of your life in which to write," Miss Hazell reminded her.

"But I shan't always be young."

Miss Hazell was pouring out more coffee.

"Youth is a very necessary quality in a sponge cake," she remarked with a half smile, "but not necessarily so in an author. I think you have probably got a great future before you, Lindsay; you may writhe later on to see your early attempts in print."

"I think I must risk that." Lindsay dutifully returned her smile. "Besides, Miss Hazell, Knoxton Jervis have taken an option on my next two books."

"They will wait for them if they think they are worth waiting for, but the school can't wait. The school needs *now* the leadership which I believe you only at this time can give it. This is not a problem that can be solved by staff interference, although, of course, we shall be behind you. I want you to tackle it, but you can only do it successfully, unburdened by this hobby of yours. You failed badly last term because you were trying to do too much." She leaned back wearily in her chair. " As I said just now, the school needs you. The children are a little out of hand. They want inspiring leadership, not the mere discipline which the staff and other prefects can look after. The fifths are in a silly mood; they need inspiring too. Rachel has made a conscientious head girl, but she is no leader; that she is the first to admit herself. We have had some splendid prefects in the past. You have gained a great deal from their leadership. Now is the time to pay your debts, Lindsay."

Lindsay had gone to the window, where she stared out at some first-form children playing in the garden. They sang as they played, and their voices droned on and on and up and down unbearably.

" I am not going to pretend you have not disappointed me," Miss Hazell was still speaking quietly at the other side of the room, " but I am being patient with you because I know if you are persuaded to accept this work you will see it through triumphantly. Last term you failed because you sacrificed your responsibilities to your hobby. Now I am asking you to reverse that process. If you agree to do this I know how soon you will pull yourself round and you will pull the school round with you."

" But I can't leave off writing for a year—I'm sorry." Lindsay's voice trembled. Miss Hazell was being so kind. She hated to disappoint her.

Miss Hazell rose.

" Then if that is really your decision there is no point in discussing it further. Please think over what I have said, Lindsay. I shall appoint no head girl for the last half of this term. If you change your mind come and tell me. I feel sure that you will."

Lindsay, feeling utterly wretched, went upstairs to her bedroom. In the doorway, pale with anger, stood Lois, holding a half-unwrapped parcel in her hands.

" It's my book," she cried at once, " they've sent it back and it's your fault, Lindsay. I couldn't concentrate. You wouldn't let me use your study, and then when you did there was never peace; all that fussing with those wretched children."

Lindsay leaned against the wall. She couldn't remember ever having felt so queer before. First Miss Hazell—now Lois, and she was too tired to cope with either of them.

" I'm sorry, Lois. I know how you feel."

" You don't know. Your book was accepted, and of course everyone knows why. Your father has influence, or else he is paying to have it published. Olive said so from the first, but I was loyal to you and wouldn't listen to her. Now I know how right she was——"

" Lois——"

" Don't speak to me. Don't speak to me ever again. It's your fault. You've always made me feel so inferior that I couldn't do my best work. I never really liked you and now I know why. You're a humbug—you're a hypocrite."

" Lois, don't—please don't."

Lois was tearing the brown paper into little pieces, knotting and re-knotting the string. Her jealousy poured out in words, words, words. Lindsay heard only a few of them, but those she heard made her glad she had not promised Miss Hazell to leave off writing for a year.

" Don't ever come running to me for help again, because you won't get it, and you'll never finish a book without my help, not to mention having it accepted. Oh, I could scream with the unfairness of it all!"

And quietly Lindsay accepted the challenge.

" You are screaming already," she commented, rigid and white with contempt. " I have started another book and I shall certainly finish it. Will you let me pass, please?"

CHAPTER XXII

Ragging Olive

" You see, you've got to work the jib," Pam explained, mouthing the words, as if Jennifer were not only deaf but more than a little half-witted.

" That is the little sail in front," Gretchen put in helpfully.

Jennifer turned very pink.

" I know what the jib is, thanks most awfully," she retorted, nibbling furiously at a piece of grass.

" Ah, but knowing what it is and being able to work it are not *quite* the same thing," smirked Pam, looking so intolerably arch that for a couple of corking pins Jennifer would have punched her head, which was so invitingly close. Instead, her rage took the form of extreme politeness.

" Thanks so much for your kind interest. I'm touched *and* flattered by it, but as it happens I can work a jib."

" Yes, with Lindsay at your elbow to tell you exactly what to do and when to do it. When she's racing *Whitewings* she just shouts ' Ready about ' and leaves the rest to you."

In spite of her anger Jennifer thrilled. " When Lindsay is racing *Whitewings* "—she scarcely thought of anything else day or night, and, in spite of her discretion, the form had guessed. Possibly because they all wanted so much to crew for Lindsay themselves, jealous rivalry had sharpened their wits.

" *And* if you don't mind my mentioning it, Jennifer," Pam was continuing, still with the patient lucid air Jennifer found so infuriating, " we all think it pretty good cheek of a new girl even to think she has a chance of racing *Whitewings* with Lindsay."

" I—I—don't think so; who said I did?" Jennifer was protesting when Caroline lazily interrupted.

" Look here, I vote we don't argue; it's too hot," she yawned, rolling over on the grass and blinking at the sun. " Whatever Jennifer thinks, Lindsay certainly won't choose her. Why should she, when you, Pam, and I and Anthea have been here for three sailing terms?"

Why indeed? Jennifer knew she was being a fool, but with her usual extravagance, and in spite of a reproving nudge or two from Muggy, she had already decided that she would die of grief if Lindsay didn't invite her to crew for her. There was positively nothing else to live for.

Summer had come early to Broadland that year, bringing, besides the long sunny days, trails of flowers in the riverside gardens, good sailing winds, and the usual rush of holiday folk on their hired yachts or motor cruisers.

At River Place the best term of the year was at its height; sailing, swimming, tennis, occupied the long afternoons. Many of the morning classes were held in the side garden, where the boats passing on the river, with their gaily dressed crews and noisy radios, could not attract wandering attention.

The lower fourth, while throwing themselves with all their usual gusto into the term's special activities, were still a little subdued. Miss Hazell had been very seriously angry with them after the midnight picnic on the *Junk*, and her anger had been all the more impressive because she refused to treat the matter as what she called a childish prank. Deliberate disobedience had very nearly ended in a tragedy too terrible to contemplate, and the fact that courage of a high order had been shown brought no indulgence for the culprits. Their sentence emphasized the wholesome impression already made by the interview in the sitting-room. It was sickening to have to sleep in the first-form dormitory under the strictest supervision until half term, while the first form, odiously triumphant, were moved up to Rotten Row. No more ragging on that scale for the lower fourth; it simply did not pay.

Something of the sort was in Pamela's mind when she spoke again.

" Only another week now until Rachel leaves. If Olive is head girl, and, you see, she will be, we shall have to be rather *subtle*—you know, unbearably irritating without doing anything bad enough to bring in Miss Hazell."

" Rather."

" We can manage that all right."

" Wasn't it jolly good at prep last night? She was *seething*."

There was a thoughtful, grass-nibbling pause while they remembered in silent rapture Olive's discomfort.

" She showered so many lines all over the place," Gretchen went on presently, " that she couldn't possibly remember who she gave them to."

Pam nodded comfortably.

" We'll pool them, and all do a few."

" We'd better pool the answers to those beastly problems too. Nobody had time to do more than about one," Geraldine suggested lazily.

" Oh!" Pamela frowned quickly. " Pooling our work is different."

Geraldine shrugged.

" We certainly can't force Olive to resign *and* do our prep. And we don't want to upset Miss Matthews."

" No."

" And if we *could* prevent Olive being appointed head girl we'd be doing the school a lasting good. We've got to think of that."

" Yes—Jennifer, you're best at maths. How many did you get out?"

" Three."

" Help! I didn't get any." Pam, having fought and utterly vanquished her conscience, sat up suddenly. " After all, I suppose it doesn't matter specializing in some subjects. As a matter of fact, I think schools should do much more of it. Look here, Jennifer, if you will just give us some tips about those problems, quite casually, you know, I'll run through your French essay and Caroline——"

" There's Lindsay sailing with Prue again," somebody interrupted, as Prue's little red-sailed boat swept round the curve of the river. " I don't believe she ever speaks to Lois now, do you? I *do* wonder what can have happened?"

Nobody knew and nobody cared. In some queer way Lois had spoiled Lindsay. Now that they were friends no longer, Lindsay was just too sweet for words again.

" She's writing another book," Jennifer told

them impressively. " In the library, every evening. Several times I've just peeped in as I've passed, and she's scribbling away, sitting on the corner window-seat."

The others nodded.

" I've seen her too," Anthea murmured.

" Well, remember, nobody is to disturb her," Pam commanded in her sternest tone. " Not even you, Jennifer."

" *Me?*" Jennifer echoed feebly.

" Yes, you! You've got much more cheek than the rest of us put together where Lindsay is concerned."

Jennifer coloured brightly.

" Have I?" She did not know whether to be indignant or flattered.

" Yes, but you'll go too far. You'll get a fine snub one of these days, you see," Pam informed her, scrambling to her feet as the sound of the tea-bell came faintly from the house.

It was a few days later that Lindsay, passing the lower fourth's form-room during evening preparation, noticed several pieces of chalk hit the glass in the upper part of the door. Glancing through before strolling on, she saw Olive standing in front of Gretchen's desk, obviously holding an investigation of some sort, while at very frequent intervals more chalk flicked against the blackboards and stationery cupboard.

At the end of the corridor she met Jennifer, scuttling along with a furtiveness which not only roused Lindsay's suspicions, but in a vague way made her uneasy for Jennifer's sake. Jennifer might be, and was, a prize little ass, but the furtive air was new and not attractive.

" What are you doing, Jennifer?"

" I—well—I——" Jennifer could not conceal the sheet of drawing-paper in her hands, but she was careful to hide what was written on it.

" Why aren't you at prep?"

" I—had something to fetch."

" For Olive?"

" Oh no."

" What did you have to fetch—that paper?"

" Yes, Lindsay, please, I must hurry—or Olive will notice I'm not there."

" I hope she does. And you can't go yet. Why is all that chalk flying about your room?"

Jennifer, looking very bland, smothered a giggle.

" We've got a poltergeist in the form-room, Lindsay. It's awfully funny. He chucks things about, but no one has ever seen him. It's only when Olive is there—he especially doesn't like her —yesterday he threw pins."

Lindsay was looking down at her steadily, and Jennifer, meeting her eyes, quaked before their level gaze.

" That's pure cheek, Jennifer, not the sort of answer I want from you."

Jennifer pulled herself together.

" I'm sorry; I didn't mean to cheek you, Lindsay."

" Right. What have you got written on that paper?"

" Oh—please!"

" Turn it round. I want to see."

Jennifer obeyed, colouring furiously, and **Lindsay** glanced at it with contempt.

" What are you going to do with it?"

" Only pin it on Olive's back—just for a bit of fun."

" Tear it up."

" But, Lindsay, I can't. *Actually* it—it isn't mine."

" I don't care whose it is. Tear it up."

Once again Jennifer obeyed. No junior—not even the most brazen—had ever been known to defy Lindsay in this mood.

" Go and put the pieces in the basket on the landing and then come back, please."

While Jennifer had gone Lindsay thought rapidly. When she came back she was ready for her.

" Jennifer, very little preparation has been done in your room during this last week. Hasn't Miss Matthews complained?"

" Well, no—she hasn't."

" Surely that's very odd?"

" Well, you see—we've managed somehow."

" You mean you've cheated."

Jennifer's wits—or what there were of them as Pam remarked afterwards in deep disgust— deserted her.

" Oh, Lindsay, how did you know?"

" I didn't know for certain, but I do now. Jennifer, what is all this about? You and Pam and Anthea and all the others are much too nice to

cheat over your work. Besides, it's a thing that
never has been tolerated at River Place. Public
opinion has always been so dead against it."

Jennifer said nothing. She could have remarked
with truth that public opinion had changed a lot
—in other forms as well as her own—but she
didn't, and Lindsay noticed her restraint with
grim satisfaction.

" We only help each other a little—just to prevent getting into rows," she murmured presently.
" And, Lindsay, I didn't mean to—to let it out."

" I know."

" I can't think why I did."

" It wasn't your fault; I made you. Why did
you all start this wretched business?"

" It was because of Olive. We want to—well,
to sort of dissuade her from being made head girl,
and we can't rag in prep *and* do our work. Nobody
could."

" But the choice doesn't rest with Olive; nor
with you. If Miss Hazell appoints her head
girl——"

" We thought she might refuse if she knows how
we feel about it. It isn't only us. All the juniors
hate her."

" I don't want to hear your opinion of Olive or
of anybody else," Lindsay interposed crisply.
" Perhaps when you are old enough to criticize
without abuse, what you have to say may be of
some value."

Jennifer swallowed rather loudly before attempting to speak again.

" You are being awfully hard, Lindsay."

" I've got to be. But," Lindsay relented a little, " it isn't all meant for you. A great deal is meant for myself. Look here, Jennifer, this cheating over your work because you have wasted time ragging in prep has got to stop."

Jennifer stared at her feet.

" *I* can't stop it. I do it myself. I hate Olive as much as anybody. More, really, because——"

" It's so mean to blame Olive."

" But it's her fault. We don't want her to rule us. English people choose their own government and English schools should be allowed to choose their own prefects. If we chose our own prefects we'd obey them."

" Would you? I wonder. Are these your own opinions, by the way, or are you just quoting what you've heard the others say?"

" They are mine *and* theirs. We want you for our head girl."

" Well, that, I'm afraid, is impossible."

Jennifer looked at her anxiously.

" Do you mind if I ask you something?"

" Of course not. Why this sudden delicacy?"

" Are you going to do anything about what I told you just now?"

" I haven't decided yet. I can't do anything officially because I'm not a prefect." It was only as she said the words that their true meaning came to her. Things were happening in the school, beastly things, and she had no official authority to deal with them.

Seeing the relief in Jennifer's eyes she made a quick decision. If she had no official authority she could at least prevent Jennifer, whom she liked, from being spoiled.

" In the meantime I want you to promise that you will do your own work fairly, even if you can't persuade the others just at first."

Jennifer shuffled her feet, dropped her fountain pen, picked it up and dropped it again.

" If you're asking me specially——" she began in an awed voice.

" I am."

Jennifer's smile must have met at the back of her head.

" Oh, then, I will! I'd love to. It will be heavenly being a martyr for——"

" Good. Go back to your form-room now, Jennifer."

Jennifer looked hurt. Lindsay might have let her finish. After all, martyrs weren't ordained every day.

Lindsay went thoughtfully downstairs. Jennifer was being spoiled—so was Anthea, so was Pam, so, probably, were many of the others. They were getting a wrong attitude towards the things that mattered most, and she could do nothing officially about it because she was not a prefect. She could drop a hint to Prue, of course, but Prue was already uneasy about the dangerous spirit abroad in the school; so, no doubt, were the other prefects. Knowing something was wrong, and being able to cope with it successfully, were two very different matters. Rachel and Co., she knew, were getting more submerged every day.

For the rest of that evening Jennifer's face haunted her. It stared up out of her soup plate at supper. It danced over the pages as she tried to write afterwards in the library. She saw it in the moonlight as she lay wakefully in bed. All round Jennifer there were other people. Pam, Anthea, Pat, some of the first-form children, but Jennifer stood out most clearly.

" In the morning I'll go and tell Miss Hazell I have changed my mind," she decided, and immediately afterwards she fell asleep.

In the morning on her way to Miss Hazell's study Lindsay passed the post table. Lying there, addressed to herself, was a parcel which she took and opened mechanically. Probably something unimportant from home. She'd just—she cut the string and out fell a bundle of printed paper. It was cut up in long narrow strips. The slip proofs of her book.

She stared at them, too thrilled at first to move. She read the opening paragraph. It looked absolutely professional in print. She ran through the proofs searching for the bits she liked best. There they all were, but just as miraculously improved as the first paragraph had been. Ambition surged so that she thought it would choke her.

Thank goodness she hadn't gone to see Miss Hazell before opening that parcel as she so easily might have done. The school must manage without her now. The children wouldn't come to much harm.

Probably she had worked herself up about nothing
at all and she would certainly keep an unofficial
eye on them. Whatever happened, she must finish
that second book now. It was idiotic of Miss
Hazell—and unfair—to suggest that she was the
only competent leader in the sixth.

CHAPTER XXIII

A Meeting in Hall

Lois wandered disconsolately down to the river.
It was a glorious afternoon, one of June's best, but
as she felt bored and lonely the sunshine only
seemed to mock her. She glanced round the
deserted garden looking, not very hopefully, for
someone to amuse her. She knew the whole school,
having apparently gone mad about their absurd
regatta, were at Windrush Broad either on or in
the water. Since Lois could not shine as a swimmer
or as a sailor, she had no patience with their foolish-
ness. She preferred to read, she told herself,
sitting down on the towpath with her back against
a willow tree.

Presently Lindsay passed, sailing one of the tubs
with a crowd of juniors on board. She was evidently teaching them the rules of the river, because
after a motor boat had gone by with a single blast
of its horn, a shrill chorus recited enthusiastically:
" I am directing my course to starboard," obviously in answer to a question from their skipper.

They all looked intensely serious, Lois noticed, and quite idiotically happy, especially that pushing red-haired child who was grabbing the main-sheet as if she were afraid it would get away from her.

Lindsay was always very busy these days, and very polite to Lois, and maddeningly aloof. Lois had made two determined attempts to recover her friendship and both had been rebuffed with a competence she did not care to remember. Oh, well, it was fortunate that Lindsay was not the only member of the sixth, although she often behaved as if she supposed she was. Olive had made several very friendly advances lately, and Olive certainly would not require in her friends that lofty moral standard demanded by Lindsay. Besides, Olive was becoming very important these days. Since Rachel left she had been unofficially running the school and there was very little doubt in anyone's mind that she would be appointed head girl. Rather an achievement for the new sixth-former to be recognized as the special friend of the captain of River Place. She was pleased by Olive's notice without realizing that nothing more flattering than their common jealousy of Lindsay Dysart was drawing them together.

Prudence's little red sail came sweeping round the bend with Anita's *Swansong* racing after her. They waved as they passed and Lois waved back enviously. Her father had refused to buy, or even to hire her a boat for one short summer term. Schoolgirls did not need such a luxury, he maintained, and no argument that she could produce would alter his opinion.

Her big share of *Whitewings* was one of the things she missed most since her quarrel with Lindsay. She sailed with Olive sometimes, but Olive was not a good enough sailor to have much patience with beginners. Life was very difficult, Lois sighed to herself, but it became a little easier the moment she noticed Olive sailing towards her.

" Catch! " shouted Olive, throwing a rope. " Come and have tea with me in the study," she invited as she tied up. " Nobody will notice. They are all having theirs down at Windrush. I'm quite worn out with it all. It is so hot and there is always so much to do before the regatta. Heats and practice races and all the rest of it."

" Which of the juniors are you having to crew for you?" Lois asked, as they strolled back through the garden.

" My dear, what a question! Her highness has the first choice."

" Lindsay? But why? She isn't even a prefect."

Olive laughed without amusement.

" That makes no difference. The children are not compelled to crew for us, you know, and it is distinctly annoying to be informed with a smirk by Pamela or Caroline, as I was last year: ' Oh, Olive, I'd love to crew for you—if Lindsay doesn't ask me.' "

" Well, really! The cheek of the modern child!"

Olive agreed with regret for those good old days

when juniors were juniors in outlook as well as in age.

" I assure you that happened to both Anita and me last year. But in any case the crews aren't chosen until nearer the time. It keeps all the children up to the mark, you see."

" Oh, well, you won't have any trouble this year. You'll be head girl by then," Lois reminded her.

Olive smiled complacently.

" Who do you think Lindsay will choose?" Lois asked, as she helped to get tea in the cool study.

" Oh, Anthea probably—or Pamela. They are the best; and when her highness races, she races to win."

Outwardly the school ran smoothly after Rachel left—smoothly enough for Lindsay, engrossed in her second book, to be able to forget her anxiety about the juniors and concentrate, when she had time, on helping to make sure of the regatta's success. She did keep an eye—when she remembered—on Jennifer, but Jennifer, while she thought she was unobserved, seemed fairly cheerful; at other times she wore an air of dark depression which was not very convincing. Jennifer, in fact, was finding martyrdom a rather difficult business; difficult because her form were so horribly tolerant.

" We're helping each other, not cheating," Pam coldly informed her when Jennifer tackled her, " and we shall do it as long as we want to. You need not. Nobody cares whether you do or not."

That was the difficulty. Nobody cared. And you couldn't be a martyr if your friends simply refused to persecute you. Nobody could.

They didn't even tease her about trying to make up to Lindsay, for she had never dared to mention that part of the conversation in the corridor. They thought, when she refused to give or accept help with her work, she was showing off or trying to be clever. It was sickening. Her spirits rose, however, when certain plans began to be discussed by her form to do with the big general meeting about the regatta. At last, she thought she saw an opportunity for a really agonizing coup.

The meeting, an annual affair, was held towards the end of each summer term, the head girl usually taking the chair. This year, however, it was Olive who signed the notices, and Olive who magnificently took the chair, with the other prefects grouped about her on the platform, when the whole school had assembled in hall.

The girls seemed in an unusually orderly mood. Not a movement could be heard as Prudence read the minutes of the previous meeting. The points arising from the minutes were discussed quietly and in a business-like way. And then, as Olive stood up to speak, something happened. Still the silence was unbroken. Still there remained that atmosphere of acute devotion to duty, but before she had finished her opening remarks every junior, having produced a book from under her chair and settled herself lazily with her feet on the rail of the chair in front, had started to read. The first form, who had no chairs in front, stretched themselves out on the floor with their backs to the platform and their books propped up before their faces. The perfect timing and precision of the demonstration was so impressive that the seniors simply stared in admiring bewilderment. Only Jennifer, a stiff, flaming-cheeked figure, glorying in martyrdom, had no book. Jennifer's eyes were fixed slavishly on Olive's face; her painfully stiff back emphasized the sprawling attitudes of the others. She was being a martyr now all right, and Lindsay, unless of course she had gone suddenly blind, could not help being impressed. So thought Jennifer.

Lindsay, however, deeply shocked by the demonstration, was too busy grappling with a sudden onslaught of conscience to have any interest in martyrs. The school was not running smoothly after all. This frightful affair not only showed the juniors' dislike of Olive; it showed too, and much more seriously, the unwholesome spirit abroad in River Place. Never had anything like this happened before. Poor Olive! But in spite of her sympathy it was with a slightly contemptuous interest that Lindsay waited to see what Olive would do.

Olive, having no doubts about her capabilities as a leader, stepped determinedly to the edge of the platform.

" Put your books away at once, please. We have a great deal to get through and must not waste time."

Nobody moved. Nobody raised even an eyelid. The fifths looked amused. The prefects, lacking Olive's faith in her powers, glanced mechanically at Lindsay sitting with the rest of the sixth at the back of the hall. She looked pale and very strained, they noticed, almost as if this frightful affair concerned her personally.

" I shall not speak again," Olive announced rashly. " Put your books away at once, please, and attend to what I have to say."

Still nobody moved except to turn a page over with a nonchalant flick, or to relax a little more luxuriously in her chair.

Olive looked hard at her watch to hide the angry colour flooding her cheeks. The other prefects made uneasy, irresolute movements. There were only five of them against fifty juniors. Something must be desperately wrong with the school that numbers should suddenly matter so much. The prefects, armed as they were with tradition and an unusually elastic authority, had always been impressive figures. Never before in the long history of River Place had one of them been publicly defied.

" I will give you one more chance to obey me," Olive announced, in a voice that quivered oddly. " You refuse? Then every junior will leave the hall immediately. And I need hardly add that this is not the last you will hear of this disgraceful exhibition."

Still nobody moved except Pamela, who, with an artless smile, leaned over to show Caroline something in her book. As the two tittered and giggled with their heads together, a spatter of blackboard chalk arrived, apparently from nowhere, on the platform. Olive, feeling desperate, turned back to the other prefects.

" What shall we do?"

" Oh, let's go away quickly; it's so undignified to sit here being defied," Mary wailed.

" Let me get at them." Anita was in a seething rage.

" Hadn't we better get Lindsay up here?" Prue murmured. " She's the only one who can save our faces—if it isn't too late."

" But Lindsay's gone away," whispered Vivien, after a quick glance over her shoulder. " How odd! She was here just now, I'm sure."

More and more chalk was pitting itself against the wall, the table, and the prefects' legs. One piece actually bounced on Olive's head. Giggles came from the middle of the hall, but still no junior moved a muscle.

" Oh, do let's go away! I can't bear it," Mary was beginning again, when the door at the back of the platform opened and Lindsay came through. She still looked pale, but there was a grim determination under her confident manner—that much-criticized manner which, for the first time on record, was welcomed by the baffled prefects. After some whispered words with Olive she went to the front of the platform. As if by magic every book was closed and every junior sat up alertly. Lindsay pretended not to notice them. The situation, she knew, called for desperate measures. Nothing could retrieve it now, yet she must manage in some way to prop up the prefects' battered prestige.

" I have two messages for the seniors," she announced, addressing a tennis shield on the wall behind the sixth form. " Miss Hazell wishes me to tell you that she has appointed me head girl. She will make the formal announcement herself this evening." Terrific sensation—yells of delight from the lower school, beaming smiles from the upper, Lois's face outstanding in its anger and astonishment. " The second message is about the regatta meeting. Or would you "—Lindsay turned and spoke clearly to Olive over her shoulder—" would you rather make the announcement about the altered arrangement yourself, Olive?"

" Not at all. Please carry on," murmured Olive, struggling between astonishment, relief and dismay. Lindsay, head girl! Lindsay, that quite impossible prefect, in a position to patronize and command them all!

Lindsay turned back to her still cheering audience.

" Quiet, please! Olive asks me to tell you that she is holding the meeting to discuss regatta plans in the gym in five minutes' time. Seniors only will be admitted. Every junior will remain where she is until she has learnt by heart the first fifty lines of the book that she has found so engrossing earlier this evening. When she is certain she knows the lines—and it might be as well to take no risks— she may go to bed. Thank you, that is all."

Her glance awed and chilled the long lines of juniors who hurriedly stared at their knees. Only one had the courage to speak in a shrill, officious voice.

" Please, Lindsay, Jennifer Windgate hasn't *got* a book."

" Then she must share her neighbour's," curtly answered Lindsay, showing a wisdom which Jennifer, bursting with thwarted martyrdom, rage and self-pity, did not appreciate until long afterwards.

Having settled that small point, seen the seniors quietly leave the hall, and the juniors start to learn their lines, Lindsay left the platform by the way she had entered. She had several things she must do, but one was outstandingly important. She must send the book she was writing home immediately, so that she would not be tempted to break the promise which she had given Miss Hazell when she had gone to her study in the middle of that dreadful meeting. Miss Hazell had been very understanding, and very glad that Lindsay had at last changed her mind. It was she who suggested that the new head girl should herself announce her appointment.

Fetching paper and string, Lindsay made a parcel of the whole thing—lay-out book, rough notes, the few finished chapters—addressed it to her mother, and carried it down to the lodge. If it were left on the post table all night the temptation not to send it away might prove too strong for her.

Scott, the school porter, was working among his flowers.

" If you are going into Horning to-night, Scott, I wish you would take this to the post office," she said, having no idea how urgently she spoke. " And please be sure to register it; it's valuable."

Scott looked at her curiously.

" Certainly, miss. I'll see it goes off for you to-night."

"Thank you. How lovely your delphiniums are!"

She hesitated a moment, smiled at him absently, and then, bracing herself for the year ahead, she went back into the house.

CHAPTER XXIV

The Regatta

Lindsay was head girl, and the school, with a few exceptions, was jubilant. The juniors were especially pleased because she was so exactly what they expected a head girl to be, and so exactly what Olive was not. As, with an air of great originality, the Duckling pointed out, Lindsay was so very super. She *looked* super. She did all the things that really mattered, such as sailing, tennis, running the Agony Inter, and writing books in an absolutely super way. She was, in fact, *super*.

The others agreed with as much enthusiasm as if all this had not been said a hundred times before. With Lindsay running the school, it was bound to be practically perfect, and if the iron hand promised to be decidedly active inside the velvet glove, which the new head girl wore so dashingly, nobody really minded.

" I think it's rather nice being kept up to the mark," Pam remarked one hot afternoon, as they collected their swim suits before going down to

Windrush. " It makes you feel sort of comfortable and secure. Doing what you like all the time really gets very tiring, doesn't it?"

Again everyone agreed.

" I'm glad we've left off all that ragging in prep and helping each other," Caroline muttered from the depths of the locker, where she was rummaging for her rubber cap. " It was an awful responsibility deciding just how far we could go without being run into the Nutkin. We know we can't go very far with Lindsay, but we can enjoy ourselves all the same."

" And isn't it lovely to see ' Lindsay Dysart— Head Girl ' in the slot on the study door?" gushed the Duckling.

It was so lovely that they all went downstairs the long way round, so that they could look at it again. All but Jennifer. She had some returned history to do, and she wasn't really sorry. She knew there would be no sailing that afternoon, and swimming was a subject at which she certainly did not excel. Besides, the sixth were going to choose their crews by to-morrow evening at the very latest, and she felt she could no longer bear the complacency of Pamela and Caroline telling each other of the meaning glances and significant remarks with which Lindsay had favoured them.

" If she's going to choose one of them I wish she'd hurry up," Jennifer muttered crossly, as she went into the cool form-room and opened her history book. " This suspense is simply too frightful."

Since the meeting in hall Jennifer had been treated, in a good-humoured way, as rather a joke by her form. At first they had been furious with what they considered her priggishness and disloyalty in not joining in the rag. They had secretly determined never to speak to her again, but when Lindsay, ignoring her saintly behaviour, had not only made her learn the lines but had chosen her as one of the three people in the form to recite them, opinion had veered. It was pretty bad luck, they admitted. Instead, therefore, of being cold-shouldered, Jennifer was merely warned in a good-natured way about the dangers of " showing off " and trying to be different.

" You'll never be happy here or anywhere else unless you try to be like everybody else," Pam informed her from the depths of her own experience.

" Lindsay isn't like everybody else," Jennifer had muttered, looking pinkly indignant.

Sniffs of derision met this rash statement.

" Well, really, you *are* conceited, Jennifer! Fancy comparing yourself with Lindsay!"

Jennifer gave it up. She simply couldn't explain to the circle of shocked, derisive faces *why* she had sat up straight and refused to read at the regatta meeting. Anyhow, she wanted to forget about it. Lindsay hadn't been a bit nice and she was sick of being a martyr. Being a martyr simply didn't pay unless one had the proper sort of audience.

She turned with a self-pitying sigh to her history, and was still reading hard when half an hour later Lindsay came into the room.

" Oh, there you are, Jennifer! Anthea said I'd find you in the form-room. Look here, we are choosing our crews this afternoon; would you care to help me sail *Whitewings* at the regatta?"

Jennifer, who had been balancing comfortably on the two back legs of her chair, fell over backwards with the shock, and disappeared from view.

" I—I—simply can't believe it," she gasped, blinking at the ceiling.

Lindsay looked at her over the nearest desk.

" But you meant to crew for me from the moment I showed you that photograph of Rita, didn't you?"

" Oh, long before that."

" Then don't be such a little humbug." She helped her to her feet. " We're having a practice race at six o'clock."

" I'll go and get ready now," said Jennifer fervently.

" But you don't need two and a half hours to get ready."

" I want to think about it," Jennifer said. " The greatest moment of my life has come."

Her own form were not merely surprised at Jennifer's new importance, they were aghast and dumbfounded.

" But if Lindsay beats the rest of the sixth, which of course she will do, you'll help her sail *Whitewings* against competitors from a real yacht club for the silver trophy, and there has never *been* a silver trophy awarded before," Pam stuttered, when at last she had grasped the incredible truth.

Jennifer smiled in a perky way, which was very hard to bear.

"You asked her to choose you," Caroline accused sternly.

"I certainly did not."

Then *why* had Lindsay chosen Jennifer? They asked each other the question helplessly and repeatedly. Nobody knew the answer. Jennifer was all right, of course, but not a bit intelligent or efficient or even reliable—a sort of promising half-wit in fact.

Nor did Lindsay's remarkable choice escape comment in the prefects' room.

"She's the last child I should have chosen," Anita remarked as they broke up after the weekly prefects' meeting, the first at which Lindsay had presided as head girl.

"She knows what she's doing, and you can't deny she is picturesque," Lindsay answered lightly.

To Prue, however, she was more expansive.

"If I hadn't chosen her she would have died of grief—to use her own expression. Besides, she's been trying very hard to do the right thing lately —in her usual intense, fat-headed way, of course."

Prue looked at her affectionately.

"You're an odd mixture, aren't you? Very tough in patches, but with soft streaks. I thought you were awfully hard on Olive all through the prefects' meeting; she wasn't meaning to be *very* nasty, and she must be disappointed about not being head girl, you know."

Lindsay was silent for a moment before answering.

"Olive is a bully," she said quietly. "If she thinks I am afraid of her—which I am, a little—she'll make things hateful for me and difficult for us all next year."

"Oh, quite. There's no doubt about that. I wasn't criticizing, only I couldn't help feeling sorry for her," Prue agreed hastily. "And, Lindsay, there is one other thing I'd like to mention."

"Do; there's no need to be so delicate. You mustn't lose your grip, Prue."

Prue grinned and, not knowing quite how Lindsay would receive her next remark, boldly plunged. "I wish you'd be more obvious about your writing these days."

"Well, really, Prue!" Lindsay studied her in mild amusement. "You spent the first two terms of this year begging me not to write at all, and now——"

"I know, but now I've a special reason for wanting you to make more *show* about the book you are writing."

"I'm not writing a book."

"Not? Oh, Lindsay, then what Lois says——"

"What does Lois say?"

"Only that she helped you so much with your first book, practically wrote it in fact, and you can't manage without her help. She's whispering it to everybody."

"I thought she would." Lindsay sounded more

indifferent than she felt. " But I can't do anything about it. I promised Miss Hazell, you see."

Prue nodded understandingly.

" I guessed that might be it. And after all Lois can't do much harm. People will know she is only jealous."

" I hope so. I wonder why people so often say ' only jealous ', though," Lindsay said. " I think it's the worst possible thing to be. It seems to make a person completely unreasonable and dishonest even with themselves. I'm sure by now Lois has really made herself believe she did half write my book. She helped me, of course, by being interested and most awfully nice at first, but that's different."

" You don't miss her too much, do you?" Prue asked, detecting a touch of regret in the other's tone. She had never asked for the reason of the quarrel, which had been so much gossiped about by everybody in quiet corners and during confidential strolls in the garden, and Lindsay had not told her.

Lindsay pulled herself together. Prue was worth a thousand people such as Lois, and yet Prue had no place in the thrilling world into which Lois had introduced her.

" Of course not, old thing. I'd much rather be with you."

Prue glowed with pleasure.

" And it will be great fun running the school next year?"

" The greatest fun in the world," Lindsay agreed

indulgently, as if humouring a favourite child.

Jennifer stuffed a big chocolate into her mouth from the box Lindsay had given her and pushed her face down into the pillow. If she started to cry she knew she would never leave off, and then she would not be able to see clearly the tiny bit of the racing which passed the san window.

The chocolate tasted like sago pudding, and Jennifer decided not to eat another one until she could appreciate it properly. Lindsay was old enough to believe that Jennifer was young enough to find in chocolates a cure for any trouble; but chocolates, even such gorgeous ones as these, could not touch a misery like Jennifer's.

Life in general had been so wonderful until the day before yesterday, and now it was simply too frightful for words. To keep herself from crying properly she thought over the good bits. There was that practice race when she had helped Lindsay sail *Whitewings* for the first time. It had been such a lovely evening, and the little boats had looked so pretty drawn up by the tow-path, and the sixth, even Olive, so dashing in their green polo-necked sweaters, embroidered with the school crest. All the lucky juniors chosen to crew had been enviously watched by the crowd who gathered to see the race start, but Jennifer had the added satisfaction of being envied by the other crews too. It had made her feel rather heady and over-important, especially as some of the staff were there.

" It's great fun to be envied," she had whispered to Lindsay, appreciating a new experience.

" Yes, isn't it?" Lindsay had agreed, busy with the sails and thinking of something else.

They had won the race, although they had started last.

" Why are we starting so far behind?" Jennifer, in her ignorance, had wildly demanded as Anita's sail, the last to leave before them, had disappeared round the river bend.

" Because of our handicap," Lindsay had explained patiently.

" Oh, does that mean that we are the best—I mean, you are the best sailor?"

" Not altogether. Miss Sedly handicaps a boat's speed, but she does consider skill too. Jennifer, don't forget what I told you about easing away the jib."

" Rather not! But this evening I'm sure to do everything wrong, I feel so excited. You won't judge me by this evening, will you?" Jennifer pleaded.

" No," Lindsay promised easily.

Then there was that almost intoxicating feeling of superiority when, after the race, skippers and crews walked over to Windrush to see how the pitiful creatures, entered only for the swimming events or the comic-craft race, were getting on. Jennifer could have wept for them. Poor, poor things, messing about with rafts and crates on the Windrush when she was helping to sail *Whitewings* for the silver trophy before an audience, not only of the school's guests, but of people from all the surrounding villages, who came to line the river banks and cheer and shout encouragement.

During the following days, every one of which contained coaching of some sort from Lindsay in the thrilling art of sailing, Jennifer's happiness seemed to lift her above the petty annoyances and restrictions of ordinary life. Walking about in a dream, she simply did not notice them, probably because they wore the glamour of everything connected with that time.

And then John's letter came.

" I dare you," wrote John, " to slide down the bannister rail on your back. It's quite easy; I've done it. Nothing less than two floors counts."

Jennifer, suffering badly from swelled head, had immediately flung herself on to the top of the longest sweep of bannisters in the building and, almost as quickly, had crashed off again. When people, hearing the fall, came from all directions, she was lying on the floor, apparently lifeless.

At the memory of that dreadful waking up to find herself made a prisoner in the san by a fractured ankle, tears started in real earnest, and she did not notice Anthea come in with a plate of raspberries and cream until Anthea spoke.

" I thought you'd like these. I can get you some more if you like. Tea has just started. The tables look so pretty under coloured umbrellas by the water."

Jennifer feverishly rubbed her eyes with the sheet.

" Oh, Anthea—I'm nearly dead of m-misery."

" *Darling* Jennifer, I know and I'm sorry," Anthea murmured, hugging her.

Jennifer gulped, sniffed, and tried to eat some raspberries. They might have been burned porridge. She pushed the plate away.

" You'll help Lindsay win the trophy better than I should have done. Sometimes I forget to ease away the jib at exactly the right second."

" Oh, I don't know. Lindsay *chose* you," Anthea reminded her.

Jennifer managed a damp smile. It was true. Lindsay *had* chosen her. Nothing—not even an earthquake—could alter that.

" Who won the comic-craft?" she asked, feeling slightly better.

" Pat won the junior race and Marjorie, of all people, the senior. You should have seen Gretchen. She capsized almost at once and everybody shrieked, she looked so funny."

" S-she must have done."

" It's an awful shame your people are in France just now," Anthea went on, trying hard to find the right thing to say. " It makes it so lonely for you. Couldn't your brother have come to the regatta?"

" I didn't want him to—it's all his fault."

" Oh!" Anthea delicately refrained from asking why. " Well, never mind. We are all coming up as often as we can to see you, but nurse says you mustn't have many visitors."

" I know, it's an awful bore; it's because I've still got a temperature and I don't feel like eating, otherwise I might have been carried downstairs and allowed to watch." She rubbed her eyes again on the sheet. " Everyone is v-very nice. All the staff have been to see me and Maddy gave me those lovely rose-buds."

Anthea was sniffing them admiringly when Gretchen put her head round the door.

" Oh, hullo, old thing. I say, you're looking awfully well. Anthea, nurse says you must go now and I may stay five minutes. I've brought you some raspberries and cream, Jennifer—oh, you've got some already. Oh, well, if you don't want them, I'll eat them myself. Pity to waste them. *Do* you want them, Jennifer?"

Jennifer, having waved good-bye to Anthea, shook her head drearily.

" Did you get very wet when your boat capsized?" she asked, watching with languid interest her visitor demolishing the gift she had brought.

" Did I not? But I was in a swim suit, of course. That interfering Olive dived in to rescue me. She wanted to show off her life-saving because she wasn't in the team, I suppose."

" Who won the relay race? You can have these raspberries Anthea brought too, if you like, I don't want them."

" The lower fifth—oh, can I? Thanks. We were only allowed a stingy amount downstairs. There are simply crowds of visitors, eating their heads right off as usual. Do you know, I saw that old bishop—who always has to tell us when to laugh at his jokes—polish off two platefuls?"

" Goodness, how could he? I think they taste like burnt porridge."

Gretchen looked shocked.

" My dear, they're divine. I suppose Anthea told you that Anita and Caroline came second in the sailing? Caroline is nearly bursting with swank, so if you hear an explosion you'll know what it is."

When Gretchen had run away, promising to come again as soon as she could, with something else nice for Jennifer, Caroline arrived with an offering of cream buns and very full of her exploit.

" Coming in second is really the same as winning," she explained complacently, when she had made polite inquiries about how Jennifer felt. " No one ever expects to beat Lindsay, and of course no one at school ever does."

"N–no," Jennifer agreed in a forlorn voice, trying not to shudder too obviously at the cream buns.

And then when Caroline had described her own part in the sailing race, with a painful regard for detail, it was time for the most important event of the regatta, and nurse came in to push Jennifer's bed up close to the big window.

It was a lovely evening, smelling of summer in a riverside garden; a very special scent, Jennifer thought, sniffing noisily. Already the guests in their gay frocks were strolling down to the towpath. At the edge of the woods on the other side of the river, strangers were standing in a long fringe. Jennifer thrilled. It seemed to make Lindsay, as the only school competitor in this special race, so grand.

Three times the little sailing boats would pass the garden to finish their race just before the river bend. From her window Jennifer would not be able to see the finish, but she could see enough to make it very exciting.

" We must have no more visitors to-night," nurse said, fetching a chair for herself.

Jennifer's heart fell. She had hoped and hoped that perhaps Lindsay . . .

" Oh, nurse, not one? If she was a very special one?"

" Not one," nurse said. " There's the gun; they've started."

In the distance they could hear that the cheering had started too. The first time *Whitewings* passed she was fourth.

" Lindsay must do better than that," nurse said. Jennifer could not speak. If only, *only* nurse wouldn't speak either.

The second time *Whitewings* passed she was third.

" That's better," nurse said maddeningly.

The last time *Whitewings* passed, lying over at a thrilling angle, she was drawing level, amid roars of encouragement, with a sleek brown boat sailed by a young man in a startling blazer.

" Now we shall see," nurse said. Jennifer bit her lips. Lindsay must win. She *must*. The roaring and the cheering followed the race, growing fainter, and then: Bang! Bang!

" Close finish," nurse said.

Jennifer stared at her in amazement. She looked,

in this world-shattering moment, exactly the same as usual. She was even straightening the counterpane. Jennifer pitied her calm and envied her and hated her.

" Oh, nurse, I feel so awful. I don't know whether Lindsay won." If nurse started fussing with her pillows Jennifer felt she would simply have to throw the cream buns at her.

" You soon will know," nurse promised. " I'll go and find out. By the way our visitors are behaving, I should think she certainly has won."

" Yes—nurse, do hurry, and if you *should* see Lindsay——"

" Well?" nurse encouraged.

" Oh, nothing. Please come back quickly."

Jennifer waited in a fever of suspense for the news, hoping against hope that Lindsay would bring it herself. But it was only nurse who presently reappeared carrying a supper tray.

" Well, Jennifer, you've got your wish. *Whitewings* won."

Jennifer felt she had known that for centuries.

" You didn't happen to speak to Lindsay?"

" No. She's having so much fuss made of her that I should think it would turn her head, if she were less sensible, or maybe, less used to it. Now you really must drink a little milk. I've put an ice cream into it. You've scarcely taken anything all day."

Jennifer obediently gulped a little down before pushing it away. She wished nurse would go so that she could gloat in peace and in misery over all she was missing. There was Lindsay's triumph. It would have been so lovely to have seen it and to have shared in it a tiny bit as Anthea was doing. There was the presentation of the cups and prizes by the bishop, who was packed so full of raspberries. There was the dance, which would follow a partified supper. Her new frock for the dance suited her so well that even Caroline, forgetting to be critical, for a moment had stared admiringly. Life was too, too sad.

Later that evening, when it was getting dark and Jennifer had been alone for a long time, she thought she heard whispering voices outside the door, which was presently opened softly.

Jennifer, wide awake, looked round.

" Here's your special visitor," nurse said benevolently. " Then perhaps you'll oblige me by going straight off to sleep."

As she spoke she opened the door wider and in came Lindsay, radiant in a frock of green chiffon decorated with velvet ribbons and tiny flowers.

" Oh, Lindsay!"

" I've brought you *Whitewings'* prize," Lindsay said. " You may keep it to do what you like with until you are well."

" Oh, Lindsay, it's beautiful! A little silver yacht. I—I——" she rubbed her eyes fiercely with the sheet.

Lindsay glanced at her keenly. She knew that neither the doctor nor nurse were quite satisfied with their patient.

" You're not worrying about anything special,

are you? Except, of course, not being able to sail with me and all that."

"No." Jennifer's lips trembled. She hadn't meant to behave like a feeble baby in front of Lindsay. "I'm just so dreadfully miserable. And it's all my fault. I can't blame anybody else, which would have been such a comfort."

"You did it for fun, I suppose?" Lindsay asked, more indulgently than was her habit of referring to Jennifer's particular brand of fun.

"No. And I didn't do any of the other things for fun either," Jennifer burst out. "Not the singing or the lights or—the booby-trap. My brother dared me, or else I dared him, to do them all. Dares have been spoiling my life for ages—I hate them and I believe I've always hated them—and now that I couldn't help you sail *Whitewings* they've absolutely ruined it."

"Oh, not quite," Lindsay mocked her gently. "There is always next year."

Jennifer looked at her in swift hope.

"You mean, you might let me crew for you next year if—if——?"

"I will let you. Of course I will, and there's only one 'if'. You really must give up this silly game you play with your brother, which even at its best is completely childish."

"Oh, I will. I promise. Actually I'm dying to give it up only "—her face suddenly clouded— "John will think I'm not brave."

"Then John must be an even bigger goose than you are, and goodness help your parents. Whatever can you imagine is brave about balancing a pair of hockey boots over a door, or trying to slide down the bannisters on your back?"

"Perhaps I used the wrong word," Jennifer murmured happily.

"I should think you must have done," Lindsay agreed. "You do mean to stop those dares?"

"Oh, rather. Yes. I'll write to John to-morrow."

"Then here's to next year's regatta," Lindsay smiled, raising the silver boat. "We'll go pot-hunting together."

Jennifer touched it reverently. "To next year!"

Then she pulled the sheet up to her chin, smiling blissfully over the top.

"What a lovely year it will be. You'll be head girl and I shall have no awful suspense about not being chosen to crew for you."

"You seem to have an obsession with suspense," Lindsay commented with a grin.

Jennifer looked intelligent. She must keep Lindsay standing there at the end of the bed as long as she could.

"An Obsession with Suspense. It sounds lovely. Wouldn't it be particularly clever for the title of your next book?"

"No. I think it would be particularly idiotic. Look here, Jennifer, I must go now. Nurse says you've hardly eaten anything all day. Could you manage an ice if I bring one—just a small one?"

"A small one? It need not be *small*!" Jennifer almost shouted. "I could eat a boatful. I've never felt so super in my life."